First Edition Romance

A Garriety Romance

First Edition Romance

A Garriety Romance

Shannon M. Harris

SAPPHIRE BOOKS

SALINAS, CALIFORNIA

Dedication

To books, chocolate, & falling in love

Acknowledgments

I want to thank Chris and everyone at Sapphire books for all that they do to bring our stories to you. Also, thank you to Linda North for helping me get this book into shape.

Chapter One

Ainslon O'Neil tapped the ink pen in her right hand, in a one, two, one, two beat on the top of the counter as her eyes scanned the list of new inventory that they'd received the previous day. With a stroke of luck, she'd acquired two boxes of books from a private collector when he decided to downsize his collection.

Her passion was finding and saving vintage children's books. Justin Bishop, her business partner and best friend, preferred to stock their comic section of their bookstore. Turn the Page had exceeded both of their expectations when they'd decided to go into business together. Though frightening and scary, they managed to pull off the transition from an online business to an actual storefront with ease.

They held themed evenings for children's story night and game nights where they provided snacks and drinks to all participants twice a month. In the first nine months of business, their in-store sales far exceeded their online presence, proving they'd made the right decision in expanding their business. Though at times trying, they would do whatever necessary to make sure their store stayed a success.

The large open space consisted of several dividers throughout the layout. A quarter of the store stocked their children's books. Another quarter housed the comics and action figures. The other two quarters were divided into the office area, a temperature-controlled room for the vintage books, and a room for book readings and game nights.

When they bought the building, they didn't know whether they would be able to fill it. Now, they were almost ready to find a bigger space.

A child's laughter drew Ainslon out of her haze. She glanced up from her worksheet and scanned the space where a small group of kids and parents milled about. A quick scan at the screen in front of her showed a few teenagers in the comic section. Sarah, their only full-time employee, currently manned that section. If the business kept at its current rate of growth, they would need to add someone part time.

She eyed the clock. It read eleven-forty-five. Justin should have gotten back already with their lunch. She wanted sandwiches, but he had insisted on tacos from a food truck, Taco Heaven, that always parked a few blocks from their store. Before going back to her worksheet, she reached for the blue and white cardigan by the cash register and slipped it on. Older buildings always seemed to have a draft, including this one. Now, she wished they hadn't spent all that money to insulate the space, considering it didn't help.

At the bell alerting her someone had entered, she looked up, grateful when Justin walked in. She slipped the pen behind her ear and joined him at the small table behind the counter after he mentioned to Sarah her lunch would be in the breakroom. "Took long enough."

He handed her a taco and a small cup of cinnamon donuts. "I know, right, but so worth it." He took a large bite of his burrito. Though patchy in spots, the beard he'd decided to grow the previous month to appear older looked good.

The rich aroma of spices that wafted out of the taco engulfed her when she unwrapped it. Thin slices of beef nestled in a flour tortilla, layered with pico de gallo, avocado, and a sauce she never could identify.

She lifted the taco to her mouth when the bell alerted them a customer had entered. Justin pushed back from his chair to stand, but she waved him off. "Eat. I've got this." He grinned and gave her a thumbs up.

She stood, straightened her cardigan, and eyed the woman as she browsed the section of pop-up books along the far wall. Even from the distance between them, the woman's height and wealth were evident.

The light blue button-down and tailored grey trousers fit the woman's trim figure to perfection. The red heels were a definite turn on. It was a far cry from Ainslon's ten-year-old jeans and black t-shirt she had thrown on that morning. Not exactly designer, but comfortable. Compared to the woman, she felt more like a teenager. In awe, she eyed the woman's dark brown, curly hair hanging just above her shoulders. Ainslon could see herself running her fingers through those curls. As curly and wild as the woman's hair looked, it probably took a load of time to complete. Whoever could pull off a move like that, so effortlessly, deserved her admiration.

Ainslon sucked in a breath when the woman turned around and walked up to the counter. Deep brown eyes combined with perfectly shaped brows, and full lips only added to the overall picture. The brown curls framed the woman's face perfectly. Ainslon figured she was in her early to mid-forties. Her heart thumped loudly in her chest when the woman smiled. *For goodness sake, Ainslon, you are a businesswoman, and it isn't the first time you have seen a beautiful woman. Get it together.* The woman looked vaguely familiar, but Ainslon couldn't place her. She put on her best smile. After all, this was a customer. "Can I help you with something today?" Ainslon bit her lip when the woman placed a well-manicured hand on the counter. Her nails were short and painted a deep red. The same color as her heels.

"You can. I am looking for a first edition copy of *Mary Poppins*." She flicked her fingers. "I could look for one, but don't have the time and I would rather put it in the hands of someone far more capable than I am in such matters. You came highly recommended by a friend."

Ainslon nodded and just stopped herself from asking for the friend's name. "All right." She picked up her iPad but knew she didn't have a copy in inventory. At least not a first edition. She clicked on several Excel documents to confirm what she already knew. Her heart thudded in her chest, but she kept her eyes on the tablet even as the woman's perfume drifted her way. Good grief! At thirty-four, she shouldn't be feeling this out of sorts, not with a first meeting. She turned to address her customer. The woman's gaze swept over her and set Ainslon's heart racing even more loudly than before. "I don't have a first edition in inventory, but I do have another copy that will give you an idea of condition."

"Wonderful."

Ainslon stepped away from the counter, glad for the slight reprieve, and walked to a door just to the left of the main floor. The compact room had cost a small fortune to set up, but to preserve the vintage books the room needed to stay temperature controlled at sixty-five degrees. She entered the four-digit code on the lock pad on the door, entered, and quickly located the plastic bin that contained the book she needed. After exiting the room, with book in hand, and shutting the door, she walked back to the counter and placed the book in front of the woman. "As you can see, this is a nice copy. Crisp, clean pages and the spine is tight. I was fortunate to acquire this one."

"May I look it over?"

"Sure, go ahead."

The woman picked it up and examined the entire book before placing it back on the counter. "This is exactly what I want, only in a first edition. *Mary Poppins* is my nephew's favorite movie and I wanted to get him something special for his eighth birthday."

"I can check with my resources and try to find a first edition for you. Would you like to start the process?"

The woman regarded her evenly. "You're not the only vintage bookstore in the area." A smile quirked up her lips. "Even though my friend recommended you, what do you have to offer me?"

The question seemed innocent but Ainslon's mind couldn't help but conjure up all kinds of naughty scenarios. When the woman smirked, Ainslon leaned forward and rested her hands on top of the counter. *Get it together.* This was a business transaction. "We are the largest comic book and children's store in the area but finding and selling vintage and rare children's books and comics is a passion of mine and I, along with my business partner, Justin, have made a business out of it. I can assure you, I am good at what I do, and I have never turned down a challenge." While the woman did hold her attention, the idea of embarking on this challenge intrigued her. "You won't be disappointed."

While seeming to make up her mind, the woman hummed quietly. "How much will the book cost me?"

"Depending upon the condition," she clasped her hands together on top of the counter, "probably around three thousand…maybe a little more." It was a lot of money for a gift for an eight-year-old, but Ainslon couldn't afford to turn down this woman's business.

For a few moments, the woman studied her. "How do we start the process?"

Ainslon grabbed the clipboard off the corner of the counter with the fill out sheets and pulled the pen from behind her ear. She would input the information into her digital files at the end of business. "Name?"

"Lauren Millán."

Ainslon masked her surprise as she wrote the name down. Lauren Millán owned C and C, one of the most popular businesses in the city. The store carried thousands of different types of candy and gourmet chocolates. On top of that, C and C made the list of Garriety's top ten businesses of the year for the past ten.

Not only was Lauren Millán one of the most eligible lesbians in the city, but she had also been named one of the top five most influential women of color in Garriety the previous year. No wonder she looked familiar. The pictures in the papers didn't do the woman's beauty justice. She wrote the name of the book next, then looked up. "Phone number?"

"If you hand me your clipboard, I'll write it down

for you."

Ainslon slid the clipboard toward her and waited while she filled out the rest of the information. She did a double take at the date; the eighteenth of August. That was under three months away and a month before the annual Garriety food festival where Turn the Page would present the children's story hour.

When she gave her presentation speech to be considered for this year's festival, she'd included a copy of an LBGTQ book, because she felt, as a lesbian, it was important to include one. Thankfully, no one had objected to her choices. She knew Garriety was an inclusive city; however, there were a few conservatives on the board this year, but they hadn't objected either. Teresa Thatcher ran the food festival board and tried to recruit her to sit on the board as an ambassador for Ireland, but Ainslon had vetoed that idea. Mrs. Thatcher still bugged her from time to time, but Ainslon held steady on her choice.

"Is this date firm?" Ainslon asked.

"It is. Is that going to be a problem?" Lauren glanced at her watch.

Ainslon had to tear her eyes away from the vision in front of her and look at the clipboard instead. "I'm not sure. Most of the time, circumstances are out of my control. I normally like a little more time than this, but if you're willing, I will do everything within my power to find your book."

"I'm willing." Lauren sounded and looked a bit flirty to Ainslon. Then she offered her hand and Ainslon gripped it with a firm handshake. "It was a pleasure to meet you."

Ainslon held on a tad longer than necessary before releasing her hand. "The pleasure was all mine."

Smooth, Ainslon. Smooth.

Lauren tucked a stray piece of hair behind her ear. "Good luck in your search. I have a feeling you won't let me down." She winked and walked out the door with, Ainslon was sure, an extra swing to her hips.

Ainslon groaned and thumped her forehead against the countertop. Holy hell. Lauren was hot. Really, really hot. So hot her hand still burnt from her touch. She shook out her hands. *Get it together, Ainslon.*

"Ainslon," Justin whispered in her ear. Ainslon sprung up from the counter, eyes wide, as he pulled her into his side. "What was that about?" He grinned as she pulled away and sat at the table behind the counter. He followed and took a seat across from her, crossing his arms. "You seem flustered."

She glowered at him, took a bite of her taco, then wiped her mouth. "Shut up." She laughed. "Did you see her?" She fanned her face. "Good grief. To top things off, she wants me to find a first edition *Mary Poppins* for her."

Justin's eyes widened. "Wow. That's spending some serious cash." He stood and patted her on the head. "Just remember," he pointed at her, then at the door, "the quicker you find that book, the sooner you can see her again." He whistled all the way to the counter where a customer waited to check out.

Ainslon ate the last of her food, grabbed her iPad, and settled down at one of the small couches scattered throughout the layout to start her search. Justin was right. The quicker she found the book, the sooner she could see Lauren again. She'd never failed a mission and she didn't intend to start now.

Chapter Two

Lauren waited until she was an acceptable distance away from Turn the Page before she stopped and took a deep, calming breath. Ollie had been right. Ainslon's Irish accent was a thing of beauty. When Ollie first suggested the bookstore a couple of months back, Lauren had kept putting it off, but when the other two stores in the area couldn't find the book she wanted, she didn't have any another choice but to go to Turn the Page. Why had she waited so long?

The temperature-controlled room and Ainslon's professionalism told Lauren all she needed to know about how much Ainslon valued her business. Only a true collector could appreciate such a room and it told her it was a serious venture.

Even though she felt Ainslon could use a crash course in fashion, her clothing attire didn't detract from her beauty. Long black hair framed a sharp jaw line and eyes so green, she knew if she stared into them long enough, she'd drown. The flirting surprised her, but it was always nice to grab someone's attention. She seemed a bit young, but there was no harm in looking.

Getting her thoughts in order, her attention turned toward the crosswalk when she spied a tall woman headed in her direction.

Besides being a friend, A.J. was also the photographer for her new marketing campaign. The brochures would highlight a new line of custom and European chocolate. The possibility was there to add a coffee bar featuring a wide array of international coffees, but she hadn't made her mind up yet.

After two years, she'd worked out a contract with a supplier in Switzerland that had made her chocolatier, Noe, happy. Luck was on her side when she'd lured Noe, only one of five true chocolatiers in France, two years ago with the promise that he would be able to create to his heart's desire. It had been the selling point for him moving to Garriety. His work didn't come cheap, but since he'd come on board, they'd won three competitions in Vegas, and their mail order business had tripled their overseas customer base. His work was impeccable, and she had no intention of letting him go.

"A.J." Lauren accepted A.J.'s kiss to her cheek. Since their first meeting, A.J.'s sense of humor captivated Lauren and the two quickly hit it off. In the past, Lauren had asked her out, but A.J. had explained that she still grieved the death of her wife and it wouldn't be fair to either one of them. Her focus needed to be solely on her three-year-old daughter, Rosy. After that, they moved into a comfortable friendship. Lauren slipped her arm into A.J.'s and steered her to the crosswalk.

"I'm glad I caught you," A.J. said. "I planned to call later, but I have an opening for tomorrow morning. I've already cleared it with Leo, and she'll bring someone with her so I can get the shoots of the exterior I need without pedestrians marring the photos. All she asked for was money for pizza and beer. I'm working it into your bill."

Leo, Lauren knew, was a friend of A.J.'s and a police officer that helped her with photo shoots from time to time. "Of course. Is there anything you need me to do?"

"No, we'll be here at around eight thirty. That way I can get plenty of photos without anyone in the store. I'll take all the exterior ones, then the interior, your office, and the kitchens. I've got a few projects ahead of yours to finalize, but I should have everything ready by the end of the month. You worked it out with Noe, yes?"

"Yes, I did. Tomorrow would be wonderful." Noe acted like a bear when Lauren had asked him to be in a few pictures. He had agreed when Lauren said he wouldn't have to give any on stage demonstrations at the Garriety food festival. C and C was one of the platinum sponsors and would have a booth set up with a menu of not only their usual offerings, but also a few Puerto Rican staples. It was important to her for others to get a taste of her heritage, no matter how small.

"If you have a minute to spare, I'll have someone put together a bag for Rosy."

A.J. chuckled. "I see how it is," she said as she guided Lauren across the street to C and C. "All for Rosy, none for me."

Lauren arched her brow. "She is my favorite."

"She's mine too."

Once inside, Lauren instructed George, an employee, to get A.J. a bag together, then climbed the stairs to her second-floor office where Ollie should be waiting for their lunch date. She'd known Olivia Markinson for close to twenty years. Lauren loved Ollie's three children like they were her own and spoiled them rotten. She would do just about anything for all four of them. Including paying an exuberant amount for Colin's birthday present. He still hadn't taken the Lego set she gave him for Christmas out of the box and she knew he would take care of the book. She'd also bought him some art supplies for his newly shown talent.

Lauren walked into her office, shut the door, and noticed Olivia in her office chair.

"You know," Olivia said, looking up from a magazine. "When you said lunch at twelve thirty, that's what time I expected you here."

Lauren rolled her eyes and set her purse on the floor by her desk before picking up a small box and placing it on the desk next to Ollie. "Really, Ollie? I'm only," she glanced at her watch, a gift from her grandma, "two minutes late." She sat in one of the chairs in front of her desk.

"You better have a good reason." She stopped mid-flip in her magazine, pushed it to the corner of the desk, then picked up the box, gently opening the lid. "He'll love it. He's been practicing with the book you left him."

"Good." For the past three months, Lauren had taught Ralph, Ollie's eldest son, the art of Origami. She first took up the practice in college. It brought her satisfaction to finish a piece and taught her patience. "As for why I'm late, I stopped by Turn the Page for Colin's birthday present."

Ollie stopped unpacking their food and sent a disbelieving look her way. "Just now? I told you about that store months ago." She tsked and kept unpacking the food.

"Yes, well, could you blame me? One of Turn the Page's display windows is ducks and the other one is dragons." Lauren fidgeted in her seat. "The other stores looked more reputable, but they couldn't find the book I wanted. People's incompetence never fails to astound me. These people are supposed to be professionals. Ainslon promised to endeavor to find the book I want before Colin's birthday."

Ollie pushed a sandwich her way. "You're really cutting it short. She may not be able to find it."

"She said she would give it her best shot."

"Really?" Ollie smirked.

"Don't start." Lauren took a bite of her turkey and Swiss on rye with honey mustard. Lauren wouldn't be surprised if Ollie had roasted the turkey herself instead of buying it already pre-packaged. Ollie really did make the best sandwiches. Owning one of the largest real estate companies in Garriety afforded Ollie the means to hire the best nannies and cooks, but Ollie took her children's well-being seriously and tried to be there in every aspect of their lives. Including making their lunches.

"It's all right to be attracted to someone. She's beautiful with a killer accent and the sharpest jawline I've ever seen."

"Then why don't you ask her out?" Lauren took a sip of her water.

"Don't be silly. When would I have the time?" Ollie waved off the suggestion.

"Of course. Silly me." Ollie's life revolved around her children and her career, but Lauren wished she would spend some time on her own love life.

"When she finds your book—"

"If."

Ollie pursed her lips. "When. Ask her out. No harm done."

"You only mentioned the place in passing. How do you know it so well?" In fact, she'd mentioned it a lot in passing.

"Ralph and Colin compete in their game nights and Heidi enjoys the book readings. I always make it a point to speak with Ainslon and Justin when we go. I believe I've told you that before."

"I don't know." She patted her lips clean with a napkin. "I'm too old for her and don't even know if she's a lesbian."

"Thirty-four and she is. Her last name is O'Neil, in case you were wondering. I was at the festival's board meeting when she gave her presentation and stated in said presentation that she was a lesbian."

"Huh. Thirty-four?" Lauren raised an eyebrow.

"Thirty-four is only a ten-year difference. Completely doable. Stop trying to get out of it. You'll make some woman a fantastic partner."

"I suppose."

Lauren glanced at the sign above the door to her office. The original C and C sign. When her great-great grandparents had immigrated from Puerto Rico, her great-great-grandfather had opened the first C and C. It lasted fifteen years before business slowed and they had to close shop. Thirty years later, her great-grandfather opened the second C and C and used the sign, but a short ten years later he had to close shop also. Her grandpa tried a third time and opened C and C again, but it too failed. When she decided to open the latest incarnation, her grandmother had taken her into the attic and had uncovered the original sign. Weathered over the years by the elements, Lauren had the sign preserved. The sign hanging outside the store was an exact replica of the original one she had in her office.

"Earth to Lauren."

"Sorry." She shook her thoughts away. "If the book doesn't come in time, I have a back-up-plan. No worries."

"I'm not worried." Ollie gathered her trash up and threw it in the nearby small trashcan before picking up her purse and walking to the door. "In all honesty, Lauren, if the woman has you this out of sorts, after only meeting her once, you need to think about why. By the way, I love it when you wear your hair like that." Ollie blew her a kiss, then walked out the door.

Today, rather than straighten her hair, she'd decided to style her natural curls before leaving the house. If Ainslon's reaction was anything to go by, she would let her curls out more often. Lauren stood and plopped herself down in her office chair. She would take Ollie's words to heart, as always. If, upon their second meeting, the pesky feelings continued, she would, maybe, do something about them. Maybe.

She enjoyed being in a relationship and her last one had ended on a good note, but she hadn't wanted to get back out there. Casual dating had its moments but turned stale after a while. Settling down with someone and planning a future together filled her with warmth, but the thought of putting herself out there held no appeal.

She opened her laptop and did a quick search of Ainslon O'Neil. There wasn't much. Seemed like Ainslon stayed out of the limelight, considering her business partner, Justin Bishop, did most of their PR. She clicked on one of Ainslon's pictures found on their store's Instagram page. In it, she was sprawled out in a picture window with a scarf around her neck and wearing glasses. Lauren didn't think she could get any more attractive. She was wrong. The glasses added a whole other dimension. Ainslon certainly was photogenic.

Lauren exited out and shut the screen. There would be time for pointless daydreaming later. Right now, she had a business to run. Ollie had asked her to sit in on the board for the food festival, but due to the demands of her business, Lauren had turned down the invitation. However, she had donated a substantial amount of money to become a platinum sponsor.

The festival board projected at least forty thousand visitors for their third year. Feedback on how well festival goers received their new recipes would determine if they converted part of the store into a coffee bar. Besides her family, her heritage meant the most to her, but at the heart of everything, she was a businesswoman and wouldn't do anything to jeopardize her business. She vowed to not fail where her ancestors had.

Chapter Three

A week after her meeting with Lauren, Ainslon wasn't any closer to finding the book than on the first day. Justin had tried to be encouraging but failed in his usual epic way. She forbade him from helping and exiled him to the back room sorting through the several boxes of action figures delivered the previous day.

Even keeping her nose to the grindstone, she'd still exhausted almost all her resources. It didn't help that her mind always wandered toward Lauren with her perfect hair, amazing smile, and her killer sense of style.

Out of curiosity, she had googled Lauren, with her cat, Shady, curled up next to her. She didn't want to be a creeper but couldn't bring herself to care when looking through all the pictures of the striking and dynamic businesswoman. As closely as the Garriety Gossip website followed Lauren's life, no mention of a significant other ever appeared or was even hinted about. Most of the photos revolved around Lauren at business functions or with her family.

Ainslon had refrained from telling Easton, her sister, about everything that happened the previous week. Easton owned Brew and Bake, a bakery, located only a block away from her store. She loved Easton dearly but knew she would hound her if she found out about her crush. Easton was having trouble in the love department and liked to live through Ainslon's dating life, but lately, Ainslon's was as non-existent as her sister's. They had made plans to have dinner together the following night.

Easton wasn't her sister by blood. When Ainslon was fifteen, her parents caught her making out with her best friend Deirdre. She confessed to her parents she was gay, and they refused to accept her. A few months later, her grandmother, Edna, had flown across the world to pick her up from Ireland.

Edna was born in Ireland but had immigrated to the United States when she was twenty, where she met, fell in love with, and married Clive, another Irish immigrant. Greg, Ainslon's dad, and mom, Eileen, were born in the United States, but when Ainslon was almost two, her parents decided to move to Ireland to learn and live the culture.

It wasn't until Ainslon and Edna were back in the states that Ainslon found out Edna had also taken in another girl. Easton was a year younger than her, and both of her parents had died in a car crash. Edna had known Easton's parents and when CPS couldn't find a placement for her, because of Easton's age, Edna was granted custody. They'd grown up together and their bond was unshakeable. Ainslon didn't know what she would do without Easton by her side and hoped to never find out.

They were opposites in looks with Ainslon's black hair and green eyes compared to Easton's blond hair and brown eyes. For some reason, no one ever had a problem seeing them as sisters. It didn't matter that Ainslon had an accent and Easton didn't.

She scooped up a handful of sunflower seeds, mini chocolate chips, and peanuts to eat. While chewing, she searched her mind for any other leads for the book but drew a blank. When her cellphone rang a familiar tune, a grin split her face and she hopped off the couch, grabbed her phone, and swiped it before her nana could hang up. If it wasn't an emergency, Edna would only call once and would refuse any calls after the fact.

"Hi, Nana."

"Ainslon, would you like to have dinner with me tonight? I'm making your favorite."

Ainslon leaned back against the counter and counted to ten quietly in Irish. When she'd moved in, Edna had made sure Ainslon never lost sight of her heritage and one of those things was keeping up with her Irish. They only used the language from time to time, but Ainslon was thankful Edna had kept up with it.

"Ainslon, I can hear your breathing over the phone. You know, I'm an old woman. No telling how much time I have left on this earth. You could at least pretend to want to talk to me."

Ainslon groaned. "Nana, don't be silly. I always enjoy talking to you and I would love to have dinner with you."

It always amazed her how such a sweet, frail looking, eighty-eight-year-old woman could be so manipulative. Her Irish stew was the stuff of legends. Ainslon may have left Ireland behind but Edna made sure she always had a piece of it with her. Either in the language or the family dinners. Ainslon's favorite meal was bacon with cabbage and turnips and mash. No matter how many times Ainslon made it, she never could match Edna's.

"That's the spirit, dear. Dinner's at seven sharp.

Grá gheal mo chroí thú."

Ainslon let the words wash over her, 'you are the bright love of my heart,' then she came back to reality. Edna only spoke Irish when she felt sentimental. "I love you too."

If dinner was at seven that meant she would have to be there by six thirty at the latest. When Justin came back with lunch, she filled him in on her conversation and he agreed to lock up for the night.

❧❧❧❧

Lauren pushed the flatbed shopping cart through the aisles of Sadlers, Garriety's one big box store, as Patricia, her mother, kept piling items on it. Lauren eyed the cart, overflowing with supplies, to make sure nothing fell off. Once a month, Lauren accompanied Patricia on her grocery shopping to load up on necessities. One, because Lauren didn't want her mother loading and lifting so many heavy items, and two, because she loved spending time with her. Though, she never understood why her mother bought so much. It was only her, Callie, Jeffrey, her brother-in-law, and nephew, Charlie. Lauren had a feeling her mother bought so much so she could make meals for her neighbors that didn't get around as well as they used to.

Patricia still lived in the small three-bedroom home Lauren had grown up in. The house, located in a modest neighborhood on the outskirts of the city, didn't have any of the hustle or bustle of the city. It was a wonderful place to grow up and Lauren wouldn't trade her memories of it for anything. She loved vacationing around the world, but Garriety was and would always be her home. Not every child grew up in a loving family, and Lauren knew how lucky she was. It still pained her to walk into the home and not see her papa sitting in his recliner in the living room.

Eleven years ago, he'd died unexpectedly, and the hole he'd left in their lives still ached from time to time. Her parents had almost reached their fiftieth wedding anniversary. After her mother's grieving process, she'd started living again, like her papa would have wanted. Between cooking and gardening, Patricia liked to visit with her neighbors and had a weekly appointment for bridge and chess at the community center. Just like her mother, Lauren liked to keep busy. Where she learned love and patience from her papa, she learned passion and drive from her mother.

Lauren nodded at a few people she knew but kept pushing the cart per Patricia's instructions. They stopped at the produce section, where Lauren would be picking up some items for herself. She had a visit to the farmers market with her sister planned for Saturday, but, as much as she liked the farmers market, the prices on the produce here were too good to pass up.

"Grab a box of the plantains and a bag of mangoes," Patricia said, as she surveyed the berries. "And a container of strawberries and a bag of grapes." At her last check up, Patricia's cholesterol readings were a little high, so she added more fruits and vegetables and less meat into her diet.

Patricia deposited her picks on top of the largest box. "How have you been, *little duck*? We haven't talked much this week." She eyed the cart, even though Lauren had carefully packed as they went along.

Lauren smiled at the term of endearment her mother had always used for her. She laid her bounty beside her mother's as they made their way to the vegetables. "Good. Revenue was up three percent last quarter and we're almost done with the planning for the food festival. I'm still looking into purchasing the empty building beside ours, but the owner is being stubborn." She plucked a package of zucchini and a bag of green beans up but stopped when Patricia placed a hand on her arm. "Momma?"

"I'm happy your business is doing so well, but how are you doing?"

"Fine. You know I'm a creature of habit." Lauren turned away from her mother's penetrating gaze.

"I know. There isn't anything else?"

"Why? Is there something specific you want to know?" Patricia had a sixth sense for this stuff.

"Well, Ollie and I talked, and a certain name came up in the conversation. Ainslon." Patricia lifted her eyebrows in question.

Lauren should have known Ollie would say something. Before answering, she surveyed around to make sure no one lurked nearby to overhear. "There is nothing to tell, Momma." Lauren grasped her mother's hand. "Honestly, there is nothing to tell. If, and that's a big if, she finds the book I'm looking for, I might, I might consider asking her out."

"Good." They went about their shopping. "I want you to be happy. That's all. You'll never make it the fifty years your father and I did, but I'm sure there is someone out there for you."

Lauren stopped in the middle of the aisle, her tone dry and a bit hurt. "Thanks, Momma, for putting everything into perspective for me. Way to make your daughter feel good."

"Oh, stop. You've had love and that's more than

a lot of people can say. I want to see that smile on your face again."

"Momma, I smile all the time."

"True, but you know what I mean."

"I do." She knew arguing with her mother would be a wasted endeavor, so kept quiet as they finished their shopping.

Back at Patricia's house, they worked in tandem to put the groceries away. When Patricia refused her help with lunch, Lauren relaxed at the table with a cup of coffee. They would always have lunch together on their shopping days and Patricia always insisted on cooking. Today, lunch was a simple, but delicious tomato soup with some of their newly acquired purchases.

As she sat across from her mother, Lauren intended to always make the most of their time together. One never knew when life would be cut short and it was never guaranteed that she would outlive her mother. "So, Momma, tell me about your week?"

Chapter Four

Far sooner than Ainslon would have liked, the time arrived to leave for dinner with Edna. She waved bye to Justin and walked the few blocks to her apartment. Once inside, she greeted Shady with plenty of cuddle time and treats.

After Shady received adequate attention, Ainslon stared at her closet and contemplated what to wear. She knew what she wanted, but also knew Edna would throw a fit. Instead of the first choice of sweats and t-shirt, she opted for a gray sheath dress, a red belt, and a pair of black flats. She grabbed her blue cardigan out of the hall closet, patted Shady on the head, exited her apartment, then rode the elevator to the underground parking garage. Her trusty Jeep Wrangler, Belle, was a comfort and as she sat behind the wheel, she vowed to get out more often on her days off. Belle was her one big purchase when Turn the Page's sales had taken off.

The drive to Edna's was quick and easy. After parking, she opened the kitchen door and the sight of not one, but two women greeted her.

Edna and Easton stood by the stove with their backs to her when she walked in. Great. The two of them together usually equaled trouble. She let the door slam shut, and Easton jumped, but Edna kept her cool.

"Ainslon, you know how I feel about slamming doors."

"Sorry, Nana." Ainslon scowled as Easton smirked. She kissed Edna's cheek, slapped Easton on the arm, then walked into the living room, slipped her cardigan off, and hung it up on the coat rack. After shutting the door, she turned around and almost bumped into her sister, then pressed both hands on her chest and squeaked. "Jesus, Easton."

"Don't be such a baby."

Ainslon bypassed her. "What are you even doing here? Didn't you have plans?" At the entranceway to the kitchen, she spun around. "And where's your car?"

"In the garage."

"And your plans?"

"Cancelled. I'm all yours tonight."

"Goody."

"Ainslon," Edna said. "Set the table. Easton, pour everyone a glass of wine."

Once they were all seated, Ainslon kept her mouth shut while waiting for one of the other two to say something first. It wasn't unusual for them to have dinner together in the middle of the week, but something smelled off.

The atmosphere was tense, but not as tense as the disastrous blind date from 2014. To this day, she and Edna refused to speak of it again. They had sworn on a blood oath never to tell Easton about it.

"So, I asked you two here for a reason," Edna said. She sipped her wine. "I worry about you both, and I'm not getting any younger." She held up her hand to ward off their questions. "I know you two don't like to hear that. I'm old and all I want is for you both to be happy. I know you're both fulfilled in your jobs, but I still worry."

Ainslon and Easton shared a look even as Ainslon

reached across the table and took Edna's hand. "Don't worry about us. We're good."

"Ainslon's right, Nana. Our dating lives might be shit but everything else is running smoothly."

"Be that as it may," Edna said, "I know you both work better when you're in relationships."

"True," Easton said.

Ainslon finished off her food that tasted as good as it smelled, then dabbed her lips with a napkin. "Nana, it's not as easy as putting yourself out there. I want something more than that…and that takes time."

Easton eyed her, causing Ainslon to squirm. "What aren't you telling us?"

"Nothing." Ainslon downed the rest of her wine. Edna always bought the good stuff. Good wine is like a good lover, Edna would tell them. Once you find one, don't ever let them go. However, if they start to sour, throw them away. She and Easton had taken that advice to heart. Last Christmas they'd both chipped in and bought Edna a case of a wine she liked. The lover part, they were both struggling with that.

"Now, don't lie to us," Edna said.

Ainslon sighed. "It's really nothing. I…" She took a deep breath. "I have a tiny crush on someone. She commissioned me to find a book for her. I'm having a bit of trouble finding it." She frowned into her empty glass.

"You dog," Easton said. "Mixing business and pleasure."

"I'll get back to the woman in a minute," Edna said, "but I might have a lead on some books you can look into."

Ainslon turned to Edna. "Really?" Thank God for Edna and her nosiness.

"Old Man Collins' granddaughter, Shelly, moved into his house a few weeks ago. He left everything to her when he died. As you know, his book collection was extensive. The next time I see her, I'll invite her to dinner and see if she's willing to sell and ask if you can take a look."

"Nana, that sounds great." Old Man Collins never let anyone see his book collection, but he used to brag about it all the time. It would almost be a miracle if he had her book, but it was the only lead she had at the moment. Hopefully, his bragging held substance.

"Now, let's clean up, then head into the living room with some tea and talk about this crush of yours," Edna said.

Once settled in the living room, Easton wasted no time grilling her. "Do I know this woman?"

Ainslon took a sip of tea to bide her time.

"Now, don't be shy, dear. What's this woman's name?" Edna asked.

"Lauren." Ainslon set her teacup and the saucer on the coffee table.

"Lauren, huh," Easton said, narrowing her eyes. "What's her last name?"

"Millán," she said quietly.

"Wait," Easton said. "I couldn't have heard right because it almost sounded like you said Lauren Millán."

"I did." Ainslon flopped back against the couch and lay her arm over her eyes.

"Good grief, sis. She is one of the most eligible people in the city." Easton whistled. "She's a looker. That's for sure."

"The name rings a bell," Edna said.

"She owns C and C." Easton took out her phone

and pulled something up before showing Edna.

"She's in the papers quite a bit, isn't she? And if I'm not mistaken," Edna said, "she's a bit older than you."

"Only ten years." Some intel from her recent cyber stalking. "I'm aware that the crush is pointless, but I can't help it. She's…she's…"

Edna chuckled, then patted her knee. "She must be something if she's got you so flustered. I haven't seen that in a while."

Ainslon sat up. "She is, Nana. I've only met her the one time, but I can't get her out of my head."

"When I first met your grandpa, I was the same way. Love wants who it wants."

"I've never felt that way, but it's something I want," Easton said, softly.

"Love?" Ainslon laughed. "Nana, at this point, it's only a crush. I'm sure half the town has a crush on her."

"Still, I've never seen you act this way, even with your ex. This Lauren must be something special."

Ainslon picked up her teacup and took a tentative sip. "There's something there. At least I don't think I'm imagining it."

Easton spoke up. "I go to her store from time to time and have spoken a few words in greeting. She's not my type, but I know she's yours. The business suits are nice, but I'll take a woman in jeans and a t-shirt any day of the week. Have you ever been to her store?"

"No. Justin goes." Ainslon licked her lips. "The last thing I want is to make an ass out of myself. I'm giving it time to stew."

"Don't let it overcook," Edna said.

They finished their tea in silence.

"By the way," Easton said. "Since you never go to C and C, you wouldn't know but the building next to their store is for sale. I know you're looking for a bigger building to move into." She shrugged. "It wouldn't be cheap, but it might not be a bad idea to check it out, and when you do it will give you an excuse to explore C and C, and maybe run into Lauren."

"That's not a bad idea." It was, in fact, an excellent idea. Being next to a chocolate store could have its perks. Besides their usual patrons, people shopping at C and C, out of curiosity, might check out their store.

"I'm proud of you both."

Easton jumped up and joined them on the couch. "We love you too, Nana."

Ainslon held back the emotions that swirled around her. "I love you too, Nana."

Edna kissed them both on the cheek. "Now, since I am old, would one of you go into the kitchen and plate us some rhubarb crumble and ice cream?"

"Of course." Ainslon laughed.

"And don't forget before you two leave to take a bunch of leftovers for yourself. That's why I made extra." Before heading to the kitchen, Ainslon leaned down and kissed Edna on the cheek. "You've always been a good girl. Go, now."

As she cut them each a slice, it hit her how old Edna was and that she wouldn't be around forever. She hadn't talked to her parents in close to twenty years and they never tried to get in contact with her. It took a lot of years to come to terms with what they did, and she hoped to never see them again.

Edna chuckled when Ainslon handed her the plate with the largest piece of crumble topped with ice cream. "If it's okay with you, it's late and Shady's already been fed, can I stay here?"

"Your room is always ready for you. You know that, dear. You don't have to ask."

"Thanks," she said around a mouthful of ice cream.

"After I eat this, I need to get going, but Ainslon, call me if you need anything. You as well, Nana," Easton said.

"Don't I always," Ainslon mumbled.

"You're a good girl too, Easton," Nana said. "And since you're staying the night, Ainslon, you can make us both breakfast. I like to eat by seven." She had a twinkle in her eye that Ainslon would never get tired of seeing.

"Seven it is."

Chapter Five

Thursday morning, Ainslon adjusted her backpack as she walked down the sidewalk. The cool breeze refreshed her more than her morning shower. As long as rain wasn't in the forecast, she preferred to walk to work. Getting in a bit of exercise never hurt anyone. She greeted familiar people along her route and fifteen minutes later, opened the door to Turn the Page. Justin waved at her from behind the counter.

"Good morning." She bounded over to him.

"Morning." He slid a cup of coffee toward her.

As she walked around the counter, she slipped her backpack off, then took a sip of her coffee. Two sugars and a good amount of milk, the way she liked it. She eyed the papers laid out on top of the table. "What's all this?"

He clapped his hands together. "This is our plan for the next several story nights. I want to try and expand on what we already have. I've been researching children's book authors and illustrators as well as comic book authors and artists and was thinking about some ways we could get them here to do a reading. Sign some books, interact with the kids. Maybe once every three months or so. I've been looking into the costs."

He'd clearly done his research as she leafed through the papers. "That would be great and may attract people that wouldn't normally come to the store. At the festival we can put out a survey and see what kind of feedback we can get."

"That's good. We could hire someone to hand out flyers or offer them a voucher for the store."

"I like it." Ainslon tapped her thumb on the counter. "I mentioned to Easton and Nana last night about moving to a bigger location. Easton said the store beside C and C is for sale."

He relaxed back against the counter. "I heard the owner is being an…" he looked around the room, then whispered, "ass."

"That's what Easton said." She crinkled her brow. "It's out of our price range."

"Definitely." He crossed his arms and smiled at a customer that entered. "But sales have been fantastic the last two quarters. Game nights are growing, and I've had, as has Sarah, a lot of people tell us they come from the next town over to buy comics and things from us because of the atmosphere we have. Besides, if not now, when? The place would be perfect for us and it won't hurt to look into it and get the numbers."

"I know. It's a big step. We've only been here a little under three years and I'm afraid we would be pushing it."

He shrugged. "Maybe, maybe not. This is our dream and if we have the chance to expand now rather than later, we should at least look into it. That building would be enough space for us for years to come. And the traffic that area receives is ten times what we see here."

She waved at one of their regulars, then turned back to Justin. "You're right. We should at least look at the numbers."

"That's the spirit. I'll look into the building if

you want?"

"No," she all but shouted. "I can check it out."

He squinted at her, then snapped his fingers. "You've never been to Ms. Millán's store, have you? Which is sacrilege." He shook his head. "All right. You check out this new building, then check out her store. And that's not a request. Go into her store."

"I'll think about going into C and C. I haven't seen the other building but know what those buildings on that street could offer us. We could house the comics and competitions on the top floor and expand our children's sections."

"It would be awesome. I'll look up the listing later, so you can at least get a look at it, but it will give you a better feel seeing it in person."

"All right." She knocked three times on the countertop. "If you need any help with figuring out the authors, let me know."

"Will do, Chief." He saluted her.

At twelve-thirty, Ainslon walked out of the store with Justin and Sarah's lunch orders in hand. She enjoyed the crisp air and in no time stood in line for her food order.

Less than thirty minutes later, with her food bag in hand, she turned to head back when she caught sight of Lauren walking down the sidewalk in her direction. Her eyes traced every curve of Lauren's body. Beautiful didn't even begin to describe how good Lauren looked.

"Ainslon, hi," a small voice said from behind her.

Ainslon turned and took in Kat and Emma, Kat's girlfriend's daughter, both regulars to her store.

"Hi, guys. Don't you look pretty today, Emma. I love that dress."

"Thanks." Emma twirled. "Kat bought it for me."

"Well." Ainslon winked at Kat. "She has good taste." She turned her attention to Kat. In her mind, Kat's muscles, while impressive, didn't hold a candle to Lauren's slim frame. "What you ordered came in."

"That's great." Kat put her hands on Emma's shoulders and drew her back against her legs. "We'll swing by after lunch and pick them up."

"Sure thing." Ainslon knew a few months back that Kat and her girlfriend, Dylan, looked into buying one of the buildings on the same block as Turn the Page, but the deal fell through. Dylan, and Kat's sister-in-law, Leah, wanted to open a florist shop and Kat wanted an office in downtown Garriety for her tiny house business.

She didn't want to get Kat's hopes up, but she figured getting a feeler out wouldn't hurt. "Listen, Kat, I know your deal fell through with getting the building for a florist shop and office, but I might have a place for you in mind."

Kat perked up. "Really? Briley and I've looked everywhere for the size of building Dylan and Leah want and, so far, nothing."

"It's a big might, but..." She motioned for Kat and Emma to follow her to a more secluded spot on the sidewalk. "It's not a done deal and I don't know when things will work out, but Justin and I are looking at bigger buildings for our store and if that happens, we won't be able to keep our current store."

Kat ran her fingers through her hair. "Seriously?'

"Yep, but we're only in the talking stage and I wanted to give you a heads up. If you're interested—"

"Are you kidding? We're interested. If everything pans out for you, I would definitely be interested."

"It's a long shot for Justin and me, but fingers

crossed our plan works out."

"We'll have all of our fingers crossed as well. The size of the building would be exactly what Dylan and Leah are looking for."

"When I know, you'll know."

"Sounds good. We'll see you after lunch for our books."

"You ladies have a good lunch."

"You too," Emma called out as they walked away.

When Ainslon turned back around, Lauren was gone. Oh, well. Maybe next time. Ainslon took a deep breath, then pivoted and headed back to her store with a spring in her step.

Chapter Six

After grabbing lunch from the food truck, Lauren made her way back to C and C. The quick glance she got of Ainslon brightened her morning. She entered the store, then deposited Carrie's lunch on the counter. "Have Mark take over while you eat lunch."

"Yes, ma'am." Carrie saluted her.

Lauren looked at the semi-crowded room, then headed up the stairs to her office. After dropping her food on her desk, she walked to the interior window that overlooked the store's main floor. She'd been terrified when she first opened the store, but her family had a legacy and she wanted to be able to carry on the family business name. It ranked as one of the scariest endeavors in her life, but she'd pushed on with the support of family and friends and created something she was proud of. It didn't hurt that it was also lucrative.

It hadn't always been easy, but it had always been worth it. Seeing the look in her grandma's eyes when she saw the finished product would always hold a special place in her heart. Her grandpa had died seventeen years ago, and she wanted to make them both proud.

The family's heritage was extremely important to them and they'd passed that on to her. She could trace her line back to Jamestown around 1663, and San

Juan even further back.

Having the recognition of the town was nice, and it would be a lie if she denied enjoying the awards, but what she really loved was the expression on her customers faces when they walked around the store.

Everyone enjoyed candy or chocolate, or at least they should. Her family made sure she and Callie could speak fluent Spanish and it was one of the best decisions they could have made. She loved seeing the looks on her customers' faces when she spoke to them in their language. In college, she learned enough French and German to get by. One never knew when they would need it in a business setting. She was currently studying Mandarin, but it was harder than expected, but she would plow ahead. She might be a lot of things, but a quitter wasn't one of them.

The one thing she hadn't expected, and didn't enjoy, was the frenemies made along the way. No one had a problem with her opening a business, no; everyone had been supportive until her business flourished, then they turned jealous. She and the mayor still didn't get along after he tried to get her into bed and failed. She grew a thick skin after that and tried to avoid him at all costs. It didn't seem to matter to his wife that he was a lying, cheating bastard. She had a feeling he wouldn't be reelected. She sure as hell hadn't voted for him. For protection against anything he might try to pull, she kept the video surveillance from her store of the night he came in just as she was closing and made advances toward her.

A knock on the door grabbed her attention. "Yes."

Carrie poked her head around, a nervous look on her face that reflected in her voice. "Lauren, do you have a minute?"

"Of course." Carrie had turned nineteen last month and had worked for Lauren for close to two years. Her evaluation was coming up and, along with that, a raise. Lauren directed her to the chair in front of the desk. "What's on your mind?"

Carrie sucked in a deep breath. "Okay." She clutched the armrests of the chair, her knuckles turning white. "I love this job. I don't want to lose it."

The girl looked on the verge of tears. "Carrie, you've done nothing to warrant getting fired; in fact, you've exceeded my expectations. The customers love you, especially the children."

She shook her head. "You won't want me on the front line anymore."

"What is it?"

Carrie took a deep breath, then blurted out, "I'm pregnant."

Lauren started. That's not what she'd expected. She schooled her expression to neutral. "How does that make you feel?"

"Scared." Her eyes teared up. "It was stupid. I was stupid."

"If you're throwing out stupids you should also give one to your boyfriend."

Carrie chuckled. "We both were."

"Does he know?"

Carrie nodded. "I told him last night. He was surprised, but he wasn't angry. He vowed to take care of us both, but we're so young. I don't know if I can do this. I love this job, and you just helped me sign up for courses at the community college. I don't want to throw all our hard work away. Then there's my mom." She dabbed at her watery eyes. Lauren knew Carrie's mom was a strict Christian. "She's not going to like this. Larry's looking for an apartment for us now. He's working at the lumber mill, but they're getting ready to lay off and he was the newest hire. I don't know what we're going to do." She stood abruptly. "And here I am throwing all this on you. My boss. Oh, God." She headed toward the door.

Lauren caught up with her at the door, then guided her back to the couch and sat beside her. "Take a deep breath. Another. Good." She rubbed Carrie's back until she calmed down. "I'm going to ask you a few questions and all I need are yes or no answers. Can you do that?"

"Yes."

"Do you want to go to college?"

"Yes."

"Continue working here?"

"Yes."

"Do you want to move in with Larry?"

"Yes."

"Do you want to keep the baby?"

"Yes." She buried her head in her hands. "Oh, God."

Lauren wrapped an arm around Carrie's shoulders. Lauren was fond of the girl. From what she'd seen of Larry and from what Carrie had said, he was a good boyfriend and he loved her. "You don't have to worry about your job. I'm not going to fire you because you're pregnant, and if you want to keep working the front register, you can, but if you want to move to another position, we'll figure something out. As for an apartment. Let me talk to Ollie and see if she knows any budget apartments that are available. Also, your health insurance package covers your pregnancy. You're not alone, even if it feels that way."

"Why," Carrie hiccuped, "are you doing this for me?"

"Because I like you. And everyone, at some point in their lives, could use a hand. If Larry ends up being laid off, I can ask around and see if anyone I know is hiring. From what you've said, he's a hard worker."

"He is." She raised her head up and sniffled, accepting the tissues Lauren handed her. "He wants to be a pastry chef but doesn't have the time or the money. He was turned down for the two culinary grants he applied for."

That gave her a few ideas for Larry, but she wouldn't mention it to Carrie in case they didn't pan out. "First things first. Are you going to tell your mom right now?"

"No. She would flip out to know Larry and I are having sex."

"So, let me call Ollie and see what she says, then I'll ask around and see if anyone is hiring. Now," Lauren stood and pulled Carrie up, bringing her into a hug, then pushed her away to arm's length, "go get yourself cleaned up and think about whether there is another position that you'd be interested in."

"I like working with the customers, but I thought it would always be neat to work in the packing department."

"Are you sure?" It was a more demanding job than working the front register.

"Let me think on it. I know it's harder work than what I'm doing now."

"Take a few days and we'll see if we can't get everything rolling."

"You're the best, Lauren. You really are." Carrie gave her a smile before she walked out.

Poor kid. Lauren sat and picked up her phone. Ten minutes later, she hung up with Ollie and opened her laptop to get back to work. The quicker she finished, the quicker she could explore Noe's new creations.

Two hours later, she entered the kitchen. Noe stood next to their latest hire, watching as he demonstrated a technique using chocolate. When he finished, he joined Lauren.

"His work is coming along," Noe said.

"Good. Show me what you've been working on." Noe moved them to a long counter set in the center of the room and indicated several chocolates. "When will they be ready for the store?" She bit into a chocolate and coconut concoction she'd asked him to prefect. "Delicious."

"Another week or so. I've almost got the menu for the food festival finalized. I know you wanted plenty of coconut options and I've added a guava filled chocolate and polvo de amor."

She smiled at his pronunciation of the words. From time to time, his French accent made it difficult for his words to translate through. As it did this time. "That's a good idea. Might give the lovers in the crowd a bit of a boost." Polvo de amor, or love powder, was made from grated coconut meat, mixed with sugar, then placed in a kettle to cook rapidly. It was served crisp and golden.

"I plan on serving it alone or as a topping on the chocolate custard I'm making."

She only planned to sell candies and chocolates at the event, but Noe made it clear that they needed to get a read on how well desserts they offered would sell.

"I have complete faith in you." She plucked up a couple more chocolates from the counter on the way out of the kitchen and popped one in her mouth. As she walked into the store, she stopped, spotting a familiar face.

Briley, one of her most frequent customers, and her daughter, Griffin, were browsing the jellied candy section. Griffin never failed to lift Lauren's spirits, even if they didn't need lifting. She handed Carrie the other chocolate, then headed in Briley's direction.

"See anything you like?"

"Lauri." Griffin squealed, then held up her arms for Lauren to pick her up. Lauren usually only allowed her sister to call her that but made an exception for Griffin. Children would always be her weakness.

Lauren picked the eager child up. "Hello, Reinita." Griffin giggled at the nickname, meaning little queen. "Briley, what brings you two by today?" They last came in the store a couple of days ago.

Briley groaned. "Evan and his friends ate all of my chocolate and Griffin wanted to tag along. And I promised Leah I would bring her back some spicy chocolates."

"Follow me." She carried Griffin securely in her arms until they entered the chocolate section, where she handed her to Briley. Lauren walked behind the counter and picked up a pair of tongs. She normally didn't wait on the customers, but Briley was one of her best. "How many and what kinds did Leah want?" Leah usually didn't come in with Briley, but the one time she did meet the other woman, she knew exactly what drew Briley to her. The significant age between the two women gave her pause, but their love was evident and the last thing she would ever do was judge such a successful relationship.

"Give me a dozen of the dark chocolate and a

dozen of the other mixed spicy chocolates." Lauren picked and filled a medium sized box, then put it aside. "Give me a dozen of your fruit filled ones, and two pounds of your mixed nut chocolates." Briley turned her attention to her daughter. "Griff, do you want something?" Griffin made grabby motions at the milk, dark, and white chocolate shaped animal ones. "Give us half a pound of those."

Lauren had been unsure about the plain shaped zoo animals, but they were a huge hit with the children. "Anything else?" she asked, handing a grinning Griffin a giraffe shaped piece.

"I need to put in a custom order for my normal amount of assorted chocolate dipped fruit for our house opening next Thursday. It's been a good year so far. We're on track to flip a half dozen more houses before December."

"That's wonderful." Lauren grabbed the pen and pad and waved George off. Every time Briley had a house opening, she would order from them.

"Dark, milk, and white chocolate. Strawberries, oranges, bananas, pineapple, and cherries. You choose what combination of chocolate and fruit works best."

"No blueberries this time?"

Briley looked sheepish. "No, the last time I ate them all."

Lauren chuckled as she calculated Briley's total with her business discount. Briley tried to object when Lauren included the business discount to her regular order, but Lauren insisted. "You're one of my best customers."

"All right," Briley conceded, then set Griffin down. She watched as Griffin ran to the corner of the room housing the chocolate lollipops and stared up at the display. Briley leaned closer to the counter and said softly, "Leah and Evan will be in next week to order things for Griff's birthday. I'm not sure what they're after but be forewarned, I believe they're going all out."

"I can't wait." Lauren handed over Briley's bag and kept her eyes glued to them until they were out of sight.

"She's a pistol, that one," George said. Apparently, he'd watched the transaction.

"Griffin is a sweetie."

"I'm talking about Briley."

Lauren chuckled. "Yes, her too." She made her way to her office, then slumped into her desk chair. Seeing Briley with her daughter made her remember when she'd come out to her parents. They hadn't taken the news as well as she'd hoped, but they'd quickly educated themselves and were, along with her sister, her number one supporters. However, her mother had made it clear that being a lesbian didn't mean she couldn't give her grandkids. When younger, Lauren had argued that her focus needed to be on business, and in the last few years that she was too old, but her mom had insisted she wasn't.

Days like today, or when she spent time with Ollie's children, or her nephew, made her want children, but when she was at home, curled up on the couch with a glass of wine and watching true crime documentaries, she wasn't sure about wanting her own. For now, she would continue to shower her nieces and nephews with all her attention and not worry about children of her own yet.

Chapter Seven

On Friday morning, Ainslon ventured across town to check out the building for sale. She kept her eyes averted from the colorful sign that hung above Lauren's store. For the moment, she needed to stay on track. *Stay focused.* She took a few up-close photos of the building, stepped back to take in the full effect, and snapped a few more. Easily four times the size of their store, Ainslon couldn't help but be impressed. The mix of wood and red brick lining the outside made the exterior pop.

The front of the building consisted of six large windows, in contrast to the top floor that only had three. The building sat on a corner lot and had a side entrance with a staircase leading to the second floor. That would be perfect for game nights. They could close the first floor and concentrate on the gamers. It would be an amazing purchase, but even with their current profits, she didn't know if it would be possible. First, they needed to call the owner and inquire about their stipulations since it seemed they were being difficult to deal with.

Instead of fighting the draw of the store next door, she turned toward it and glanced up at the large C and C sign. The larger purple swirling Cs on a gray with black background instantly drew her eyes. She walked a few feet to her left and took in the colorfully decorated windows. If she had to describe them, she would settle on whimsical. It was a bad idea to stay here and gawk. While her exhaustive internet search of Lauren gave some information, it couldn't tell her all she wanted to know. Good grief, she only met her once. How could a simple infatuation get out of hand so quickly? Maybe she should go back to the bookstore. She had the information she came for.

She adjusted her backpack straps, glanced through the window one last time, and turned away from the store, only to run straight into Lauren. Ainslon clung to Lauren's forearms to keep them both from falling. When she realized where her hands were, she jerked them back.

"Are you all right?" Lauren asked, holding her hands out, ready to catch Ainslon if she slipped.

Lauren looked even better than the first few times Ainslon had seen her. She wore those damned tailored pants again, today in black, and a light gray long-sleeve t-shirt. The material felt as soft as it looked. Today, Lauren wore her hair pinned up in a clip.

Ainslon pushed her hands into the pockets of her jeans. Lauren studied her with, what she deemed, concern and caution. "I'm fine." She waved a hand in the air. "I should be asking you if you're all right. I ran into you." She flashed what she hoped was a sincere smile.

"I'm all right." Lauren took a step back. "Are you coming in or going to look through the window?" She arched her brow.

Ainslon wanted to kick herself. She should have never come here. Seeing Lauren in front of her, in the flesh, only solidified her crush even more. Not to mention, she'd been on her mind since their first meeting. "Sure. I mean. I was going in."

Lauren smiled and opened the door to allow her in. Ainslon walked through and stepped to the right before she stopped in awe at her first look around. Why hadn't she been to the store before? The place was amazing and the smell, divine.

The hardwood floor was stained in numerous shades of purple, yellow, and green. Dozens of large-scale replicas of famous candies hung from the ceiling and hundreds of different types of candy adorned the walls. A dozen rainbow colored candy dispensers were built into the opposite wall. Hanging above the wall, behind the counter, were two different characters; a lollipop and a chocolate bar, wearing matching plaid coveralls. From all her research, the two characters had been associated with the store since it opened. Even the kids running around didn't deter from the overall atmosphere. The smell alone would invade her dreams. She was utterly charmed. "Wow!"

Lauren came to stand in front of her. "Have you ever been here before?"

"No, but now I wish I had. This place is amazing! No wonder Justin loves it so much."

"Would you like a tour?"

"I would love one." The words slipped out before she had time to think about them.

Lauren grinned, walked to the corner of the room, and motioned with her hand around them. "The building is divided into several different areas. This one deals mostly in candy, the other one in chocolate, and we have a kitchen in the back. My office, storage, and packing are located on the second floor. If the candy or chocolate has our logo on it, we make it in house. We pride ourselves on everything we offer. If we don't have it, we will find a way to make it, or order it. My mother helped me decorate this room. She's a colorful character and I let her have free rein."

Ainslon touched the nearest package of cherry hard candies. "Who designed the characters?"

Lauren slipped the package off the hook. "I did. Choco and Lollie. My nephew helped me name them. This entire endeavor has taken me by surprise. I never, in my wildest dreams, thought that people would take to it like they have. I am floored by all the awards we have received from the city."

"That's how I felt when the online bookstore took off. When Justin and I decided to open a physical store, it was scary, but we've been open almost three years and so far, so good. One of the biggest draws for us is the readings we have twice a month. We offer snacks for the kids and encourage them to dress up according to that night's theme." She smiled, thinking about the last one where all the kids dressed up as their favorite Winnie the Pooh character. She turned to Lauren, expecting to see boredom written across her face, but all she saw was interest.

Lauren turned her gaze back to the store. "We also offer all kinds of different parties; receptions, birthdays, baby showers, or whatever a client wants. I don't have children, but our clients seem to enjoy the parties we throw for them. Do you have children, Ainslon?"

Ainslon almost forgot to breathe when Lauren said her name. "I don't have human kids, but I do have a cat, Shady McQuinn."

Lauren nodded. "I lost my lab, Mickey, last year. He was twelve." She motioned with her head toward the back. "Follow me." They walked through several aisles and Ainslon tried to avert her eyes from the trousers hugging Lauren's ass, but failed miserably. As she raised her eyes, the woman working behind the cash register busted her. Her name tag read Carrie.

"Ms. Millán, good afternoon," Carrie said.

"You as well, Carrie." She walked over to a picture that hung on the wall, Ainslon following. In it, Lauren knelt on the ground and had one arm around a black lab; a pair of Aviators hid Lauren's eyes. The smile on her face was breathtaking. Whoever was taking the picture was lucky to have that smile directed at them. "That's my Mickey."

"He looks like Oisín, my Nana's dog. He died five years ago."

"It's hard when we lose them, but the time we spend with them well makes up for the pain when they are taken from us." Lauren motioned with her hand to another room and winked. "Let's check out the chocolate room."

Ainslon's head screamed at her to decline and get the hell out, but her feet seemed to have a mind of their own. As soon as they entered the room, the chocolate aroma hit her full force and she groaned.

Lauren laughed. "Would you like a sample?"

"Yes, I would." She held Lauren's eyes and sucked in a breath when she took a step in her direction. Did she miss something? They were talking about chocolate, weren't they?

"Do you have a preference?"

Ainslon wanted to scream, "you," but clamped her mouth shut. She didn't trust herself to speak so she shook her head.

Lauren stepped around her and behind the counter. "The filled chocolates are my favorite. There is no better feeling than when you bite into the chocolate and the burst of flavor erupts on your tongue."

Ainslon shivered and nodded. What was wrong with her? She stepped up to the counter and surveyed the assortment, trying to get her bearings. Chocolates of all shapes and sizes, filled with everything from chocolate to apricots took up an entire level. Her eyes landed on an assortment in the middle row, the fruit filled ones. "I would like to try a fruit filled one." Somehow her voice came out sounding normal. At least she hoped it did. At this point she didn't know what the hell she was doing.

"What kind?"

Ainslon grinned. "Surprise me."

"Turn around."

"What?" She blinked.

"Turn around if you want me to surprise you." Ainslon did as instructed. A moment later, Lauren stood in front of her. "Close your eyes," Lauren said softly.

Ainslon followed Lauren's instruction.

"Open your mouth," Lauren said.

Ainslon thought she was going to die when Lauren placed the chocolate in her mouth. The thought did enter her mind to bite down on Lauren's finger, but she refrained. When she opened her eyes, Lauren had a coy smile on her lips.

The taste of chocolate melting on her tongue was exquisite, but when she bit into the morsel, the burst of raspberry filling was almost orgasmic. The sweetness and tartness balanced with the milk chocolate and dash of sea salt was an amazing experience.

"Wow!" She wasn't sure if it was the chocolate or the smiling woman standing in front of her that elicited such a response.

"That's the second time you've said that." Lauren grinned and motioned them both away from the counter. "I take it you like it here."

"You have no idea." Ainslon turned to their left when a woman walked up next to them and slipped her arm through Lauren's. Lauren melted against the woman's side with a touch of familiarity and the brilliant smile she displayed transformed her.

Ainslon thought the woman looked familiar. Perhaps she was one of the women in Lauren's family pictures she'd viewed in her Google search.

Ainslon cleared her throat. "Lauren, thank you for the tour, but I should be getting back. I told Justin I would pick up lunch. He's probably wondering where I am."

"Lauri," the woman said. "I didn't mean to interrupt. I only need a minute, then you can get back to your friend." She looked from Ainslon to Lauren.

"Ainslon, this is my sister, Callie. Callie, Ainslon."

Ainslon held her hand out to Callie. "It's nice to meet you."

"You as well." Callie squeezed her hand.

As soon as Callie released her hand, she took a step back and regarded Lauren. "I do need to be getting back. You brightened my morning, Lauren. Thank you for the tour. I enjoyed myself immensely."

"Ainslon," Lauren said, shaking off Callie and taking a step toward her. "She only needs a minute. Are you sure you have to go? I can show you the kitchen and we can sample some of the new chocolates."

"As tempting as that is, I can't." Ainslon hated seeing the disappointment on Lauren's face, but she couldn't stay. "I really do have to go. Today is my day to grab lunch, and Justin and Sarah will be wondering where I am. I'll take a raincheck on the rest of the tour."

"That can be arranged. Let me walk you out."

At the entrance door, Ainslon turned to Lauren. "Thank you again."

"It was my pleasure. You're welcome any time."

"I'll keep that in mind." She would definitely be back.

Chapter Eight

So. Who is Ainslon? I can't recall ever hearing that name before," Callie asked after she dragged Lauren back to her office and shut the door.

Lauren loved her sister, but at times she could be trying. They'd been mistaken for a couple a few times and she'd wanted to make sure Ainslon hadn't come to the same conclusions. While she and Callie both had their papa's brown eyes, Lauren's complexion and hair were dark like his, but Callie took after their mother with a lighter complexion.

"Who is she?" Callie asked again.

"She owns a bookstore and is looking for Colin's birthday present." Lauren paced in front of the window, disappointed that Ainslon had left so abruptly. It took all her restraint not to kiss her instead of giving her the chocolate.

"And?"

Lauren watched the customers down below. "Honestly, there's nothing to tell. This is only the second time we've met."

"But you want more. Come on." Callie grabbed Lauren's hand and dragged her down onto the loveseat beside her. "I could feel the fireworks coming off you two. *Boom!*" She made an explosion motion with her hands. "Tell me."

Lauren groaned. "I don't have time for this. I have to work, and you still haven't told me why you came by.”

“You can give me a few minutes. You were going to show her the kitchen and you know how much Noe hates to have visitors sprung on him, and the reason I came by isn’t as important as this.”

She knew she wouldn’t be getting out of this without giving her sister something. “Yes, I like her, but she’s doing a job for me right now. That’s it. There really isn’t anything to tell.”

“From where I was standing, she’s interested in you too.”

Lauren lay her head back. “She’s gorgeous and awkward, and I would really like to get to know her better. I wished she hadn’t left.”

“She needed to get back to work.” Callie pushed on Lauren’s shoulder. “Go on.”

“Her accent sends chills through me. I don’t know what a relationship with her would look like, but I would at least like to have dinner with her.” Admitting it aloud felt good. She and Callie had their differences growing up, but after she graduated college, they’d reconnected, and she couldn’t have a better sister or friend.

“That’s more like it. I can tell you’re taken with her. I haven’t seen you look this way since Gabby.”

“Yes, it’s taken me by surprise. I don’t even know her, and Google was no help. She really doesn’t have an online presence.”

Callie blinked in surprise. “Cyber stalking, are we now? You must really like her. Tell you what. Tonight, we’re going out.” Callie cut off Lauren’s protests. “We are. I’ll pick you up at nine-thirty for drinks.”

“Nine-thirty. Couldn’t we go earlier?” She was usually in bed by eleven.

"No. You're too much of a homebody as it is. Dress nice."

She didn't want to go out but knew she couldn't deter Callie.

By the time nine-thirty rolled around, Lauren was, by no means, ready to go drinking. But she'd dressed nice, per Callie's instructions.

She paired skinny jeans with a short black jacket, white sleeveless blouse, and her favorite pair of black Louboutin's. She kept her hair down. She always thought her eyes were her best feature but received the most compliments on her smile.

A text from Callie alerted her she'd pulled up outside. Lauren slipped her license and credit card into the front pocket of her jeans, along with the spare key to her condo. She had no intention of getting drunk, or any intention of losing her purse. That had happened once and she vowed it would never happen again.

She snatched her phone from the kitchen table, locked the door behind her, and walked to the elevator. The ride down was quick, and she waved at the night guard, Bruce, as she stepped out onto the busy street. She'd bought the condo eight years ago, when this part of town was still growing, for a little under six hundred thousand.

A few months ago, Ollie had tried to get her to sell because the market had boomed, encouraging her to find a place closer to her store. Ollie tried tempting her with the price of close to four million, but she loved the condo and had no plans to sell it. At least, not at this point in her life.

She climbed into Callie's car and buckled in.

"At least it's not workwear."

Lauren rolled her eyes. "Where are we going?"

"NightCrawlers."

She should have known since it was Callie's go-to bar. It was in the top three of the most popular bars in the city. Every other Saturday, they had live music, and a signature drink on the weekends. She hadn't been there in a few weeks and the closer they got, the more her excitement grew. Maybe this is what she needed.

Once inside, they were escorted to a table for two and their drink order quickly taken. Lauren slipped off her jacket and Callie whistled.

"See, that's what I'm talking about. The ladies and gentlemen will be all over you. Just send the men my way."

"You're married."

"I'm joking. I can admire a fine-looking man, but Jeffrey knows he has my heart."

Callie and Jeffrey, married for close to twenty years, had a fifteen-year-old son named Charlie.

"I'm surprised Jeff didn't come with you tonight." Lauren took a sip of her apple martini, letting the flavors dance on her tongue. Tonight, she was starting off with a martini before moving on to the craft beer on special that night. Tonight's choice, the Blushing Cowboy, was a salty, sour German beer made with coriander and strawberry. She couldn't wait to try it.

"He declared it a father and son bonding night. They've been playing classic Mario for hours and were expecting pizza when I left to pick you up."

"That sounds like fun."

"I know, but we needed some time together." Callie reached across the table and enfolded Lauren's hand. "I've missed spending time with you."

"I've missed spending time with you also." The

moment she looked away from Callie, her eyes locked with Ainslon's, whose eyes were locked on hers. She was seated with three other people, a man and two women. "Mierda."

"What's wrong?"

"Ainslon's here. Why is it that I keep running into her?" Lauren gulped down half of her drink.

"Slow down, tiger." Callie turned toward Ainslon, then back to Lauren. "Go say something to her."

"You can't be serious. She practically ran from my store today. I'm sure the last thing she wants is to see me and she's with people. Maybe one of them is her date."

"Not likely, the gentleman has his arm around one of the other women, so that's probably his date. The other woman looks familiar." She squinted, then snapped her fingers. "She works at Brew and Bake."

"So, you don't know if they're dating?"

"No, but it won't hurt to say hello."

"I don't know." Lauren finished her drink, then ordered a Blushing Cowboy, fried mushrooms, and pulled pork sliders. She might as well drown her sorrows in good booze and food.

"They're just now getting their appetizers. You have time."

An hour and twenty minutes, two beers, and two appetizers later, Lauren still hadn't worked up the nerve to approach Ainslon.

"Go on, Lauri, I have faith in you."

She knew Callie was goading her, and it was working. "You're right." She took a deep breath, made to stand, but sat back down when Ainslon and another woman moved to the dance floor. The other woman looked familiar, but Lauren couldn't place her.

Ainslon laughed as the woman dipped her, then spun her around the dance floor. Great. Just great.

"So," Callie said, throwing a twenty on the table. "How about we get you home? I've only had one drink since we arrived." She slipped her arm through Lauren's. "You're obviously not ready and that's fine. I'm sorry for pushing you."

"It's all right. I know you meant well, and I am tired."

"We do have to get up early for the farmers market tomorrow."

"I can't wait."

Callie rolled her eyes and escorted her toward the door. On the way, they passed by Ainslon and the woman. Ainslon smiled at her but quickly turned her attention back to her dance partner.

For some reason, Ainslon had made a deep impression on her. Now she had to get her body to catch up with her mind. The last thing she wanted to do was to rush into anything, but she also didn't want to miss her chance. Hopefully, tomorrow she could come up with some sort of game plan.

※ ※ ※ ※

Ainslon let Alice, a barista at Brew and Bake, steer her around the dance floor. After the dance, they made their way back to their table. Ainslon flopped into the booth as Easton left the table to dance with Alice.

She couldn't get the sight of Lauren out of her mind and knew tonight her dreams would feature Lauren in that top. She accepted the beer Justin handed her.

"So, that's Lauren," Brandy said. She and Justin had been dating for a little over eight months and they seemed to make a good match. Ainslon had never seen him so happy.

"It was."

"Do you know who the woman is that was with her?" Justin asked.

"Her sister. Lauren introduced us when I was at her store." She took a sip of her beer. The Blushing Cowboy was amazing, and she would be ordering it again when it was offered.

"She's beautiful," Brandy said. "You should have asked her to dance."

"I'm with Brandy on this one," Justin said. "All she could do is say no."

"No, she could have also called off our business dealings. In case you've forgotten, I am doing a job for her."

"I haven't forgotten, and from what you've told me about her, she doesn't strike me as the type to do something like that." Justin finished his beer, stood, and held out his hand for Brandy. "Dance with me."

Once Justin and Brandy left to dance, Ainslon buried her face in her hands. She kept her eyes closed even as she heard a body plop down in the seat across from her.

"You look troubled," Easton said.

She looked up and into Easton's eyes. "I don't know what's wrong with me."

Easton rested her elbows on the table. "Yes, you do. You like her. Just let it ride. What happens will happen. This is what? The fourth time you've seen her in the last few weeks. You're bound to run into her again."

"I know, and that's what scares me."

"Don't be scared." Easton stood and held out her hand. "What you need is to dance out your insecurities."

It always helped when they were teenagers, so why not now. Ainslon finished her beer and stood, slipping her hand into Easton's. "Let's do this."

Chapter Nine

Bright and early Saturday morning, Ainslon arrived at Edna's house. Twice a month, they visited the farmers market and Ainslon would never miss it.

She'd made it home relatively early the night before but had tossed and turned for a good hour, thinking about Lauren. She tended to overthink things but couldn't help it. Her nana always said overthinking would be her downfall.

The farmers market first, then her thoughts could stray to Lauren later.

Before she could even get out of the car, Edna was walking down the steps. Ainslon jumped out, kissed her on the cheek, and opened the passenger side door for her.

"Stop staring at me, dear. I'm not dead yet."

"Nana." She groaned. "I wish you wouldn't say things like that."

"It's no secret I'm old."

"I know." After fifteen minutes of driving, Ainslon flicked her blinker and pulled into the semi-full parking lot. After shutting off the engine, she unclipped her seat belt, climbed out, then opened the passenger door. "Ready to get started?"

"I'm ready to shop, if you're ready to carry my things."

Ainslon reached behind the passenger seat,

grabbed the two tote bags she kept stashed there, slipped one on her shoulder, then handed the other to Edna. Ainslon rolled her eyes at the look Edna gave the bags.

"Don't worry. I'll carry them both when they're full. Like always."

Edna slipped her arm through Ainslon's and they walked from one end of the market to the other. Edna liked to check out all the vendors' offerings before she made her final decisions, even though she always bought from the same vendors.

On the way back to the front of the market, Ainslon's eyes widened when she spotted Lauren and Callie ahead of them. She wanted to play off what had happened, but Edna was way too perceptive.

"Who's that?" Edna gestured toward the women.

"Nana, no," Ainslon warned.

"Tell me." Edna narrowed her eyes at the two women, then her face lit up.

Ainslon knew honesty was her only way out of this. "The one in the jeans and white t-shirt is Lauren."

Edna arched her brow. A smile played on her lips. "Your Lauren?"

"Well, not my Lauren, but the Lauren I'm finding the book for."

"Yes, dear." Edna patted her arm. "Your Lauren."

Ainslon knew when not to argue. "Yes."

"Let's go."

"Nana, no."

But it was too late. Edna whirled around faster than a woman her age should be able to. "Now you listen to me, young lady. I didn't raise you to be a coward. We are going up to them and you are going to introduce me."

"I...I...fine." She huffed, knowing arguing with Edna would be a losing battle. As their steps took them closer to their goal, her heart beat double time, and her legs felt weighed down by lead. Edna didn't seem to have that problem and dragged her along. She thought about fleeing, but at that exact moment Lauren turned, looked at her, and smiled.

"Ainslon." Her smile lit up her face and didn't fail to cause Ainslon's heart to pound. She was sure the other women could hear it.

When words weren't forthcoming, Edna pinched her. "Lauren." Another pinch. "This is my nana."

"Edna, dear." Edna extended her hand toward Lauren.

Lauren stepped forward and accepted her hand. "Edna, it's so nice to meet you."

"Well, aren't you sweet? Like you were dipped in honey and rolled in sugar." Ainslon groaned and Lauren chuckled, but Ainslon could have sworn she saw a twinge of pink blossom on Lauren's cheeks. "You're much more attractive in person than in the pictures they print in the paper."

Ainslon could feel her face heat up, but Lauren only grinned and winked. "That's what I've been saying for years."

Edna gave a nod toward the woman beside Lauren. "Introduce me to your friend."

Lauren slipped her arm around the woman's waist and pulled her into her side. "This is my sister, Callie."

"Edna, it's nice to meet you," Callie said, then offered her hand to Ainslon. "Nice to see you again, Ainslon."

Ainslon shook Callie's hand. "Same here." Then

stuffed her hands in the pockets of her jeans, trying not to fidget.

"Isn't this nice?" Edna clapped her hands together, then pulled Callie away from Lauren and slipped a hand through her arm. "Why don't you show me around? I have this big tote bag to fill up."

Callie looked between Lauren and Ainslon, then shared a look with her sister, before nodding. "Let's go. This is one of my favorite places to visit."

"Wait." Ainslon reached for Edna's arm. "What are you doing?"

"Shopping. Isn't that what you do at these types of things...or am I mistaken in my old age?"

Ainslon looked upward and groaned. "Nana."

"I have the phone you bought me. I'll be fine and if this nice woman does happen to kill me and stuff my body someplace, I am sure Kelly would still be able to make me look acceptable at my viewing."

Ainslon threw her hands up. "Oh, dear God, Nana." Kelly was the funeral director hired to take care of Edna's funeral plans.

"Okay. Okay. We're going," Callie said, pulling a smirking Edna away.

Ainslon stood rooted to the spot as Edna and Callie got farther and farther away. She let out a relieved breath and turned back around. "I'm sorry about that. When she gets something in her head..." She let the words hang in the air.

"Exactly what are you sorry for? The fact that Edna claimed my sister, or the fact that you are standing here with me?"

"I...I...guess neither. The fact is, Nana can be—" She waved her hand in the air and Lauren chuckled.

"She seems wonderful. They'll get along great."

"Probably, but she ambushed your morning." The awkwardness she expected never materialized. Fuck. Lauren was so easy to be around.

"Nonsense. Now, I'll spend it shopping with you."

The flutter in Ainslon's stomach, when she first spotted Lauren, turned into a free for all. "Lead the way."

They had only taken a few steps when Lauren spoke. "Do you come here often?" Ainslon's steps faltered and she fought the urge to laugh, but that didn't stop Lauren from chuckling.

Ainslon decided to cut her some slack. "We come twice a month. Nana likes to look around and it gives her a good bit of exercise and we get to spend time together. A win-win for everyone."

"Yes, a win."

Score one for Ainslon.

"Are you looking for something particular today?" Lauren asked. "I usually shop at the market near my condo, but Callie always drags me along with her." She smiled. "It usually takes me a while to find something I need, but not this morning." Lauren gave her a knowing look.

"Is that so?" Lauren nodded. Okay, so Lauren was interested. Score two for Ainslon. "I was planning on picking up some potatoes and sweet potatoes," Ainslon said. "Maybe a couple of acorn squash. Besides that, who knows. I'm not a make a list kind of girl."

After Ainslon had purchased her potatoes, Lauren directed her to an empty picnic table, and they sat down across from each other. "Is the vintage book scene competitive?"

Ainslon laughed. "Yes. Especially with children's books. Most don't survive well and those that do are few and far between. Of course, books in the condition that you want sell well, but those aren't the only books I sell. Not everyone can afford a first edition vintage book, in pristine condition. But buyers that can't afford them are usually happy with what they can find within their budget."

"Do you get a lot of competition from eBay or other online auction sites?"

"I don't attract those buyers. The people that come to me want to know that I am actively looking for what they want. That I will take the time to make sure the book is in the condition that they want, and they want to inspect the book before they buy it. It's true we started off online, but I would Skype with my customers and show them the book they wanted. They got to see firsthand what the book looked like. In this business, once you've earned someone's trust, you're golden, but if you ever lose that trust, your reputation could be destroyed. I have never bought a book off eBay for a customer, but if I've seen a book that might meet the criteria, and a business and not an individual is selling it, I'll contact them outside of eBay and try and set something up."

Lauren looked astonished. "It's cutthroat?"

"Last year in Washington State, I can't remember the name of the town, a local historian killed an elderly man for his first edition, first printed copy of Gone with the Wind."

Lauren faltered. "That's…Are you serious?"

"The book was in amazing shape. The dust jacket only had a minor tear on the bottom right edge. I don't think anyone ever opened the book. I wouldn't have killed for it, but I would have been tempted."

"Oh my. That tempting?"

"Us book people are pretty serious about our trade."

The look of interest on Lauren's face charmed Ainslon. "What happened to the book?"

Ainslon frowned. "The police confiscated it, and by the time it was handed back over to the rightful owners, it wasn't in pristine condition anymore. Where it once would have sold for up to ten thousand dollars, they would have been lucky to get five for it."

"Really, that much of a difference?"

"The dust jacket was torn in several places and the spine of the book was broken. That plays a huge part in the selling price. Thankfully with children's books, a lot of them didn't have dust jackets. How about your world, is it competitive?"

"It can be. Especially if you're trying to branch out. It's taken me almost two years to convince a small Swiss chocolate company to sell to me. I've also made a few frenemies in town because my business has done so well."

"Now, that I understand. People that are nice to your face but behind your back hope for you to fail."

"Garriety is an amazing place to live, but the business world can be trying at times."

"That's for sure."

The two stared at each other, neither saying a word, until Lauren's cheeks flushed, and she dropped her gaze, then abruptly stood. "The vendor across the way is selling acorn squash."

Ainslon smiled and followed beside her. Seeing Lauren so flustered was a turn on. It was nice to know there was a little insecurity behind her flawless looks.

When Lauren touched her arm to lead her toward the vendor, Ainslon could only nod, because of the tingles Lauren's fingers sent throughout her body. Her touch only lingered for a moment, but she felt it all the way to her toes.

"So." Lauren rubbed her hands together. "I come here a lot and know for a fact," she gestured off to the left, "right through there is the best face painter in all of Garriety."

Goodness. Ainslon did love a playful woman. "The best, huh?"

"The best."

Ainslon slipped her arm through hers. "Then what are we waiting for?"

Twenty minutes later, Ainslon lifted her phone and snapped a picture of a grinning Lauren. A purple and blue butterfly adorned her right cheek. Ainslon had opted for a black cat on hers.

Lauren directed her toward the artist's mirror. "I think we look awesome."

Ainslon smiled. "I think you're right." She stepped to the side when a couple and their kids walked up. "No text from Nana, so what's next?"

"How about a picture together to show off our ink?" Lauren held up her phone. Ainslon nodded, then held her breath when Lauren slipped her arm around her waist and brought their faces together. It took all her restraint not to turn her head and kiss Lauren on the cheek. After the picture was taken, Lauren squeezed her side, then pulled away. "How about you lead the way to our next destination?"

Ainslon brushed her hands down her pants. "I'm good at leading."

"I kind of had a feeling you would be."

Ainslon was sure the smile on her face would become permanent as much as she used it. In no time, they both had a small bowl of ice cream in hand and were standing side by side, people watching. Ainslon thought they fit together perfectly. Ainslon slipped her spoon in her mouth and savored the rich vanilla taste. Where she had opted for vanilla with a caramel drizzle, Lauren had chosen something as exotic as herself, coffee ice cream with a dark chocolate drizzle and chopped hazelnuts. She would remember that.

"So, where to next?" Lauren asked.

Ainslon was about to answer when she spotted Edna and Callie headed in their direction, Edna's ice cream cone firmly in hand. She got one every time they visited the market. She was a bit disappointed their time together would be ending but even from the distance between them she could tell Edna was tired. Although she'd enjoyed her time with Lauren, she would never jeopardize her nana's health for it.

Lauren huffed beside her. "Callie told me this morning she wouldn't be caught dead eating an ice cream cone here."

Ainslon knocked their shoulders together. "My nana has an uncanny ability to get people to do things they wouldn't normally do. She's a manipulative old bird." She gave Lauren a sly smile. "Besides, we got our ice cream."

Lauren nodded her agreement. "You bet we did." She placed her hand at the small of Ainslon's back. "Let's not keep them waiting. I can tell Edna's tired from here."

Ainslon's heart warmed at her words, but the smile on Edna's face meant trouble.

"Nana, I see you've done some shopping." The tote Callie carried looked about half full.

"We had a great time. Learned a bit about each

other." The sparkle in her eyes put Ainslon on edge.

"That's nice," she answered.

"I thought you didn't want ice cream?" Lauren accused her sister.

"I changed my mind," Callie said, then quickly changed the subject. "I see you've done a bit of getting around." She stared at Lauren's cheek.

"We did," Lauren said.

"You only live once, dear, is what I say," Edna said. "Why hold back on what you really want, when it's right in front of you."

Ainslon bit her lip, but kept her mouth shut.

"Now, I want a few of those zucchinis, then we need to go home," Edna said. "Mildred is coming over for a late lunch today." She walked off, leaving the three of them alone. Ainslon accepted the bag when Callie handed it over.

"It was nice to see you again, Ainslon. Edna spoke highly of you."

"Thank you, but she's biased."

Callie patted Lauren on the hand. "I'll meet you at the car."

Lauren fondled her necklace and smiled shyly. "I had a nice time this morning."

"So did I." Ainslon nervously gnawed her bottom lip for a second. Then thought, *what the hell* as she leaned forward and kissed Lauren's cheek. She took a step back.

"Well." Lauren grinned. "I'll see you around."

Ainslon returned the grin. "You will."

Lauren tilted her head, then did a slow appraisal of Ainslon from head to toe. "My book notwithstanding, I look forward to it."

Ainslon sputtered but Lauren only grinned and

bid her a goodbye before walking off. Ainslon took a moment to get her bearings before joining Edna. "Ready?" she asked as she accepted the zucchini and slipped them into her bag.

"Yes." A few moments later Edna spoke up. "I like that Lauren put that smile on your face." Ainslon breamed and knew she would sleep well that night, having her nana's seal of approval. Besides Easton, Edna's was the only opinion that mattered.

⁂

Lauren did a quick spin when she was out of Ainslon's line of sight and pumped her fist in the air. A teenager held up his hand and she high-fived him as she passed by. The boring day she'd expected with Callie turned out amazing. Ainslon was exactly what she was looking for. Beautiful, smart, sexy, and a dash of awkward.

The grin wouldn't even leave her face if she wanted it to. As she approached her, Callie lifted her phone and took a picture.

"What was that for?" Lauren asked.

Callie smiled softly. "I want you to always remember the moment you started falling for her."

Lauren came to a complete stop. "Don't be silly."

"Let it happen naturally. There is no rush. It's clear she likes you." She gripped Lauren's shoulder. "Being happy looks amazing on you."

"Really?"

"You bet." Callie kissed her unpainted cheek.

"For once, I'm going to heed your advice. I won't fight it but I'm not going to push it either." The last thing she wanted was to make Ainslon nervous or scared.

"I don't think you're going to have to push it. I have a feeling everything is going to fall into place."

"Be that as it may, I'm going to let Ainslon set the pace. I have this feeling. I know she likes me, but…"

"I agree."

Callie tossed her keys in the air and Lauren caught them. "You're driving." Callie stopped with her hand on the door. "What time do you have to pick Colin up for tonight?"

Tonight was the official opening of the astronomy section of the Garriety Science Center and she'd promised to accompany him. It had been in the works for two years, and Lauren was just as excited as Colin to see it completed. It was set to open a year ago but was delayed because of funding. "Ollie's bringing him by at five, then she, Ralph, and Heidi are going to the Eatery." The Eatery, a family friendly buffet style restaurant, served everything from chicken wings to ceviche.

"Have fun."

"I plan on it."

Chapter Ten

Ainslon glanced in the mirror later that night and smoothed out the sides of her black, knee length, sleeveless dress, and adjusted her red belt. Satisfied with what she saw, she slipped on her heels and made her way to the living room. A glance at the clock showed ten minutes until Justin was set to arrive. After patting Shady on the head, she locked up, rode the elevator down to the lobby, and stepped outside to wait. She nodded at the security guard, noting the dip of his head with satisfaction. It had taken her almost three years to get any sort of acknowledgement out of him.

She didn't know what surprised her more, the fact that Edna had ditched her earlier at the farmers market, or that Lauren had wanted to spend time with her. Just thinking about Lauren sent chills down her spine. How could she be so smitten after only a few times in Lauren's presence? The feelings, though unexpected, made her feel alive and happy. A long time had passed since she felt this way, but she wasn't going to push things.

She stepped toward the sidewalk when Justin pulled up outside her building. She slid in and pulled her seat belt on. Justin had on a black pair of pants, white dress shirt, gray vest, and a red bowtie.

Justin glanced from her to himself, then pulled the car back into traffic. "I see you stole my fashion choice."

"Great minds think alike." She laughed and settled in for the twenty-minute drive. She perked up when he slowed, and her eyes grew wide when he pulled up to the entrance that included a red carpet and several photographers. She hadn't expected the opening of the astronomy section of the Garriety Science Center to be so extravagant.

"This is so neat," he whispered.

"Why are you whispering?"

"I don't know." He grinned and stepped out, giving the valet his car keys before walking around the car and opening Ainslon's door.

Ainslon accepted his hand and stepped out. Only a few flashbulbs went off, thank goodness. She wasn't used to going somewhere so fancy. At the door, she handed the doorman their tickets.

"Have a good evening." The doorman tipped his cap.

"Thank you."

As soon as her feet crossed the threshold, Ainslon let the full effect of the atmosphere wash over her. "This is so cool."

"I know." Justin held out his arm and Ainslon slipped her hand through it. "Look at us." Ainslon laughed and scanned the area when she came to a complete stop. "Ainslon, what?"

Her eyes zeroed in on Lauren talking to a man in the corner of the room. "It's Lauren." The blue, knee length, long sleeve dress hugged her body to perfection.

"Let's go say hi." Justin squeezed her hand.

"She's busy; we can catch her later."

He frowned, then brightened as his sight fixed on something across the room. "There's Colin from game night. Let's go say hi to him." Ainslon was fond of the boy. He and his siblings, Ralph and Heidi, made it to just about every game night.

Ainslon nodded, followed beside him, and walked up to Colin. "Hi, buddy." She couldn't help but be conscious of the fact Lauren stood only a few feet away, but she kept her attention on the boy in front of her.

"Ainslon, how cool is this?" He wore a pair of black trousers, blue button-down, and a black tie with the planets on it.

"That's what we were talking about," Justin said.

Colin looked at their intertwined arms and squinted at them. "Are you dating?"

"What?" Ainslon adjusted her belt. "Me and Justin. No. We're friends who love astronomy."

"I'm going to get us something to drink," Justin said.

"Okay." She surveyed around them. "Fancy, huh?"

"It is. Have you seen the observation deck yet?" A voice said from behind her.

She turned around and came face to face with Lauren. "Hello."

"Fancy meeting you here."

Ainslon just about swooned when Lauren pecked her on the cheek. "You look beautiful."

"As do you."

"It's Ainslon, Aunt Lauren," Colin said. "From game night. I won the tickets. Remember?"

Aunt? "I didn't know he was your nephew."

Lauren smiled and stepped up next to him, placing her hands on his shoulders. "He's my best friend's son. He was excited to get the tickets."

Ainslon beamed. "I was excited to get mine as

well."

Colin fidgeted. "There sure are a bunch of people here."

Ainslon glanced around, noticing the space filling up fast. She knelt next to him as Justin walked up to them. "Don't even worry about them. This is such a cool experience and most of these people don't even care about that. While they're talking it up with each other, we'll be checking this place out. What do you say?"

"Sounds like a plan."

She stood and turned warm and fuzzy when Lauren gave her a smile, then accepted the glass Justin handed her.

"Ms. Millán," Justin said. "I'm Justin Bishop, Ainslon's business partner."

"Justin, it's nice to meet you." She raised her glass to him before taking a sip.

"You as well. Let's go check out the observation deck." Justin took the lead and set his empty glass on a tray by the door to the deck. Ainslon and Lauren followed suit. Justin held the door open for them and they walked out onto a ten-foot wide by seventy-five-foot long observation deck with a telescope spaced every five feet apart. The five telescopes on either end, Ainslon had read, stayed locked in place on different points, but the five in the middle allowed the guests to adjust them.

All glittering polished steel beamed back at them. No wonder the center cost close to twenty million to complete. It was one of the most expensive additions to Garriety in recent years. Ainslon was looking forward to checking out the planetarium at a later date. It was the one exhibit that wasn't open tonight.

Ainslon looked up and watched Colin and Justin walk to the end of the deck. She turned around and blushed when Lauren, sitting on a bench, patted the spot beside her. Ainslon joined her. "It's a beautiful night." Her eyes scanned the floor made up of bricks, engraved with the names of donors.

"It is. The stars have always fascinated Colin and he was so disappointed when I couldn't acquire tickets. So, thank you, Ainslon, for the tickets."

Ainslon couldn't take her eyes off Lauren's hand resting on the bench between them. She didn't know what possessed her, but she reached over and placed her hand on top of Lauren's and breathed a sigh of relief when Lauren didn't pull away but held tightly to it. "It was a bit of luck," she said after a moment. "The kid that usually wins was out sick." For game nights, they relied on businesses to provide the prizes given away. They'd lucked out when they received four tickets to the opening.

"He was excited when he won. He said the players are getting better and he has me playing with him as often as possible."

"That doesn't sound so bad."

Lauren squeezed her hand. "It's not. I love spending time with him and his siblings." She paused, seeming to think over her words. "I was wondering if you were seeing anyone?"

Ainslon jerked her head around and caught Lauren's eyes. She didn't know where the courage came from, but she went with it. If Lauren could be brave, so could she. "Well, there is this one woman who caught my attention."

Lauren squeezed Ainslon's hand again. "Do tell."

Ainslon leaned back against the bench and

decided to take her nana's advice. "She's beautiful and smart. Funny, caring, and," Ainslon leaned toward her and whispered in her ear, "the sexiest woman I have ever had the pleasure to lay eyes on." Ainslon mentally patted herself on the back when Lauren shivered next to her and blushed. "She's successful, good with kids, and loves animals."

"She sounds like a catch."

"I'm starting to think so," she said, quietly. "I really am."

Lauren looked uncertain. "Have you known her long?"

"From the first moment we met, all the pieces seemed to click even though we haven't been on a date or spent that much time together."

"That's a nice feeling. As for the date part, that can be easily rectified." Lauren stood and offered Ainslon her hand. Ainslon grasped it, noting how soft the skin was. They moved toward the boys when they motioned them over. "Let's go see what all the fuss is about."

As they walked hand in hand past Justin and Colin, Justin winked; she grinned back. As Lauren leaned down to look through the eye of the telescope, Ainslon fixed her gaze on Lauren's shapely rear. Lauren looked up and caught Ainslon's blatant ogling.

"Enjoying the view?"

Ainslon felt her face heat. "Yes. Yes, I am." She wanted to ask Lauren out, but wouldn't even consider that an option until she handed over her book. For now, Lauren led her to the next telescope. An hour later, they'd explored the rest of the exhibits. By the time they made it back to the observation deck, Justin and Colin were waiting for them with expectant looks on their faces. "You two look up to something."

"I agree." Lauren squeezed her hand.

Colin nodded at Justin as he started to speak, "While you two were looking, we checked out the food and it…"

Colin butted in. "It's mostly seafood, like from mom's last work party."

"I see. So, what you're saying is you want to get out of here and get something to eat?" They both nodded. Lauren turned to Ainslon. "Are you hungry?"

"I could eat." Truth be told, she hadn't eaten anything since the farmers market that morning.

Lauren rolled her eyes. "What did you two want to eat? Or do I even have to ask?"

"Pizza," they both said.

"Pizza." Ainslon chimed in as her stomach growled.

"I see I'm out voted even before we took a vote. Colin, so I can tell your mother I fed you properly, you will also be eating a salad." He nodded.

"Lauren, did you drive?" Ainslon asked as they made their way to the entrance.

"We took a cab."

Ainslon looked at Justin and he smiled. "You can ride with us and we can take you two home."

"Are you sure? It won't be a problem for us to grab a cab."

"It's really no trouble."

A short drive later, they were all seated at a table by the window in Ainslon and Justin's favorite pizza place, By the Slice. Lauren and Colin deferred to Ainslon and Justin to order for them. Lauren's eyes widened by the amount of food the two ordered. Ainslon looked sheepish for a moment, then shrugged.

Better for Lauren to find out now how much she ate, rather than later.

"So, Colin. Your aunt tells me you've been practicing playing Settlers of Catan."

"Yep. Aunt Lauren plays with me. She's good."

"Really?" Ainslon didn't think Lauren could be any more charming, but she proved her wrong at every turn.

"There is a lot you don't know about me. Even before Colin started with your tournaments, we'd have game night a couple of times a month."

"Justin and I have game nights once a month with a few of our friends."

"I wouldn't recommend playing with Ainslon. She's competitive," Justin added.

"I'm not that bad," Ainslon muttered, then shut up when she felt a slight pressure on her knee. Lauren's hand. "Whatever. Don't ever let Justin be your partner in Charades. He's awful."

He nodded. "I really am." The waitress placed their pizza, chicken wings, and onion rings on the table and a small salad for each of them.

Ainslon pondered where to start. She grabbed two pieces of pizza, a few chicken wings, onion rings and at the last second slid her salad close by her plate, then winked at Colin, who giggled. "What? I'm hungry." She waved her hand. "Dig in."

After Lauren finished eating, her hand found its way back to Ainslon's knee. Ainslon found she didn't mind that one bit.

"I do believe it's time for us to go home," Lauren said, when Colin yawned.

Ainslon jumped up before Lauren could protest and paid their bill.

"Ainslon, I would have taken care of that."

Ainslon waved her off. "Nonsense. I didn't mind." She shrugged. "Next time you can get the bill."

Lauren's eyes sparkled. "All right. Next time."

Ainslon sat quietly while they dropped Lauren and Colin off. She breathed a sigh of relief when they pulled up outside her apartment building.

Justin shut the car off. "Ainslon?"

She turned in her seat and faced him. "What do you think of her?"

"I like her, and I believe she likes you too." He reached for her hand.

"Really?" She bit her lip. Lauren was sending out signals, but Ainslon didn't want to mess this up.

"Yes, really. Give yourself some credit."

She leaned over and kissed him on the cheek. "I'll see you tomorrow."

"Too right, you will."

She laughed and waved at the security guard before bounding to the elevator. Maybe. Just maybe she would work up the nerve to ask Lauren out properly on a date after their business concluded.

Chapter Eleven

The next morning, Ainslon woke refreshed and ready for whatever her day off had in store for her. After a quick shower, she dressed in a pair of jeans, a white tank top, and slipped on a pair of white Converses. Before she left her apartment, she fed Shady, and snatched her Wonder Woman ball cap off the hook by the door. On her way to her weekly visit to the park, she stopped at Brew and Bake for breakfast. As soon as she stepped inside, she thanked the universe when she spotted Lauren in line.

"Fancy meeting you here," Ainslon said, walking up to Lauren.

Lauren turned slowly with a bright smile on her face. "What can I say, their coffee is addictive."

"I know. I've asked Easton countless times how they do it, but she never tells me."

"Easton?"

"My sister. She owns Brew and Bake."

"I hadn't realized."

"I would introduce you, but she doesn't work on Sundays."

"Another time."

"Of course."

"Ainslon, the usual?" Alice asked from behind the counter.

"My usual coffee but add a couple banana nut muffins and chocolate chip cookies." With coffee in hand, Lauren turned to leave.

"Lauren, wait." Ainslon touched her forearm. "Would you like to join me at the park?" The invitation was spontaneous but worth it when Lauren smiled.

"I would like that."

"Order up, Ainslon." Alice placed her order on the counter.

Ainslon put her change in the tip jar and turned back to Lauren with her coffee and bag in hand.

"What do you usually do at the park?" Lauren asked.

"Nothing much. It's a chance for me to unwind from the week. We're closed on Sundays, and it gives Justin and me a chance to have a day to ourselves. We alternate Saturdays off."

"You sure you want me to join you?"

"Yes. Did you drive? My Jeep is this way."

"I walked."

Once the Jeep was on the road, it only took a ten-minute drive until she pulled into the park. "Let's see what this day has in store for us."

Lauren grinned and walked beside her until Ainslon found an empty picnic table where they both sat. Today Lauren wore a pair of black shorts, and a blue t-shirt with a pair of sunglasses tucked into the v of her shirt. Her hair was put up, and she was the most gorgeous creature Ainslon had ever laid eyes on. It would be a struggle to keep her hands to herself today. "It's a beautiful morning." She handed Lauren a muffin.

"I agree." Lauren picked up her coffee and took a sip but didn't take her eyes off Ainslon. "I enjoyed last night."

After swallowing a sip of coffee, Ainslon

answered. "Me too. The growth Garriety has seen in the last five years alone is amazing. And I'm so glad they've decided to start cleaning up the communities around downtown."

"It's been a pleasure to watch the town expand. Not only business wise, but also culturally."

Ainslon sipped her coffee. "When I moved back to the states with my nana and started school, I was afraid that my accent would make me stand out and I tried to hide it, but thankfully it made me stand out in a good way. It was certainly a culture clash coming to the United States, but Nana made it an easy transition for me. I have lived in the US more years than in Ireland, but I cannot shake my accent."

"Thank God for that," Lauren blurted out.

"Well, now." Ainslon held up her coffee cup and waited for Lauren to lift hers. "Here's to us. May we always be who we are and curse those that try and change us."

"I'll drink to that."

Ainslon quickly added, "May your troubles be less, and your blessings be more, and nothing but happiness come through your door."

"I will also drink to that."

"Nana is always spouting off some Irish proverb, but more times than I can count, her words have struck a chord with me."

"Edna sounds like a character."

"That she is."

"What's another one?"

"Let's see." Ainslon bit her bottom lip. "May the best day of your past be the worst day of your future."

"That's...deep, but man, it's wise words to live by. You know what that means, Ainslon?"

"What?"

"That today is going to be better than yesterday and I thought yesterday was great."

Ainslon chuckled. "I think you might be right." As soon as the words left her mouth, she noticed a flyer stapled to a nearby tree. Then a lightbulb went off. "Oh, I forgot about that."

Lauren looked around.

"Be right back." Ainslon hopped up and ripped the flyer off the tree. Sundays in the park had started back the previous week.

Sundays' adventures in the park.

Today's adventure: Axe throwing.

Age 17 and up.

$15.00 for four throws.

Now this was something they could do.

"So, Lauren." Ainslon held the flyer to her chest so Lauren couldn't see the writing. "Up for an adventure with me?"

Lauren stood and approached her. "Adventure, huh?" She rocked back on her heels.

"F.U.N."

"I suppose so," she replied nonchalantly.

Ainslon held the flyer up and turned the printed side toward Lauren. She fidgeted as Lauren read the words. She couldn't read the look on her face and hoped she hadn't messed up.

"Well, since you paid for dinner last night, I'll pay for our adventure."

"Really?" At Lauren's nod, Ainslon threw her arms around Lauren's neck. She knew it was a mistake the moment she felt a rush of arousal from the fragrance of Lauren's skin and perfume. She pulled away and took a step back. "So, axe throwing?"

Lauren chuckled. "After you."

Fifteen minutes later, they stood side by side, watching the festivities in front of them. Easton had told her how popular these Sunday activities were and now she believed her. She usually stayed away from this part of the park, preferring to relax closer to the water feature at the entrance. It was easy to see why these events were so popular. A dozen stations, separated by fencing, along with as many vendors, stood out against the blue of the water and the green of the grass. A glance at her phone confirmed it wasn't even ten yet and the place was swarming with people.

"I think we've arrived at the right time," Lauren said, then turned to Ainslon and crossed her arms. "Ready to lose?"

Oh, so that's how she wanted to play this. "Lose. Look, lady, I don't lose."

Lauren snorted. "I'll buy you an ice cream after I win."

"That's…that's…" Ainslon spluttered. "Deal." She held her hand out and Lauren clasped it. "I'll buy you lunch when I win."

"I can live with that." Lauren rubbed her hands together. "I've never done this before. Should be fun. Let's get in line."

Forty minutes later, they'd paid their fee and had heard all the safety rules with a group of people. The system seemed efficient.

"I'm going to win, you know." Ainslon bounced on the balls of her feet.

Lauren leaned forward and whispered in her ear. "We'll see about that."

"Ladies, over here." Their attendant, Margo, was friendly and engaging.

Three minutes later, Lauren lost the coin toss, and handed Ainslon an axe. Its weight felt nice in her hand, and she grinned as she lifted her arms over her head, then let the axe fly. Her heart pounded as it flew toward the target.

"Bullseye," Margo said. "Good job." She held up her hand for a high-five and Ainslon obliged.

"Hey, Lauren," Ainslon said, twirling an imaginary gun and holstering it.

Instead of watching Lauren throw, Ainslon did a slow appraisal from her feet to the top of her head.

"Earth to Ainslon," Lauren said. "Tied you. Your turn."

Fifteen minutes later they walked away, Lauren proudly displaying her winner's ribbon around her neck. "I'm not saying it was luck," Ainslon said. "But I'm pretty sure it was luck."

"Don't be a sore loser. Besides, I think your Irish luck rubbed off on me when you hugged me. So, this is partly your fault. I am buying you ice cream, after all," Lauren slipped her arm through Ainslon's. "I'll even buy you a double scoop."

"Who can say no to that?"

"Exactly. Two scoops are just too tempting."

"Oh, I'm tempting you now?"

"You better believe it."

Lauren's laugh delighted her and Ainslon didn't want to stop hearing it.

Once they had their ice cream, they settled back against a tree to people watch.

"I've enjoyed myself today," Lauren said. "I say that a lot with you."

Ainslon finished her ice cream. "I concur. It's nice."

"That it is." Lauren shifted to rest her shoulders against the tree, then faced Ainslon, her expression and voice sincere. "I think we could be on to something."

Ainslon took a deep breath. This wasn't what she had expected for today, but she wasn't about to deny the pull between them. "I think so as well. Lauren, I like you."

Lauren groaned. "But?"

"No." Ainslon grasped Lauren's arm and had to stop herself from swooning when Lauren slipped her hand into Ainslon's and squeezed. "No buts. I haven't had a good track record with dating, and I don't want to mess this up." She swallowed. "You feel this too?"

"I do. I told my sister I wasn't going to push for anything, but I don't want to miss my chance either. I don't want to jump into the deep end, but I would be more than willing to wade for a bit until we get our footing."

"I would love that." Ainslon beamed. "I really would. We take things slow and when we're both ready, we can take the next step."

"I agree." Lauren squeezed her hand.

"I'm surprised you're interested in me."

"Don't be silly." Lauren pulled her a little closer. "What's not to like?" She pushed the hair out of Ainslon's eyes.

Ainslon looked from her lips to her eyes, then took a step backward when the urge to kiss Lauren was overwhelming. "Yes, I agree, but there is one other thing."

"I'm listening."

"I don't even want to consider anything beyond friendship until our business is concluded."

"Phew." Lauren sighed dramatically and slumped

back against the tree. "I really thought it was going to be something horrific."

"Should I call you Ms. Dramatic?" Ainslon took a step closer and slipped her arms around Lauren's waist. "I think I'm going to like this arrangement."

"I am too." Lauren kissed the tip of Ainslon's nose. "Would you like to have dinner with me tonight?"

Ainslon shivered, groaned, and laid her head on Lauren's shoulder. "I can't. I'm having dinner with Nana tonight."

Lauren pushed Ainslon up and cupped her cheeks. "It's fine. How about coffee tomorrow morning at Brew and Bake?"

"Now that's something I can do."

"Good." Lauren kissed her cheek, moved back a step, and slid her hand down Ainslon's arm to clasp their hands together. "Do you have time for a walk?"

"I have time. Do you mind if we talk while we walk?"

"Nope."

"Why chocolate and candy?"

"When Callie and I were young, our grandma would gather all her grandchildren together and bake with us. She was amazing. Could make something out of nothing. When I was younger, I would watch her in awe. The way her hands kneaded the dough, and the way she would work the chocolate. She would spend hours teaching us her techniques. Even today, I'll see one of my employees working in the kitchens, and even knowing they were trained to work that way, it feels wrong, because it's not the way Grandma taught us. She had the patience of a saint."

Lauren took a deep breath. "As I grew older, I would still watch her in awe, but in a different light.

By the time I was in my twenties, her hands were weathered, and arthritis had set in. She would watch and direct us, but I could see the longing in her eyes to get her hands dirty, so to speak, but the pain was too much for her."

Lauren's face took on a faraway look. "I was twenty-eight when she died. She'd been sick for months. The week I spent in the hospital with my family watching her breaths become shallower and shallower was the worst week of my life. Even worse than when my papa died. There was just something about Grandma that drew everyone to her." Lauren squeezed Ainslon's hand. "Don't let a day slip by that you don't tell Edna you love her. It's over much too quickly. When she died, it felt like a piece of my heart went with her." A soft sigh escaped Lauren. "Sorry, that took on a sadder note than I'd planned. Like I was saying, I started the store because her love of chocolate rubbed off on me. I wanted to succeed where my ancestors didn't." She went on to tell Ainslon about the previous incarnations of the store. "I wanted to carry on their legacy. My great-great-grandfather named the store after his granddaughters, Carmella, and Charlotte. You've never been in my office, but the original sign from his store hangs on the wall across from my desk."

Warmth spread throughout Ainslon with each word out of Lauren's mouth. There was no way she was letting this woman go. No way at all. "I would love to see that sign."

Lauren smiled. "That can be arranged. How about you? Why'd you start your store?"

"I've always enjoyed collecting vintage books. Mainly children's books and I'm good at finding them.

When I met Justin, he had the same passion but for comic books. We became fast friends and after only a few months of knowing each other decided to go into business together. We started out online but knew we could do so much more with a storefront. We still have our online store and selling vintage books is a big part of our revenue. We wouldn't be able to make it without it. That's why I go to a lot of estate sales and auctions. I've found a lot of books that way."

"I enjoy estate sales as well. We'll have to go together some time."

"Name the time and the place and I'm all yours."

"I like the sound of that."

Chapter Twelve

Dinner, Ainslon decided, wasn't too bad. Shelly had flirted with her, but it wasn't anything Ainslon couldn't handle. Easton had texted her at lunch that she would be joining them for dinner, so it wasn't a surprise to see her standing in the kitchen. Over dinner, Edna had even gotten an invite from Shelly that after dessert they could browse through her grandfather's books.

Ainslon held Edna's arm as they crossed into Shelly's yard and climbed the few steps that lead into the kitchen of her house. The space was worn, but well looked after. Ainslon ran her hand along the kitchen table. Maple, if she were to take a guess, and gorgeous. She wanted to ask her about it but shelved that question for later.

At the end of the hallway, Ainslon held her breath when Shelly opened a door to their left and motioned for them to enter. Shelly flicked a switch and it took a moment for Ainslon's eyes to adjust to the bright lights. The moderate sized room had floor to ceiling bookshelves on all four of the walls and shelves above the door. The vast number of books sat upright and loosely packed into the bookshelves. Thank goodness. She knew, without even looking at the spines, that Old Man Collins had been telling the truth, and that the bulk of these books would probably be worth a small fortune. She quickly scanned the shelves and zeroed in on a shelf on the far wall.

After Edna waved off her offer of help to sit on the couch, Ainslon proceeded in the direction of the shelf she wanted to check out. At first glance, a minimum of three shelves held all the children's books. As her sight latched onto the spine of a certain book, her heart raced, and she had to fight the urge not to jump up and down and pull it down off the shelf. Out of the corner of her eye, she saw Shelly walk in her direction. "Do you know if these are all the children's books he has?"

Shelly leaned against the shelf. "They are. He liked to keep similar books grouped together." She pointed to the shelf across from them. "Those are mysteries and anything that would resemble them. Every shelf had a purpose. Can I ask why you would be interested in children's books?"

Before she could answer, Easton said, "She owns a children's bookstore."

Shelly slid her fingers along one of the shelves. "Really?"

"It was my dream and I made it happen." Ainslon scanned the rest of the titles. There were at least ten she wanted right off the bat. The room's temperature felt cool enough, so she wasn't concerned about their condition, only about their edition. "You said you would be willing to sell some?"

"I would consider it. Yes." Shelly pushed off the shelf.

"Do you care if I pull some down and look at them?" If she said no, this would be a wasted trip.

"I don't mind."

Ainslon reached for the *Mary Poppins* that had caught her eye. What would the odds be that he had her book? As she turned it in her hand, her fingers shook. It was in excellent condition. She prayed to whoever would listen and opened the book and flipped through, scanning the page for what she was looking for. For a moment, she shut her eyes as she took in a deep breath, closed the book, slipped it back on the shelf, and moved on to the next book. It was a first edition, but she didn't want to seem too eager. She continued to look through dozens of more books and made notes on her phone of the ones that held her interest.

She ran her eyes along the other titles on the rest of the shelves. His collection was amazing. There were several she would love to add to her private collection. She turned to Shelly sitting with Easton and Edna on the couch.

"Did you find some you were interested in?" Shelly asked, then stood.

"I did, and I know of another buyer who would take a few of these other books off your hands, but I don't want to call him unless you really do want to sell them. I found seventeen I wanted." If she was able to purchase them, she would already have six sold and their selling price would pay for the rest of the books.

Shelly seemed apprehensive and Ainslon could sympathize. This was her grandfather's collection. "You seem eager and I like that. Edna was telling me a little bit about your store."

"I will pay top dollar for them, but I won't pay retail price. I can't do that, but I will give you a fair price. Just think about selling them. If you give me your email, I'll send you a list of the books I'm interested in. You can do research on them and it will give you the cost breakdown. I'm not going to cheat you." She really needed that book, but she didn't want to beg. In the end, the decision was solely up to Shelly.

Shelly crossed her arms. "Would you like to have dinner with me to discuss it?"

"While I'm flattered by your offer, I can't."

"I had to ask."

"I'll give you that," Ainslon said and walked behind Edna and Easton out of the room. She really didn't want to leave the book, but she needed to bide her time. She knew if she offered her a fair price, there would be no way Shelly could turn it down, but she needed to make a few phone calls first. She accepted the card Shelly handed her with her email address on it. "We'll talk soon."

"I look forward to it."

"Goodnight, Shelly."

As soon as they walked into Edna's house, Ainslon threw the lock on the back door and helped Edna fix them each a cup of tea. "Ainslon, you could have gone out with her." She gave her a knowing look.

"Nana's right. One date and you would have had what you wanted," Easton chimed in.

"No, I couldn't have. After one date, she could have stipulated more dates before she would sell." She didn't want to tell them about her and Lauren yet. She wanted them to have a little time to themselves before she announced it to her family. "That's not how I do business." They settled in the living room. "I believe she wants to sell, but it was her grandfather's collection. One he'd collected his entire life. I would be hard pressed to sell. I can appreciate her reluctance, but I hope she does."

"She has your book," Easton stated and kicked her feet up onto the coffee table.

"She does, and sixteen more I want."

"How much are you willing to pay for the seventeen you want?" Easton asked.

They usually steered clear of talking about their business dealings. Ainslon ran her fingers through her hair. It would take a huge chunk out of the store's business account, but it would pay off in the long run. "I want to pay seventeen thousand, but I would be willing to go up to twenty if all the books I want pan out."

Edna's eyes widened. "I didn't expect that much." Easton's face was blank.

"If she lets me buy them for seventeen, I will already have six sold and I will make back what I paid for all seventeen. I know for a fact my friend James will be interested in a lot of the other books she has. He would pay top dollar, and if the books pan out like I am expecting them to, he would probably pay tens of thousands for them. Old Man Collins has an amazing collection. If she wanted to send them to an auction house, she would make more, but there would be fees to pay and they may not all sell at the same time. This way she would be getting paid right now."

Easton whistled. "Wow, sis. I had no idea you were making that kind of money."

"We're doing fairly well. Our vintage books make up forty percent of our sales. Last quarter we saw a ten percent increase and I'm confident it will continue to rise. We've added a lot to our comic section and have a few ideas to expand the children's book section. But we're quickly outgrowing our space. Justin and I have talked about the building beside C and C. It would be perfect."

"That's great," Easton said.

"Easton, what's been happening with you?" Edna

asked.

"Nothing much." She lay her head back on the couch. "Business is good, my dating life sucks, but what's new."

"You make it sound so bleak," Ainslon said.

"Right now, my prospects are null. It would be nice if the right woman would fall into my lap."

"Real life isn't a Rom-Com."

"No." Easton nodded. "But, wouldn't it be cool if it was."

Chapter Thirteen

It sucked when breakfast with Lauren Monday morning didn't happen. Unexpected issues arose for both of them, and they'd had to reschedule three times already this week. The feel of Lauren's arms around her was both exhilarating and terrifying and wasn't something Ainslon could get out of her head. However, the point still stood; Ainslon didn't want what was happening between them to move forward until their business concluded.

"Shady, I really like her." Ainslon looked to the cat sprawled out on the bed, legs spread, cleaning her nether regions. "The least you can do is look up when I'm talking to you." Ainslon lay her head back down on the bed and stared up at the ceiling. "It's like this all-consuming feeling, Shady." She swung her arms in the air, as her foot tapped the bed. "It's like this heat that spreads through me. Rushing through my veins. I get tongue-tied around her." Ainslon giggled and moved to sit up when she noticed Shady wasn't on the bed anymore. A quick look around confirmed the cat was long gone. "Well, see if I listen the next time you talk to me about your feelings."

A glance at the clock had her scrambling up and rummaging in her closet until she pulled out a pair of jeans and a vintage Harry Potter t-shirt, proudly proclaiming her Hufflepuff house status. At the front door, she almost went back and changed since she was having breakfast with Lauren. But she'd promised a little boy that always came into the store on Thursdays that she'd wear the shirt for him. Lauren liked her and would have to get used to the clothes she wore.

Ainslon would always choose comfort over expensive clothes, but she could see herself dressing up for Lauren. Lauren always looked amazing and dressed to impress. Though, she never came across to Ainslon as snotty or better than anyone.

With a kiss to the top of Shady's head, ignoring the cat's protests, Ainslon ambled out of the apartment and down the elevator to the parking garage. A quick five-minute drive later, she parked and made her way to Brew and Bake.

When she walked in, Lauren sat at a table in the back, beckoning her over. Her hair was put up today, but a few curls had broken loose and hung around her face. She wore a blue sleeveless blouse with the first few buttons undone, showing an impressive amount of skin. A thin gold chain hung around her neck.

The flutter in Ainslon's belly sent tingles throughout her whole body when a smile blossomed on Lauren's face. Even the butterflies in her stomach couldn't stop her from accepting Lauren's hug. Her nerves be damned.

"What a welcome," Ainslon said, after they sat. "I'm glad to see you too."

Lauren chuckled. "Can you blame me? I've looked forward to this all week."

"No, I can't blame you. I've looked forward to this also."

"Good. I'm glad we were finally able to meet. It seems a lot longer than four days."

The nerves building in Ainslon all morning

vanished at Lauren's relaxed state. "It does. I was telling Shady that this morning."

Lauren took a drink of her coffee. "How long have you had Shady, and if I may ask, how did you come about her name?"

"I adopted her four years ago. She was two. At the time, she was named Quinn, and while I liked that name, it didn't seem to fit." Ainslon scrunched up her nose in thought. "I figured once I had her for a while that a name would come to me."

"Go on."

"One evening I made a grilled cheese sandwich when my phone rang. I wrapped the sandwich in a paper towel and put it on the kitchen counter, then went into the living room to answer my phone. When I went back into the kitchen, Quinn was seated on the counter and the paper towel was torn and a bite taken out of the sandwich. The first thing that came to my mind was that was some shady shit. She waited until I left the room to eat my sandwich. So, that's how Shady McQuinn was born."

Lauren laughed. "Sounds about right."

"What about you? I know you said you had a dog, but do you have any pets now?"

"No." Lauren pushed her saucer away. "I've thought about it but haven't had the time to look into it. And now, I spend more time at the store than I do at home. My mother's always getting on to me about working too much."

"Nana does too. She knows that in order for the store to succeed I have to put in the time, but what would they do if not worry about us?"

"You got me there." Lauren leaned forward and laced her fingers together on the tabletop. "So, this

Sunday is another day at the park. Would you like to join me?"

Ainslon leaned forward. "What's the activity?"

"Does the activity determine whether or not you will say yes?"

The smug look on Lauren's face kicked her competitiveness into high gear. "I would love to join you. You know I can easily look it up, right?"

"I know. Do you not like surprises?"

"I love them. I can wait."

"Good." Lauren glanced at her phone. "I do need to get to work. As for Sunday, I'll meet you here at say, eight o'clock."

"I wouldn't miss it." Ainslon accepted Lauren's hug.

"Now, for Sunday, make sure you wear something you don't mind getting dirty in." Lauren winked and walked away. Ainslon's eyes stayed glued to Lauren until she turned a corner.

Halfway to work, what Lauren had said hit her. *Something you don't mind getting dirty in.* "What the hell have I gotten myself into." She knew two things; one, all Sundays in the parks revolved around families, and two, there was no way she was going to miss out on their next friend date. If only to see what Lauren considered clothes that she could get dirty in.

Chapter Fourteen

Bright and early Sunday morning found Lauren pacing in her bedroom, her thoughts on the one woman she couldn't seem to get off her mind. Ainslon O'Neil had swooped into her life and Lauren wasn't sure what to make of her feelings toward her. Lauren couldn't seem to get the smile off her face, but she didn't mind. Ainslon was a breath of fresh air that rushed into Lauren's life at the best possible moment.

Lauren tipped her head and regarded her reflection in the mirror. Aging used to bother her, but now at forty-four, it didn't anymore. Gray sprinkled her dark brown hair, but Lauren liked it. The lines around her eyes could easily be covered with a smidge of make-up or sunglasses.

Though her body wasn't muscular, she'd kept it lean over the years. Thank goodness her breasts still held their small shape beautifully. While not toned, her stomach was semi flat, with a hint of a pouch. She'd have to work on it. Maybe take up cycling again with Jeffrey. She knew it wouldn't take much to drag him out on the weekends, considering he had complained the previous week about getting lazy in his workouts.

A quick turn allowed her to take in one of her best assets. Her ass. She'd chosen these specific athletic pants to highlight said asset and she knew Ainslon would appreciate them, considering she'd caught her staring at her ass countless times.

After putting her bra on, she slipped on a black, short sleeve, light-weight t-shirt. During their last conversation, she had mentioned to Ainslon not to wear white today, for today's activity would be a water balloon fight. Per the flyer, some balloons would be filled with water, while others would be filled with paint, and some shaving cream. Considering most people saw her as an uptight businesswoman, she hoped Ainslon enjoyed seeing this more playful side of her. True, Garriety's gossip sites followed her around, but they always seemed to paint her in the worst light.

She needed to have a talk with Ainslon about it. She was by no means a celebrity, but for some reason her name seemed to always be in some article the Garriety Gossip printed. Although she didn't want Ainslon dragged into that mess, there was no way she wanted to stay away from her. After the astronomy opening, a picture had surfaced of them, but nothing had come of it. After their outing last week, a picture of them had popped up on the Garriety Gossip site, but there was only a short description of their time at the park. Of course, speculation ran rampant, but Lauren knew the Gossip site would never cross the line of interacting with either one of them. They did, at least, respect people's boundaries.

She jumped as the alarm on her phone went off. Time to go. She swiped the Meerkat ball cap from the shelf by the door, slipped her sunglasses on, then headed out.

She was still early, so she settled down at what she had come to think of as their table at Brew and Bake and waited. She didn't have to wait long when Ainslon strode in, dressed in a pair of jeans with a hole in one knee, and a long sleeve gray and red striped shirt. Her hair was put up and she looked good enough to eat. All Lauren thought about since meeting Ainslon was running her tongue along her jawline.

"Lauren."

Lauren snapped out of her daydream, stood, and slipped her arms around Ainslon. "Sorry. My mind was elsewhere."

"It's all right." Ainslon chuckled.

Lauren felt a spark of joy when she caught Ainslon's eyes, for a split second, linger on her ass. Score one for her.

"I'm glad you took my advice to heart."

"Well," Ainslon said, sitting down. "Your text that said don't wear white in caps was a big clue. I can honestly say I'm intrigued, and I did not look up what this Sunday's activity was. When I mentioned it to Justin, he smirked at me and walked off, announcing that I would enjoy it."

"I hope so." Lauren looked up when Ainslon covered her hand with her own.

"You look good as well."

Lauren arched her brow at the coy smile on Ainslon's face. "That's what I was going for." Lauren squeezed her hand once before pulling hers away. "Now, let's eat. The first activity starts at ten."

"Sounds good to me."

Forty minutes later, Lauren and Ainslon stared into the crowd after registering. Lauren couldn't read the look on Ainslon's face and it left her uneasy. "We don't—"

"Of course we are." Ainslon turned to look at the sectioned off portion of the park. "There's no winning in this, is there?"

"Just a good time." Lauren took the chance and

wrapped her arm around Ainslon's waist. "It will be fun to blast everyone with the balloons."

"I agree. I saw a woman who complained my vintage book prices were too high register a few minutes ago. I would love to pelt her with one."

Lauren pulled back and smiled. "That's the spirit." She cleared her throat. "I can do fancy. I will do fancy, but I also like to have fun."

"Oh, I can do fancy too. Fun now, fancy later."

Lauren turned to the right when their names were called. "Ready for this?"

"Better believe I am."

Three hours, a shower, and a change of clothes later, Lauren and Ainslon sat side by side on top of a picnic table overlooking the water.

"I felt great satisfaction popping that one guy in the chest with that paint filled balloon," Ainslon said.

"Your excitement was palpable." The morning had been fun, and Lauren felt more than once that there was something decidedly beyond friendship about her feelings for Ainslon. She would wait it out and after their business concluded, then ask her out. It was inevitable at this point. "I had fun as well." Lauren drummed her fingers on the tabletop. "Can I ask you something?"

"Yes, though I reserve the right not to answer."

"That's fair." Lauren took a deep breath. "Where did you learn to throw like that?"

Ainslon tilted her head back and laughed. "I played softball in high school. I was good too, but it wasn't something I wanted to do in college. I wanted to focus on my academics."

"Looks like your aim was true, Ms. O'Neil." The pink hue at the tips of Ainslon's ears was about the cutest thing ever. Everything about Ainslon made her pulse race. "How about some food? After that, I'm afraid we'll have to part ways. I have dinner plans with my best friend and her family tonight."

"Food sounds great." Ainslon stood and held her hand out. Lauren latched onto it.

"I am free tomorrow morning if you'd like to have breakfast together."

"I wouldn't miss it."

Lauren was in trouble, she knew it, but at this point she couldn't bring herself to care. Ainslon was a fire she definitely didn't want to put out.

Chapter Fifteen

Thursday came far sooner than Ainslon expected. Her plans to get breakfast with Lauren Monday morning never surfaced. Shady hadn't felt well and Ainslon had to rush her to the vet. Thankfully, everything turned out all right.

Tuesday and Wednesday were jam-packed, but Lauren understood work came first. They'd texted a few times and talked on the phone once. She needed to work on getting her book. That's how all this started.

The Monday night meeting with Shelly had been postponed. Tonight, she would meet with Shelly at Edna's house. Hopefully, she'd be able to close the deal on Lauren's book.

On Monday, she'd called the realtor about the building she and Justin were interested in and arranged a meeting with him at one at the building later today. She had her fingers crossed that everything would work out.

Ainslon glanced at the clock on the wall and paced behind the counter with all their financial papers clutched in her hand. They'd met with the bank on Tuesday and had everything in order. It would all hinge on the sale of their current building, but she felt confident it would sell fast. Especially since she'd already talked with Kat about the sale of the building and they were still interested.

"Ainslon, please," Sarah said.

"Sorry." She ran her fingers through her hair. "This is a big day."

"I know. Where's Justin?"

"He should have already been here. We have to leave in a few minutes." As soon as the words left her mouth, he came barreling through the door. Seeing his confident swagger helped put her at ease.

"Ready to do this?"

"Yes." She met him at the door.

"We both look nice," he said.

She slipped her hand through his arm. "That we do." She'd opted for an A-line gray skirt and a red sleeveless silk top. "I'm nervous."

"Me too. We have all our paperwork, and everything checks out. All we can do now is meet with the realtor and go from there."

"I know."

"If it doesn't work out, we'll continue looking."

They had to bypass a few obstacles on the sidewalk, because of construction, but made it to the building with five minutes to spare. She squinted when she saw Lauren walk out of her store, accompanied by the man she'd talked to at the astronomy opening. They came to a stop in front of Ainslon and Justin. Lauren regarded them with curiosity.

"Ainslon, Justin, what brings you here today?" Lauren asked, her ever present smile on her face. She turned to the man beside her. "This is my accountant, Bryce Murphy."

"Nice to meet you. I'm Justin Bishop." Justin shook the man's hand.

Ainslon shook Bryce's hand. "Ainslon O'Neil." She turned to Lauren. "I would love to stay and talk, but we have a meeting." Ainslon motioned toward the vacant building.

Bryce gave them a perplexed look. "As do we."

"What?" She had to have heard him wrong. "Our meeting is at one."

Lauren sighed. "So is ours. We've been trying to get this building for the last six months."

"I..." Ainslon didn't know what to say. Lauren was their competition. Just great. Lauren hadn't mentioned anything about expanding her business, but neither had she.

"Ainslon," Justin said. "We don't want to be late."

"No, of course not."

He let go of her and opened the door, allowing everyone in. Ainslon's eyes widened at the steel and wood beams that ran along the ceiling, and the hardwood floors. Then her eyes caught a man walking toward them. He was tall, and handsome, but had an air of arrogance about him that instantly put her off.

He clasped his hands together in front of him. "Good afternoon, I'm Fredrick Morris." He motioned to the two seats in one corner or the room. "Ms. O'Neil, Mr. Bishop, if you two would take a seat, I am going to speak to Ms. Millán and Mr. Murphy first." He led Lauren and Bryce to a table with two chairs in front of it on the opposite side of the large room. Close enough to see but far enough away that they wouldn't be able to hear their conversation.

Ainslon glanced at Justin, noticing a pained smile on his face. Lauren being their competition didn't bode well for their chances. Justin slumped down beside her. Of course she would be in direct competition with her crush, and they'd been making great progress on their relationship.

After an uncomfortable fifteen minutes, Lauren

and her companion headed in their direction.

"Fredrick is waiting for you," Lauren said.

Ainslon accepted Justin's hand and stood. "Thank you." Ainslon smoothed out her skirt and accepted Fredrick's hand when he reached toward her. "It's nice to meet you."

He smiled. "You as well. Please, have a seat. I know this might seem unorthodox scheduling both meetings at the same time, but the owner was intrigued when I told her about your phone call. She can be picky at times, but she has narrowed her two choices down to you and Ms. Millán." He held out his hand and Justin handed over their folder. He slipped his glasses on and skimmed the pages. Ainslon's heart pounded when he slipped his glasses off and placed his hands on top of the folder. "Your offer is contingent with the sale of the building you're currently occupying."

"Yes."

"So, you're not looking to expand your business, you want to move it all together. Is that right?"

"Our business has grown faster than we expected. Given our recent growth we will need to move in the next year or two. When we saw this building was for sale, it seemed like the perfect opportunity and fit."

Justin nodded. "We do well in the neighborhood we're in, but this building will give us the opportunity to expand that our current location can't."

"This building is expensive. Are you sure it wouldn't be hindering your future plans by expanding too soon?"

Justin scooted forward in his chair. "We've talked about it and feel moving to a larger location is the right step."

Fredrick tapped the folder on the desk, then

stood. "It was nice meeting you both. I should have an answer for you by the beginning of next week."

"Oh," Ainslon said, standing as well. "Thank you for your time."

"I'll walk you to the others." Fredrick smiled. "I will be in touch with you. Everyone think about what I said."

Ainslon gripped Justin's arm so hard he flinched. "We will."

"Good day."

Ainslon opened the door and walked out followed by Justin, Lauren, and Bryce.

"I hope we didn't just waste our time," Justin muttered.

"Me as well."

"Ainslon," Lauren said from behind her.

Ainslon took a deep breath and turned around. Lauren and Bryce were staring at them. This wasn't Lauren's fault. None of this was anyone's fault. "Yes."

"Would you like to grab lunch since we weren't able to grab breakfast?"

Ainslon managed to squelch her anger but couldn't keep the bite out of her voice. "Right now, I don't think that's a good idea."

"For the record," Lauren said, "I've been dealing with Fredrick for months. I even offered over the asking price and she still wouldn't accept my offer."

Ainslon shook her head. "Well, isn't that great." She tried to cool her growing anger because Lauren didn't deserve it. In her wildest dreams she would have never imagined this scenario. "You have more money to offer and we barely have enough. Christ, I wonder who they'll pick now."

"I didn't mean anything by that. I..." Lauren

nervously fiddled with the belt around her waist.

"Lauren," Bryce said. "I need to get back to the office. Are we still on for dinner tonight?"

"Of course, Bryce," Lauren said.

"Good, I'll see you then." He walked quickly away.

Justin shook his head. "Ainslon, I'm heading back to the store. We'll discuss everything later."

Ainslon watched him until he crossed the street, then turned back to Lauren. "Lauren, I…" The look on Lauren's face made Ainslon's heart clench painfully.

"Ainslon, please, let's go someplace quiet and discuss this over lunch. Just hear me out."

"No, Lauren. I…I'm not sure now's a good time…or anytime for that matter." If she didn't want to move things forward in their relationship because of the book, well, this was a much bigger deal. No matter what she felt for Lauren, she had to stick to her guns. Didn't she?

Lauren frowned. "What do you mean?"

"We're both competing for the same building. Plus, your book. We have a lot on our plates right now." How had everything changed so quickly? All Ainslon wanted to do was escape back to the store. "Look, I think, for the time being, we should leave whatever this is between us on the back burner. At least until the matter of this building is resolved."

Lauren's face registered shock, then hurt. After a long moment, she sighed in resignation. "If that's what you think. Ainslon, I can't back down from the opportunity to buy this building and I will be offering my best price."

"May the best business win." The knife that had embedded itself in Ainslon's chest tightened.

"For the record, Ainslon, you look amazing today."

Ainslon swallowed hard, trying to loosen the tightness in her throat as Lauren turned and walked away. What had she done?

Was competing against Lauren in her best interests? Was a business deal worth losing what she and Lauren had between them? She didn't know, but she would ask her family for their thoughts on the matter tonight.

❧❧❧❧

Lauren strode into C and C, rushed up the stairs and into her office. She slammed her folder on her desk, slumped in her chair, and closed her eyes. What a mess. She never in a million years thought she and Ainslon would be in competition. All the progress they'd made, gone. If she hadn't already invested so much time and energy in the building, she would, maybe, consider letting it go. However, it would be perfect for her business. She'd already had plans drawn up to knock down part of the wall between the two buildings to expand into one big showroom.

She didn't even open her eyes when her door opened.

"Don't get up," Ollie said. After a beat. "What's wrong?"

She opened her eyes and sat up straight. "I had plans of ditching you for lunch, but those fell through."

"After I slaved over this meal." Ollie spread her arms above the desk.

"You would have shared with Carrie."

"Are you going to tell me what happened?"

"As you know, Ainslon and I are at the stage of getting to know each other."

"I'm aware and happy for you. She's all you talk about lately."

Lauren groaned and unwrapped her sandwich. "Ainslon and Justin were at my meeting with the realtor today. They are also after the building."

Ollie frowned. "So, what's the issue?" She took a large bite of her sandwich.

"The issue is that Ainslon was already weary about us mixing business with pleasure, since she's looking for my book. This is a bigger deal than that to her."

"I can see her point. I wouldn't necessarily consider her finding your book mixing business with pleasure, but the building is another matter. What are you going to do?"

"I don't know." She picked at her fruit salad. "But, Ainslon made it clear, as of right now, whatever we were doing is on hold."

"I hate that for you, Lauren, but I'm sure everything is going to work out." She pointed her fork at Lauren. "Just you wait and see. I do live vicariously through you, after all."

Lauren lifted her water bottle and Ollie lifted hers. "No truer words have ever been spoken."

"Hear, hear."

Chapter Sixteen

The five hours between the building meeting and the pending dinner with Edna and Shelly flew by. Justin had agreed to close for the night, and she stopped at Brew and Bake, picked up dessert and Easton, then to By the Slice and picked up dinner before driving to Edna's house.

She wasn't looking forward to this dinner, not after the day she had experienced, but hopefully, Shelly wasn't going to give her a hard time. Afterward, she planned to talk to Easton and Edna about Lauren and this building mess.

The night before, she had talked with James about Shelly's books. He had given her a number to quote to Shelly if, once he looked at the books, they were in as good as shape as he was hoping for. All in all, she hoped by the time the night was through she would have a promise of the sale of the books.

Hopefully, one thing would go right today. How in the hell, in the span of a few hours, could she possibly not only lose the opportunity to date Lauren, but the building that would be perfect for them?

"You're quiet," Easton said.

"Just have a lot on my mind. We'll talk about it after our dinner with Shelly."

"I'll hold you to that. You know you can tell me anything."

"I know. Don't worry, we'll talk."

They sat in the car for ten minutes listening to the radio until Easton mentioned Edna was on the porch watching them.

"Right." They gathered all the food and stepped through the front door Edna held open for them. Shelly greeted them when they walked in. "Good evening." Her day might have been shot to hell, but she could still salvage the rest of it.

"You look nice," Shelly said. Ainslon hadn't bothered to change out of the clothes she wore to the building meeting.

"Thank you. There's plenty of food. Let's eat before we talk business."

"That's sounds good." Edna patted Ainslon on the arm.

Ainslon found it hard to concentrate on the conversation that occurred during dinner, her mind going over the events of the day. She caught the concerned looks from her nana and Easton. After popping the last piece of pizza in her mouth, she stood and grabbed a plate to clear the table. She masked her surprise when Shelly stood to help her.

Ainslon then pulled the cheesecake out of the fridge and set it along with four saucers and forks on the table. "Why don't we each get a piece, then head into the living room and talk things over?"

"Sounds good," Easton said.

Once they were seated, Shelly spoke. "Ainslon, are you feeling okay? You seem, I don't know, distracted."

"I haven't had a great day, but we all have those. I'll be fine."

"If you're sure."

She nodded and took a bite of the cheesecake, then pulled out two pieces of folded paper from her purse and took a deep breath. "Shelly, I know we've gone back and forth on this, but I would really like to complete this tonight." She held up her hand to stop anyone from talking. She saw the looks Easton and Edna exchanged but ignored them. "I would like to take another look at the books, as would James, but if they are as good as I know they are, the plain paper has my offer written on it for the seventeen books I emailed you about, and the lined paper has James offer for six books I know he would be interested in. If you agree, he's prepared to travel here next week to look at the other books you have and give you an offer on those. I've done my research and I'm sure you've done yours. These are our best offers. You can take it or leave it." She pushed the papers toward Shelly, then leaned back on the couch with her arms crossed.

"Just like that?" Shelly said, setting her saucer on the coffee table. "Take it or leave it?"

"Don't get upset yet. You haven't even looked at them and yes, it's like that."

Shelly swiped the lined paper up first and opened it, then the other one. Her face didn't give anything away, but Ainslon could see the slight tremble in her fingers. "I did do my research, but these prices don't match what I came up with."

Ainslon kept her voice firm. "It's all I can offer. I can't pay retail."

"Stop," Shelly said. "You're taking my words out of context. This is a lot more than I figured up. Are you sure you estimated correctly? I didn't want you to cheat me, but I also don't want you to offer more than they're worth. After all, we're both trying to make a profit."

"Oh." Ainslon felt all her pent-up aggression

vanish. "Your grandpa's collection is in fantastic shape. Better than a lot I have seen, and he took exceptional care of his books. Edition and printing are a huge factor and the books I want, and a lot of his, fit the criteria I look for. I want to be upfront with you. I'm confident you could make more money if you took the books to an auction house, but there are a lot of variables you would have to consider going that route. This way you will have the check in a few days. It's your choice."

Shelly laughed. "I don't think it really is a choice. I would be a fool to turn down your offer, and a fool I am not."

"So?"

"You can come over anytime this week and look through the books." She stood and winked. "Don't forget to bring your checkbook." Ainslon joined Shelly at the back door. Shelly ran her finger along Ainslon's collar bone. "No chance for us?"

Ainslon took her hand. "No, but I have no objections to us moving toward acquaintances, then maybe friends."

"I can live with that." She paused on the porch. "Whoever she is, is lucky."

Ainslon closed the door, then leaned her forehead against it.

"Are you ready to tell us what's been bothering you?" Easton asked from behind her.

"Yes. Just give me a minute and I'll join you both in the living room."

"Okay."

When Easton's footsteps receded, she poured herself a glass of milk and joined them. After taking a large gulp, she rehashed her feelings on Lauren, and the problems with the building. "What do you think?"

"For one," Edna said. "I don't see what the problem is. You like her, she likes you. If she was to get the building, would your feelings for her change?"

"No."

"What's the problem then?" Edna patted her hand.

"I..."

"Second," Edna said. "Whoever the building ends up with, it's out of your hands. Yes, you both want the building, but this isn't Lauren's fault and at this time, neither one of you will have a say in who the building goes to. Nothing you can do about it. If it was all about money, Lauren would have already gotten the building." She picked up Ainslon's hand. "I know it's easier said than done, but let your worries go. Go home and get a good night's rest. Tomorrow you will feel better and please don't think on something so much you create a scenario that isn't there."

Ainslon finished her milk. "You're right. Is it really that simple?"

"Why wouldn't it be?" Easton said. "Nana is right. You don't have a say over the building, but you do about your feelings for Lauren."

"What would you do?"

"I would go for it. There are plenty of ways you can expand your business but finding a woman that makes you feel...that opportunity doesn't come around every day."

"I don't know why I'm feeling so out of sorts, but I'm not sure I can go on with her with this hanging over our heads. This is a big deal."

Edna finished her tea. "You're intimidated and feel like you're not good enough. But, Ainslon, you are. I've seen the way she looks at you. Don't judge her on something you think she's going to do. Talk to her. In all my years, I know countless rifts that have been created by people simply not communicating."

Ainslon threw her arms around Edna. "I know that, Nana, but I'm not sure. Yes, I like her, but this is a big deal. It's the future of my business and I can't put that in danger no matter how much I like her." Ainslon fell back on the couch. "I'm not sure. I need to sleep on it. Next Thursday, Justin and I are going to the banquet the food festival community is putting on. Maybe that will take my mind off everything and we can make some new connections."

"Then that's what you should do." Edna patted her on the knee.

"I don't want to lose her."

Edna rolled her eyes. "Don't be so dramatic. Her feelings for you won't change that much in a week. Or at least they shouldn't if she really cares about you."

"You're right." She took a deep breath and stood and decided to stop making assumptions, especially about Lauren. "Are you ready, Easton?"

"Yes." Easton kissed Edna on the cheek. "Nana, I'll see you in the morning."

Ainslon looked from one to the other. "What's going on?"

"Just my annual check-up. No big deal."

"Are you sure? Is there something we should know about?"

"No. I am fit as a fiddle for someone my age. You two should head out."

"If you're sure." Ainslon hugged her tight and kissed her on the cheek. "I'll talk to you tomorrow."

"Drive safe."

It wasn't until Ainslon pulled up outside of

Easton's apartment that she said something. Ainslon knew she had been biding her time.

"Don't let this put the brakes on you and Lauren."

"It already has."

"Don't let it, Ainslon. Trust me. Just go for it. You won't be disappointed."

"I love you."

"I love you too."

As she lay in bed that night with Shady curled up by her head, the clip that kept replaying in her mind was seeing Lauren for the first time. The feelings that memory invoked were new and she didn't want to lose that feeling, but how could she juggle Lauren and the building without one interfering with the other?

Chapter Seventeen

The blinking cursor on her screen drew Lauren from her thoughts. Yesterday hadn't gone as she had anticipated. What was, at first, so promising with Ainslon, had come to a complete and sudden stop. She wrote countless texts to send to her but deleted all of them. Ainslon insisted she needed space and that's exactly what Lauren would give her. She wouldn't seek her out but if they both happened to be in the same place, well, Lauren wouldn't pass that opportunity up. How could she? Ainslon had already wormed herself into Lauren's life and she liked it.

Since no work would be forthcoming, Lauren shut down her laptop, closed the lid, and slid it to the corner of her desk, stood, then stretched. A.J. was due any minute with some samples, so she could justify putting off the invoices for a few more hours.

Life really wasn't fair, she decided. Happiness was within her grasp, and now, she wasn't sure what would happen. For being a woman that always put her business above all else, she was having a real identity crisis. At some point it was bound to happen, she supposed.

A knock on the door had her tearing her eyes away from the picture of her and Ainslon she kept on the desk. That Saturday at the farmers market would be one of her favorite memories.

"Come in."

She sat, then leaned back when the door opened, and A.J. walked in. Lauren let her eyes wander from A.J.'s ever present cowboy boots, up her jean clad legs, over her tank top covered chest, to a smirk on those pink lips. Finally, she made it to her eyes and the sparkle there was a familiar and constant sight.

"Do I pass muster?" A.J. shut the door behind her before crossing the room to take the chair in front of the desk.

"You always do."

A.J. slid a folder out of her messenger bag and handed it to Lauren. "Should you really be checking me out? I heard you were taken."

Lauren grimaced. "Not so much."

"Oh, do you want to talk about it?" A.J. relaxed back in the seat.

She didn't. Not again, but maybe it would help. So, she detailed everything that had happened so far and waited for A.J.'s reaction.

"So, you've spent time together as "friends" and you didn't know you were both after the same building. Now that she knows, she put a hold on you two spending time together."

"Yes."

"Sounds like she's scared." Lauren opened her mouth to speak but A.J. waved her off. "Listen, you two haven't known each other long and she seems scared to me. I've been where she is. Maybe not the same circumstance but similar. Lauren, you're a powerful businesswoman in this town. Everyone knows that. I know you do, but, sometimes, I don't think you realize the power you do hold. You're admired, successful, and let's face it, the gossip sites salivate when they get a new piece of information about you. You don't lose, at least, not when it comes to your business, and I'm sure she knows that. Hell, I would be intimidated if we were going after the same venture. You're passionate about your work and I admire that. Half the town does."

"So, what are you saying?"

"I'm saying that you need to give her time. This is a big deal no matter how you split it. Have you told her you still want to see her even if she gets the building?"

"Of course I haven't. If you were listening, this happened yesterday, and she blew my request for lunch off. We haven't talked since. I haven't had the chance to tell her that. I've composed several texts but never sent them. She wanted space, and I have to respect that. I'm not going to force my presence on her. I have more respect for Ainslon than to do that." The smug smile on A.J.'s face put her on edge. "Why are you looking at me like that?"

"It's clear you care about her. Love, maybe?"

Lauren waved her hand in the air, then opened the folder. "Don't be ridiculous." A.J. reached over and closed the folder. Lauren looked up, catching a smirk on A.J.'s face. "Do you have something more to say?"

"You can deny it all you want, but it's there. There's nothing wrong with loving someone."

"I haven't even known her that long. It can't be love." What an absurd notion. "We've only been out a few times."

"I knew from the moment I laid eyes on Leslie that I would love her for the rest of my life. Just because she isn't here anymore doesn't mean I don't love her. It's cliché but our eyes met from across the room and bam." She smacked her hands together. "I was a goner. Some people have instant attraction. Some have instant lust. While others have an instant connection. That's what

Leslie and I had. We clicked on every level. I would do silly things just to see her smile. Her laugh could turn a bad day around in an instant." She snapped her fingers. "Holding her in my arms felt like I was holding everything. Sometimes it's instant, Lauren. And yes, it's scary, but it is so much fun. We laughed together. Cried. Fought. Made up. She was everything. The first time I held her hand, I was humbled. The last time I held her hand, I was grateful. Grateful that I was there when she died. Grateful she allowed me into her life. Grateful for all the memories. That this amazing, beautiful, smart, sassy woman wanted me, blew my mind. Lauren, you can't let those moments pass you by. Those are the moments that make life worth living. Being successful is fulfillment on one level, but there's nothing saying you can't be fulfilled on all levels."

Lauren opened a desk drawer to grab a Kleenex from a box she kept in there. She wiped her eyes. Even after being gone for two years, A.J.'s love for Leslie was evident. "Thanks for sharing that."

A.J. smiled and accepted a Kleenex to wipe her own eyes.

"Even after everything that's happened, would you go back and do it again?"

"In a heartbeat." A.J. clasped her hand. "It was so worth it. Love is always worth it. No matter how much it hurts." A.J. blew her nose. "Now, that's enough of that. Let's look at the brochures."

Lauren gladly accepted the change in subject. Love, no, but an instant connection, yes. There had always existed a spark between them, and it did scare her, but it also excited her.

An hour later, and after a few changes, A.J. packed up her papers. "It's going to be fine." She pulled Lauren up and into her arms. "You deserve this. Everything's going to work out. Trust me. I know these things."

Lauren chuckled. "I will. Thank you, A.J."

"Anytime. I'll have the changes in a couple of days and if everything is to your liking, I'll have the final design by the end of the week."

"Sounds good."

After the door closed, Lauren plopped down in her chair and picked up the picture of her and Ainslon again. She traced Ainslon's smile with the tip of her finger. The feelings this woman invoked in her were like nothing she'd ever felt before. Losing Ainslon wasn't an option. She wouldn't roll over and give her the building, but she would find a way they could go on even with the building hanging over them. She hoped Ainslon would agree with her plan; she couldn't fathom another option.

Chapter Eighteen

The last thing Ainslon wanted was to get dressed up and mingle with the town. After pursuing the food festival website, the night before, she realized that Lauren was a platinum sponsor, meaning she would also be at the banquet.

Numerous times, she'd picked up her phone to text her over the past week but couldn't bring herself to do it. She hoped Lauren would text her but if their positions were reversed, she wouldn't have either. The moment the words left her mouth, after their meeting with the real estate agent, she instantly regretted telling Lauren they needed to put a hold on their budding friendship. She hoped she had a chance tonight to make things right with Lauren.

With her hand on the doorknob it hit her that Lauren might not be alone tonight. She didn't know what she would do if Lauren came with a date to this event. It would hurt, but it would be no one's fault but her own.

Downstairs she waved at the night security guard, then walked out and slipped into Justin's truck. Where he had opted to wear black slacks and a pink dress shirt, Ainslon had decided on gray slacks and a green sweater. The chosen hall for the banquet always ran cold and Ainslon hated being cold.

"You look like someone stole Shady. What's going on?"

She let out a long breath. "I regret telling Lauren that we should put a hold on what we were doing."

He nodded. "It's a mess. That's for sure."

"I really like her, Justin, and I might have ruined everything. What if she never wants to see me again?"

"I don't think that's the case. Geez, Ainslon, it hasn't even been a week. Give her some credit. I've seen the way she looks at you and she doesn't strike me as a player. You trust her, right?"

Did she? Yes, she did. The thought surprised her, but it shouldn't have. Lauren had been nothing but genuine with her, and Ainslon needed to stop jumping to conclusions. "I do. She's never given me a reason not to."

"That's good. If you see her tonight, talk to her."

"You mean apologize?"

"Yes." He mimicked playing the drums on the steering wheel. "It's like we're one person. Your mind to my mind. Your thoughts to my thoughts," he dead-panned.

Ainslon burst out laughing. "You dork."

"It got you to laugh. Look," he said, as he pulled into the parking lot. "If we don't get the building, it's not the end of the world. I was frustrated but it wasn't her fault. But you'll have to make the first move. If I were in her position, I would wait for you to come to me."

"Why are you always right?"

"It's a curse I'm willing to live with."

She pushed his shoulder. "Let's go."

Inside the doors, they received their name tags. She groaned when Justin turned to her after putting on his name tag. "Tuvok. Really?"

He pulled her away from the table. "Name tags

are silly."

Ainslon stopped walking. "I remembered you can't bring a plus one so Lauren wouldn't be bringing a date here."

"A date. Geez, Ainslon, you're so dramatic sometimes." He squeezed her shoulders. "Relax." He eyed the table to their left. "Feel better?"

"Not really. All you did was squeeze my shoulders, not give me a massage."

"The full treatment isn't free." With one last squeeze, he removed his hands. "Dave's here. I'm going to go say hi."

Figures she would lose out to Dave, the owner of Taco Heaven. "Don't leave me."

"Don't be silly. I'm sure there's someone here you can talk to. Oh, look who walked in."

Ainslon turned and locked eyes with Lauren. She took a deep breath to steady her nerves enough to walk up to her when Olivia Markinson slipped her arm through Lauren's and guided her to a table set up at the opposite side of the room.

Ainslon stopped a woman wearing an apron of a volunteer server. "Is their booze in this place?" Surely, Teresa, as the organizer of this event, would supply ample beverages.

The sympathetic look on the woman's face confirmed her worst fears. "I'm afraid not. Teresa authorized soda and water."

"No iced tea?"

The volunteer grimaced. "She's on some kind of health kick. No added sugar."

"But you said soda."

"All diet." The woman winked. "Good luck tonight. Better you than me."

Well, hell. She turned to find Justin when she noticed Lauren's eyes on her, then Olivia whispered something in her ear and Lauren turned back to her. At this rate, everything was going to crash and burn. She would never forgive Easton for missing tonight. Of all nights, this had to be the one she had to go out of town. Lucky bitch.

"Ainslon, I thought that was you," someone said from behind her.

Ainslon turned around. "Teresa, hi."

Teresa slipped her arm through Ainslon's. "Let me show you around. I bet there's a few people you don't know. I'll introduce you."

"Lead the way."

Teresa started out on one side of the room and the closer they got to Olivia and Lauren's table, the more Ainslon cursed this night.

"Oh, look where we are," Teresa said. "I believe you already know Lauren, but I'm not sure you know Olivia."

Ainslon narrowed her eyes at a sheepish Teresa. Of course, this woman would look at the gossip sites. She turned to Olivia. "I've had the pleasure." She held her hand out and after a second Olivia clasped it and squeezed.

"And a pleasure it is," Olivia purred and Ainslon noticed Lauren rolling her eyes.

"Well, I have to go," Teresa abruptly said and practically ran off.

"That woman is nothing but trouble," Olivia said. "The biggest busy-body in this town."

"Hush now," Lauren said. "You're only upset because she was named the board chair and not you."

"It's still unbelievable." Olivia turned to Ainslon.

"Can you believe it?" Olivia motioned to an empty chair across the table from her. "Join us."

Ainslon slid into the chair. "Actually, knowing you both, no, I can't. She seems more the type that would blackmail someone." Ainslon shrugged. "Who knows?" She took a breath and wheeled her courage up. "Olivia, it's lovely to see you again, but may I have a private moment with Lauren?"

Olivia looked between them. "Of course." She patted Lauren on the shoulder. "I'll be back in a few minutes."

Once Olivia walked off, Ainslon moved to the seat beside Lauren.

Lauren gave a questioning lift of her brow.

Ainslon didn't like the indecisive look on Lauren's face. "I'm sorry for the way I acted last week. It wasn't your fault and you didn't deserve my snark. I was unsettled by everything and let my insecurities get the best of me."

Lauren's features relaxed. "Apology accepted."

"Just like that?" How could this woman be real?

"Yes." Lauren chuckled. "Just like that. I…I won't lie, your attitude hurt me, but I can understand it. About the building, that is."

Ainslon touched her arm. "It's business. Nothing more. I thought a lot about it this past week. I am truly sorry about my attitude. Whoever gets the building is out of our hands. I won't hold a grudge if it goes to you. I would hope you wouldn't if Justin and I get it."

Lauren covered Ainslon's hand with her own. "Of course not. I know you said it was just business, but I hope we can continue to develop our friendship and see where it goes."

"It is just business and I think the decision

we made about being friends and taking it slow is something we can continue. I'm not sure now is a good time to take it further. At least not until the business with the building is settled, then we'll see."

Lauren nodded, but her expression looked worried. "You make it sound like if I get the building that you won't want to be more than just friends. Please tell me that's not what you're saying."

Ainslon frowned. That is what it sounded like. "That sounded a lot better in my head than when I said it. Is something more than friends a possibility you would want if I get the building?"

"Yes."

Ainslon preened a bit at her answer but held steadfast. "Right now, all I can offer is friendship, and we can certainly see where it goes from there. I really don't want to mix business with pleasure."

Lauren squeezed her hand, then let it go. "Friendship first, but let me get this straight, you're not saying no to anything more developing. Right?"

"Right. More is on the table."

A pleased smile lit Lauren's face. "That's what I wanted to hear. Now, if we only had something to toast with."

"Our options are water or diet soda."

Lauren stood and held her hand out for Ainslon to take. Ainslon grasped the offered hand. "Don't be silly. If you've been friends with Ollie as long as I have, you learn a few things."

"Like?"

Lauren lead her across the room to Olivia, who'd just concluded a conversation with a woman and had turned toward them.

"Like the fact that she would never attend one of

these events without alcohol." Lauren stopped in front of Olivia.

"Can I help you with something?"

The smirk on Olivia's lips would have had Ainslon swooning if she wasn't already interested in Lauren. She'd known Olivia for the last year, from her coming into the store, but the thought had never occurred to her to ask her out. No, she had reserved that thought for Lauren and Lauren alone.

Lauren leaned close to her. "I hear you have the good stuff."

Olivia grimaced. "Not tonight. Heidi was fussy before I left, and I forgot and left the flask I was going to bring in my desk drawer. Because, God knows, it's hard enough to get through one of these events with alcohol; I don't know how we're going to survive without it."

Lauren nodded. "Ladies, it looks like we'll have to rely on our wit and water to get us through tonight."

Olivia pasted on a faux shocked look. "Water, Lauren, really? I'm going for the hard stuff. I spy Diet Coke on that table over there. It's sort of mind-boggling Teresa bought name brand. Lauren, I'll get your water." She regarded Ainslon. "Anything for you?"

"Water's fine."

"I'll be back."

Lauren knocked shoulders with Ainslon. "Just you and me."

Ainslon relaxed against Lauren when she slipped her arm around her waist. This is what she wanted. Just being comfortable with someone else. Just enjoying the silence and being together. "Would you like to have breakfast with me tomorrow morning?"

"I would love to."

Yes, losing Lauren, at this point, was not an option. She would have to come to terms with her personal life and her business colliding.

Chapter Nineteen

The night before, when Justin had brought her home, Ainslon let him know her plans for having breakfast with Lauren. He had been nothing but supportive, and she promised to bring him something back. With her backpack snug on her back, she hopped into the fray and joined the countless others on the crosswalk.

As her feet took her to the familiar destination, her thoughts strayed to Lauren and their predicament. Last night proved she wasn't ready to walk away from what she and Lauren had.

She thanked the gentleman holding the door open for her, took a deep breath, and let the smell of coffee, cinnamon, and baking bread invade her senses. She smiled at Alice, working behind the counter, and pointed to the back. Alice nodded, and Ainslon walked behind the counter and into the kitchen, then turned right towards Easton's office.

Knowing Easton got home around one last night and had barely gotten any sleep, Ainslon expected her to look tired, but she should have known better. Easton never came to work looking anything but professional and refreshed. "Good morning."

Easton leaned back in her seat. "No offense, but you look like shit. Did you get any sleep? You texted me that everything went well last night. What happened afterward?"

Ainslon flopped down in the chair in front of the desk. "Not as much as I would have liked." She shrugged. "At eight, we parted ways and I didn't fall asleep until after midnight. Do I really look bad?"

"I'm your sister. I can tell. Others, probably not. Justin will. What brings you in here? Shouldn't you be waiting for Lauren out there?"

"I had a few minutes to spare you. I promised Justin I would bring him some cinnamon rolls back." She lifted her hands.

"Well then. I'll make sure to save him some. Coffee too?"

"Yes."

"So, am I going to officially meet Lauren any time soon?"

Ainslon rolled her eyes. "If you want to meet her, you can bring Justin's order to me. Okay?" She should have seen that coming. Easton had bugged her for weeks.

"I will. Go grab a seat. We're busy this morning and I'm sure you two don't want to stand."

"Not really."

She was only in the office for a few minutes, but the dining area had filled up. She quickly snatched up one of the few available tables and sat, waiting for Lauren. She didn't have to look up when someone stepped in front of her. She would know that fragrance anywhere.

"Good morning, Ainslon."

She slipped her phone in her pocket and gave Lauren her full attention. "It wasn't, but it is now."

Lauren's voice was a teasing purr. "Do you come here often?" They both chuckled at the joke, and Ainslon felt a peace not felt since yesterday. Lauren sat across from her.

"Besides all the time I spend with you here. It's so close to the store and the fact that my sister owns it means I usually come in every morning. The banana nut muffins are fantastic."

"I enjoy them as well."

"It's Nana's recipe."

"The next time you see Edna, tell her the recipe is divine."

"I will."

The silence was only a bit awkward. Lauren broke the silence. "I'm glad you walked up to me last night. I wouldn't have done the same with you. The last thing I wanted was to disrespect the boundaries you'd put in place."

"Even if Teresa hadn't dragged me over there, I had still planned to talk with you." Ainslon nervously twisted her napkin. "I'm sorry about everything. Sometimes I let my thoughts get the best of me."

"We all do, but I hope you know you can trust me. Yes, I am a businesswoman and it's important to me, but a friend recently told me there are other things that can fulfill us. I like spending time with you." Lauren looked directly into Ainslon's eyes. "Please, don't doubt that. You mean a lot to me."

Seeing Lauren laying her feelings bare kicked Ainslon into gear. "You mean a lot to me as well. I always enjoy spending time with you."

"Good." Lauren pulled her hand back. "Now, I don't have as much time as I would like to spare for us this morning, so let's enjoy breakfast."

"Any time you have is enough."

They were finishing up when Easton walked up to them with a bag and a coffee cup in hand. "I threw in a few other things for you too." She nudged Ainslon.

"Oh, sorry." Ainslon accepted the bag and coffee. "Lauren, this is my sister, Easton. Easton, this is Lauren."

Lauren stood. "It's lovely to meet you. I recognize you from visits to my store."

"Yes, I've been there on more than one occasion." She quickly glanced at Ainslon. "And God knows, Ainslon goes on and on and on about you."

"Okay." Ainslon stood. "You've met her. So, I'm sure you have work to do."

Easton chuckled. "That I do. It was nice to meet you officially."

"You as well."

Easton turned to Ainslon. "Talk to you later, sis." Then walked toward the back.

"So." Lauren turned to Ainslon. "How often do you talk about me?"

"You're always the topic of conversation."

"I like the sound of that."

"I just bet you do."

"I would rather be on your mind than anyone else's." Lauren squeezed Ainslon's hand. "If you'll give me enough time to grab a coffee, I'll walk you to work."

Ainslon would have never asked, but it seemed like for the first time the universe was in her corner. "Of course, I'll wait." Ainslon made her way out the front door, slipped the bag inside her backpack, then rested her shoulder against the building with the coffee container in hand. There was something so intoxicating about Lauren. She looked up when the door opened, and Lauren walked out, headed in her direction. Neither one said a word while they walked toward Turn the Page.

At the crosswalk, Lauren spoke up. "How's business going?"

"Good. Yours?"

She chuckled. "I can't complain."

Ainslon tried to keep her composure when Lauren entwined their fingers as they walked the final block to her store. She pulled them to a stop outside the building. "Here we are."

"Yes." Lauren raised their joined hands and kissed Ainslon's knuckles. "I would love to stay and talk some more, but work awaits."

"Sure. Sure. How about we meet for coffee in the morning at Brew and Bake? Say seven-thirty."

"I would really like that, but I have a brunch I have to attend later, so if just coffee is okay, I would love to meet. I promise to have more time tomorrow."

"Only coffee is fine. I'll see you tomorrow." Instead of watching her walk away, Ainslon entered the store, made a beeline for Justin at the counter, and placed the coffee tray in his hand, then pulled the pastries from her bag.

"I see Lauren walked you here."

"We're having coffee tomorrow morning. We decided to stay friends for now, with the possibility of more later."

"Why are you hesitant? You really like her." He shrugged. "Just go for it."

"Really? I mean. I do really like her, and I know I shouldn't let it come between us, but I don't think I can start anything more with her while this building looms over our heads. Is that wrong?"

"No." He tore off a piece of his cinnamon roll and held it up for her. She snatched it out of his fingers and popped it in her mouth. "By the way," he called as she walked in the back room with the bag. "You look terrible this morning."

"Thanks, buddy."

"Anytime."

She sat on the stool and stared into space. She had a feeling she would never just be Lauren's friend. The pull between them was magnetic, but there were a lot of factors that could hinder taking it further. Tomorrow couldn't come fast enough.

Chapter Twenty

Ainslon would never admit to anyone how early she woke up or how many outfits she'd tried on before settling on a pair of cream-colored trousers and burgundy lightweight sweater. Sneakers would never do, so she pulled out a pair of black flats. At the last minute, she pulled her hair up and secured it with a black clip. It may be only coffee but it felt like the beginning of something and she didn't want to mess it up. She could always find another building, but not another Lauren and she didn't want to lose their budding relationship.

At exactly seven-fifteen, she pulled open the door to Brew and Bake and stepped inside, sliding to the right of the door to survey her surroundings. Lauren hadn't arrived yet, and she waved at Alice as she waited out of the way of customers. Ten minutes later, her eyes widened as they latched onto Lauren walking her way. Today she wore a black pencil skirt, pale blue silk blouse, and black heels. Her curls were out in full force and Ainslon loved it. She'd yet to work up the nerve to run her fingers through them and her anticipation grew every time Lauren wore her hair like this.

Ainslon accepted the kiss on her cheek from Lauren, and hoped she wasn't blushing too hard. Damn her pale skin. "Good morning."

"Good morning, Ainslon. You look lovely today."

"You look amazing, as usual."

"That's kind of you to say."

"It's the truth. I've liked you in everything I've seen you in."

Lauren arched her brow. "Is that right?" A smirk played on her lips.

Ainslon replayed in her mind what she said and groaned. By the look on Lauren's face, she was enjoying her discomfort. "Coffee?"

Lauren smiled. "Yes, coffee. Let's go."

It was hard not to react to Lauren's hand at the small of her back, but she held it together as they walked up to the counter and ordered.

Ainslon turned her attention back to Lauren. "If you want to wait by the door, I'll bring these over."

"All right."

Ainslon watched Lauren walk away. She had a feeling Lauren put a little extra sway in her hips. When Lauren abruptly stopped, turned around, and winked, Ainslon knew she had been caught. Lauren held her gaze a moment longer. Lauren would be the death of her.

Ainslon swung her head around when Alice said her name and placed the coffees on the counter.

"Two coffees for the lady," Alice said with a knowing smile.

"Thank you," Ainslon nodded and carried the coffee to Lauren, who opened the door for her, then accepted her cup. "Their coffee is the best."

"It is. Since it opened three years ago, I come here a few times a week."

"I don't know how we haven't run into each other before."

Lauren took a sip of her coffee. "I don't know

either. I've had C and C for the last twelve years and you've never been in my store before."

"You got me there." They'd been in such close proximity for the last few years and never met. It almost felt like a right time right place feeling. Like they weren't meant to meet until now. They fell into a comfortable silence.

Lauren spoke. "Maybe it's fate we didn't meet until now." She tapped her finger on the side of her cup.

Ainslon moved closer to Lauren when a few men passed by them. "You don't strike me as the type to believe in fate."

"I can assure you I am a hopeless romantic."

"Now, that I can see. Are you a flowers and chocolate kind of girl or does the unconventional suit you?"

Lauren stopped and leaned back against a building, holding her coffee cup between her hands. "A little of both. I like surprises. What about you?"

"I would never say no to chocolate."

"Too bad you don't know anybody who owns a chocolate store."

Ainslon grinned. "Yes, it is." They fell into an easy conversation and made two laps around the block when Lauren looked at her watch.

"Oh, my. It's almost nine o'clock."

"I guess you need to be going?"

"I do."

"Let me walk you to work."

"All right."

At C and C, Ainslon turned to Lauren. "I had a nice time."

"I did as well." Lauren reached over and straightened her collar. "We should do it again sometime."

"Tomorrow?"

"Tomorrow."

This brought a smile to Ainslon's lips. "Have a good day."

"You too."

She watched Lauren until she was out of sight then walked back to Brew and Bake to pick up breakfast for her and Justin.

She was waiting for her order when an arm snaked around her waist and a hand held out a white paper bag. "So," Easton said. "Getting lucky this morning, sis?"

Ainslon snorted. "It sure felt like it."

"From the glimpse I caught of you two, you look good together."

She turned her face to Easton. "You think so?"

"I do." She gave her waist one last squeeze. "Are you going to see her again?"

"Tomorrow. Here again."

"Nice. I'll make sure to put a little something special on our breakfast menu."

"Am I crazy? She's so…" She waved her hand in the air. "And I'm so…"

Easton placed her hands on Ainslon's shoulders. "Listen. I'm only going to say this once. Stop over analyzing everything. You like her. She likes you. You've had two dates at the park already."

"Friend dates."

Easton rolled her eyes. "Whatever. Just enjoy being with her."

"That's it?"

"Yes."

"I hope so."

"I know so."

"Okay." She kissed Easton on the cheek and stepped back. "We both have to get to work."

"I'll call you. We're still on for dinner Sunday night with Nana?"

"Nothing could keep me away."

"Not even your new, hot, almost girlfriend."

"Even that. Bye."

"Bye."

The walk to the bookstore only took ten minutes despite the crowded sidewalk. They didn't officially open until ten, but a man paced in front of their door. If Justin would have noticed, he would have let him in. She had her key firmly in hand when she approached him. "Can I help you?"

"I hope so. I have a birthday party I need to attend in," he looked at his watch, "forty-five minutes, and I need a book for my girlfriend's son."

"Sure thing." She unlocked the door and motioned him in.

"Thank you. Thank you so much."

"Not a problem. I'll tell you what. Since I've had a good morning, I'll give you ten percent off your purchase."

"Thank you," the man said, and shuffled off to find a book.

Justin motioned to the door. "I didn't even see him out there or I would have let him in."

"No problem; he was out there pacing." She plopped the white bag on the counter. "Compliments of Easton."

"I love your sister." He took the bag and walked into the back office.

As soon as the man paid for his three books, and

Justin came back out, she took his place in the office and decided it was a good time to get some paperwork done.

Time flew and she sat back in her chair and groaned when it hit her it was almost lunch time. After stretching and grabbing a bottle of water, she walked back into the storefront at the same time a delivery man entered. Her eyes automatically went to the bag he carried with an unmistakable C and C logo.

He walked up to the counter and glanced at his clipboard. "Ainslon?"

"That's me."

He handed over the bag. "Have a good day."

Before she could tip him, he was out the door. Her fingers shook a bit on the handle of the bag, and she set it on the counter, staring at it, but not touching it.

"Aren't you going to open it or at least read the card?" Justin asked.

She plucked the envelope off the bag and slid the card out.

Here's an assortment of some of my favorites and a small surprise. I hope you enjoy them as much as I do.

Ainslon couldn't stop the smile that blossomed on her face, as her heart pounded in her chest. The note was going somewhere safe.

"Nice," Justin said.

She nodded, opened the bag, and pulled out the contents. Four small boxes contained four different kinds of filled chocolates, and a small bag contained an assortment of miniature chocolate bars. Four large strawberries lay inside the biggest box, covered in four different chocolates; white, milk, semi-sweet, and dark. Ainslon's mouth watered at the sight of them. In the bottom of the bag was an index card with Lauren's delicate script written on it. The surprise in the top box blew her away. Nestled in the box was a paper squirrel. Origami. Lauren was full of surprises. She set the squirrel back in the box and slipped it under the counter so it wouldn't get messed up.

I had a good time this morning. Play your cards right and the deliveries will keep coming. From your personal chocolate supplier.

P.S. I'm looking forward to tomorrow and I hope you enjoy the squirrel. It's a hobby I took up in college.

Per Easton's advice, she didn't overthink things. She opened her messages app and quickly typed a note and hit send.

Thank you for the chocolate and the squirrel. You're full of surprises. I enjoyed this morning and am looking forward to tomorrow. I can't wait to learn all your favorites.

A moment later her phone pinged with an incoming message from Lauren.

I'm so glad you enjoyed the gift. I can't talk now, but I wouldn't be opposed to you calling me later tonight. Around nine.

Nine it is.

She set her bag under the counter and slid her strawberries to the corner of the counter when a customer set their comics and figurine down. By the looks of it, they were in for a busy day and that's exactly what she needed to keep her mind off Lauren. She usually didn't wish for time to fly, but she couldn't wait until tonight.

Chapter Twenty-one

Ainslon bounced into Brew and Bake nearly a month later, almost walking on air. Things with Lauren were progressing slow and steady, but well. The only fly in the ointment was that nearly two weeks after their meeting with Fredrick, he'd called and informed them the owner of the building hadn't decided yet and was going on vacation for three weeks abroad and would give them her decision after she returned. Ainslon wasn't happy but there was nothing she could do about it. Now, the waiting game continued.

As soon as Easton got a look at her face, she dragged her back to her office.

"Spill." She pushed Ainslon into the chair at the desk, while she leaned against the desk.

"Lauren and I have been talking and having breakfast together. It's nice."

Easton rolled her eyes. "I know that. What changed? You look different."

"Nothing." Ainslon ran over the last few weeks in her head but didn't come up with anything different. She'd met Lauren for coffee every few mornings and exchanged small gifts. Her origami collection quickly grew. Every night they talked on the phone and texted. Ainslon had also taken to sending Lauren little things from her store that reminded her of the other woman, from a Wonder Woman keychain to a story book about a chocolate store.

"So, you're dating?"

"No." Ainslon almost spit the word out. "We're friends." That stupid phrase again. It would be fine for anyone else, but Lauren wasn't just anyone. She'd brought this on herself and would do it the same way again though she yearned to take the next step with Lauren. "I called her last night and we talked for an hour like we always do."

Easton arched her brow. "Okay." She pushed off the desk, grasped Ainslon's arm, and hoisted her out of the chair. "If you don't want her to see you acting like you won the lottery, you might want to drop the blinding smile and walk like a normal person."

Ainslon wiped the smile off her face. "Is it really noticeable?"

"Yes. Yes, it is. Unless you want her to know you're willing to have her babies, you should cool it. Just friends, remember."

That stupid phrase again. "Got it." She ran her hands through her hair. The same hair she'd worked on for at least half an hour before leaving her apartment.

"I am not trying to put a damper on your joy. I am really happy for you."

Ainslon stood and engulfed her in a hug. "Your time will come. If it works out to be just a friendship with Lauren, it will have been worth it."

"Liar." Easton pushed her toward the office door. "You better get out there and don't forget my game on Saturday."

"I'll be there." Ainslon took a deep breath, walked out of the office, and crossed the room to join Lauren, who was seated at their regular table.

"Sorry, sorry. My sister dragged me to her office

as soon as I walked in."

"Not a problem. I hope what I ordered was all right?" Lauren smoothed her hand over the napkin.

"I'll let you in on a secret. I'll eat anything they sell here."

"I'll keep that in mind."

They ate in a comfortable silence.

"As much as we've talked, there is one subject that never seems to come up." Lauren pushed her empty saucer to the center of the table.

Ainslon frowned. "What subject?" They'd covered a wide array of categories thus far.

"Our dating history."

"Oh. That."

"If you don't want to…" Lauren hurried on.

"Would you mind going first?"

"I don't mind." Lauren took a sip of coffee. "I didn't date a lot in high school, but I did have a steady girlfriend my senior year. We parted when we graduated. College was a different story. I played the field but that all changed when I met Gabby. She was everything I was looking for in a partner. Smart, trustworthy, could cook a mean scone." Lauren chuckled. "I fell hard and fast but so did she. We worked well together. I'm not one to get jealous but Gabby was. I wouldn't have stood for that in any other relationship. She was different. It was the first time I could see myself spending my life with someone."

That sounded wonderful to Ainslon. "What happened?"

"Nothing bad, actually. Gabby wanted to see the world. Her dream had always been to travel. I'm surprised she even made it through college because she hated staying in one place for long. Me on the other hand, I like having a place to call home. I love Garriety and this is where my family is. A lot of young kids want to grow up so they can get away from their family and move away, but not me. That was never me. Family is everything. She got the opportunity to spend six months in Japan as an au pair. We discussed it, but I knew she wanted to go. No matter how much I loved her, I knew I would never force her to stay. We parted on good terms and stayed friends for a while. She called when the six months was up and told me she was going to Thailand. I knew, once she took the position in Japan, I would probably never see her again."

"Do you talk to her still?"

"Not as much as I would like. The last time I talked with her she was dating, in her words, a Greek goddess. I haven't spoken to her in six months. I date here and there and I'm not above casual dating, but I've always enjoyed being in a relationship. By the way, I'm clean. I was tested two months ago."

"That's good. I'm clean as well." Ainslon drummed her fingers on the countertop. "My dating history is a mix of good and bad. Even after I moved in with Nana, and I knew she was accepting, my mind would still replay the moment that my parents walked in on me and my best friend, Deirdre, making out. That stayed with me for a long while. There was the one girl in high school, but we never did more than make out. It wasn't until I was in college that I had my first real relationship. Holly and I dated for two years off and on. While it was my first relationship, it wasn't serious. It all fell apart when I found out I wasn't the only one she was seeing. I knew we weren't exclusive, but it still hurt. I met Heather, believe it or not, at the grocery store. That relationship imploded because I couldn't trust her. She hadn't done anything bad, but the trust would never come. I don't know why. I hoped I could work it out, but I couldn't. She broke up with me a week before Christmas."

"Oh, that sucks."

"It really did. I had bought her a tan leather jacket. Easton ended up getting that. She still wears it from time to time. The only other person worth mentioning is Jessica. We dated for almost a year. It was fun, but she wanted more and I…I didn't. It didn't feel right."

"That's important to you?"

"It is."

"I agree. If something doesn't feel like it's going to work, why put in the effort? A piece of me will always love Gabby. She was my first love and it took a long time to get over her. Just because it was a mutual breakup didn't make it hurt any less. I still have a photo album from when we dated. I don't think I'll ever be able to throw it out and I hope anyone I date will understand what it means to me. I don't look back on the photos and wish I was there again. I look back on them and think, man, I'm so glad I lived those memories."

That type of love sounded amazing and exactly what Ainslon wanted. She didn't know Gabby, but what a fool she was to think seeing the world would ever compare to having Lauren in her life. Ainslon leaned forward and grasped both of Lauren's hands. "So, on top of being a romantic, you're sentimental. A woman of many facets. You keep surprising me, Lauren. In only good ways, I promise."

Lauren's face seemed to light up. "I hope so. You surprise me as well."

"How so?"

Instead of answering Ainslon's question, she asked one of her own. "Our friendship seems to be heading in the right direction."

Ainslon groaned at Lauren's phrasing and the twinkle in her eyes. "Right direction indeed."

"Good. Because Callie has informed me, I should invite you to our softball game this Saturday."

Ainslon tried to hide her shock. "Our?" That hadn't come up in any of their talks.

"Callie convinced me to sponsor and be a part of it. This weekend is the first time I've been able to play this year. I might add," Lauren leaned across the table, "I pull off the uniform nicely."

"I'll be there," Ainslon said quickly.

Lauren pulled one of her hands back and tapped her bottom lip with the left index finger. "Although, you didn't let me finish."

Ainslon frowned. "Go on."

"Callie insists on everyone being present for our games if they don't have to work." Lauren let the statement hang in the air.

Everyone. Ainslon gulped. "Okay."

"You've already met Callie, but my mother will also be there, as well as Callie's husband and her son."

"Your entire family?"

"Yes." Lauren reached up and fiddled with her necklace. "Friends meet friend's families all the time."

The knowing smirk on Lauren's face set her heart racing. "Of course, I can meet your family. I would love to meet your family."

"It's settled then."

"It is." Ainslon would worry about meeting Lauren's family later.

"Edna is welcome, as is anyone else you want to

invite."

"I'll invite her."

"Good."

Ainslon stood and cleared off the table. She placed her hand on the small of Lauren's back as she opened the door and they walked out onto the busy sidewalk. Ainslon opened her mouth when a thought hit her, then snapped it shut. Lauren in a pair of tight baseball pants and a jersey was a fantasy she didn't even know she had until now. "So." She gave Lauren a half-lidded look. "Softball uniform, huh?"

Lauren laced their arms together. "You bet."

"I can't wait." Ainslon's words came out an octave higher.

Lauren chuckled and pulled Ainslon away from the people on the street and closer to the building. She leaned close to her, then whispered in her ear. "Play your cards right, O'Neil, and I might let you play catcher to my pitcher." With a smirk on her lips and a wink she quickly added, "As friends, of course." Then she kissed Ainslon on the cheek and walked away, leaving a speechless Ainslon behind.

It wasn't until Ainslon was safely seated behind her desk that it hit her. She already had plans for Saturday, and they included watching Easton play softball. No way would she miss spending more time with Lauren, even if that involved meeting Lauren's family. Besides, she had a buffer. Edna would be right there by her side. She had a few days to work out the kinks.

Chapter Twenty-two

Ainslon breezed into her store on Saturday morning, bypassed Justin helping a customer at the counter, grabbed her laptop, and got to work on updating their inventory. Normally she would have the day off, but she'd promised Justin the day before that she would go over their inventory before going to the game. She hummed and mindlessly ate from the bag of trail mix she'd brought with her. She could feel Justin's eyes on her, but she ignored him and continued with her task. Coincidently, Easton and Lauren's team were pitted against each other today, making Ainslon's choice to choose between the two unimportant. She hoped she could find a spot where she could root for both teams.

She chewed on an almond while crunching the numbers until she was sure their stock was in order. She closed the laptop, sealed the bag of trail mix, and looked up. Justin stood back against the counter with his arms crossed, staring at her. "What?" Had she missed something? She looked around the store, but everything seemed in order.

He smirked and fixed his gaze on her shirt for a moment. "Nice shirt. Bit of a change, but nice nonetheless."

She blushed. After Lauren had told her about the game, she had gone to C and C and bought one of their softball team's shirts. She shrugged. "I'm also supporting Easton." She pulled a ball cap out of her bag and slipped it on.

"I take it things are going well between you two."

She slipped the laptop back under the counter and squeezed his forearm. "It's going really good. It's going to be a pain to cheer them both on. I'm hoping to find a spot between the two teams to show support for them both."

He looked horrified. "Good luck."

"I don't need luck." They both laughed and she quickly finished her work, then collected Edna to go with her.

At the third stop light, Edna touched Ainslon's arm. "Nice shirt."

"Thanks, Nana." She quickly added, "I have on Easton's hat."

"Seems sensible. Are you nervous about meeting Lauren's family?"

"A little."

Edna patted her leg. "No need for that. Any woman would be lucky to snag you. Lauren's not bad looking herself."

"You can say that again."

"I take it everything's still headed in the right direction."

"So far, so good. I really like her, Nana."

"Oh, Ainslon, I know. It's written all over your face. Now if we can get Easton to meet someone, we'd be all set."

"You should make that your next project."

"I might do that."

It didn't take them long to reach the ballpark and find a parking space but finding a seat would be trickier than she expected.

Edna held tight to Ainslon's arm as they made their way through the grass. Ainslon didn't want to stop and talk with anyone, so she would nod at a familiar face and continue on. Edna pointed in front of them at Callie and they headed toward her. Ainslon took a deep breath and continued walking even when she took in the few people scattered around Callie. Instead of sitting on the bleachers, they had a half-dozen chairs set up in a line between the two bleachers.

Callie waved at them. "Ainslon, Edna, join us." Edna let go of Ainslon and accepted the hug from Callie.

Ainslon nervously swallowed when three expectant faces zeroed in on her. "Callie," Ainslon said.

"Ainslon, Edna, this is my husband Jeffrey and my son Charlie, and this is my mother, Patricia."

Ainslon accepted each of their handshakes and dread filled her when she turned to Patricia. Ainslon could see where Lauren and Callie got their looks from. "Ma'am."

"So, you're Ainslon. Lauren has told me about you."

"That's lovely." Ainslon shook her hand, then stuffed her hands in her pockets.

"Well," Edna said. "Lauren hasn't told us anything about you."

With bated breath, Ainslon watched the standoff between Edna and Patricia with trepidation until Patricia took Edna's hand and led her to the last two chairs in the row and they sat down.

Callie wrapped her arm around Ainslon's waist. "They'll get along great."

"When I first met her," Jeffrey said, "she scared the shit out of me, but she's not a bad old—"

"Dad," Charlie said. "Don't let Gramma hear you call her that."

"Call her what, Charlie?" Lauren asked from behind her.

Ainslon turned at the low timbre of Lauren's voice. The white with grey pinstriped baseball pants hugged her like a second skin, but the jersey held Ainslon's attention. It fit Lauren in all the right places and hugged her breasts, but was loose enough for her to maneuver in. "Wow." As she watched, Lauren slipped her aviator sunglasses off and clipped them in the v of her shirt.

Lauren kissed Ainslon on the cheek. "I'm sorry for being late. I hope Mother didn't give you any trouble? I see she's getting along with Edna."

"No trouble. Really. Everyone's nice, but we only arrived a short time ago." Maybe if she kept talking her heart rate would return to normal. She slipped her arm around Lauren's waist and held her phone up. "Smile." She would be setting that photo as her lock screen.

"Come on, Dad," Charlie said. "Let's get some snacks."

"Sure, son." Jeffrey called out, "It was nice meeting you, Ainslon."

"You as well."

"And that's my cue also," Callie said. "I need to give my team a pep talk. Although, we usually win against the team were up against. Five minutes, Lauri."

Ainslon cringed, but relaxed when Lauren wrapped her arms around her. "You look amazing in that shirt," Ainslon said.

"As do you."

"Thanks."

"Let's sit."

Ainslon sat beside Edna with Lauren beside her and laced their fingers together. She would keep telling herself friends behaved this way, while the rest of her knew it was total bullshit.

"You said Easton plays."

"She's on the team playing against yours."

A sinister grin appeared on Lauren's face. "That's unfortunate for her."

"Why's that?"

"She's going to lose."

Ainslon turned to face Lauren. "Want to make a bet?"

"What am I going to win?" Lauren slipped a stray piece of hair behind Ainslon's ear.

"Winner gets to pick what we do on our next meet up."

Lauren lifted Ainslon's hand and kissed the palm. "You're on. I know the perfect location."

"We'll see. We'll see."

Five innings later, Ainslon sat on the edge of her seat, absentmindedly eating the popcorn Jeffrey and Charlie had gotten for her. Lauren's team was up by two points. Lauren hadn't told her before today what position she played and Ainslon had been surprised when she'd taken up her spot as shortstop. Lauren was good and not one ball had gotten past her yet, but Ainslon hadn't expected anything less. She knew no matter what team won, she and Lauren would have a fantastic time together, but Ainslon hated to lose. After the end of their last inning, Lauren motioned to Ainslon and she walked to the dugout.

"Would you like to bow out now?" Lauren said, with her fingers clutching links in the dugout fencing.

"No way. They still have time to pull off a victory."

"If you say so."

In the end, Lauren's team won by one point. After the game, Ainslon hugged Easton, then introduced her to everyone. Callie asked to speak with her away from everyone.

"I'll be honest. I like you, but," Callie said, "the age difference bothered me a bit. I know it's not a lot, but Lauren has promised me that isn't a problem. It isn't a problem, is it, Ainslon?"

What was happening here? "No, it's not a problem at all. It's only ten years. I don't plan on messing this friendship up."

"Has that been a problem in the past? Messing things up."

Ainslon took a moment to consider her answer. "Depending on the situation, things have tended to go south, but I hold out hope that isn't the case with Lauren."

"She has a lot of money. Is it her money and power that attract you to her?"

Ainslon clenched her fists by her side and scanned the immediate area but didn't see Lauren anywhere. She knew she couldn't ignore the question indefinitely. She slowly turned toward Callie. "It couldn't possibly be that she's genuine, sincere, kindhearted, and by far the most attractive woman I've ever laid eyes on. Could it?"

"Very well," Callie said. "I only want what's best for my sister."

"And what would that be?" Ainslon jerked her head around at Lauren's low timbre. She couldn't help the smile that spread across her face.

"We were just talking, Lauri." Callie squeezed Ainslon's arm and rejoined the rest of the group.

Ainslon kissed Lauren on the cheek, leaned into her body, and didn't even sensor the next words out of her mouth. "Your ass looks amazing in those pants."

"Why thank you, ma'am." Lauren tipped the brim of her hat.

Ainslon swatted her arm. "You know exactly how good you look."

"I play to my strengths. As everyone should."

"And you do it so well."

"Better than Easton did today at the game."

Ainslon pressed a hand to her chest. "Ouch. That was low, Lauren. Easton did well. It's the others that could use some practice."

"I suppose I can concede that point."

Lauren intertwined their hands and lead her toward the others. "So," she paused. "How about tomorrow night I treat you to an early dinner and maybe a movie? I may be persuaded to throw in some chocolate." Then quickly added again, "A friend's dinner and a movie."

Ainslon rolled her eyes. Being only friends was the stupidest thing she could have ever said. "That's the best idea I've heard all day." Ainslon pulled her to a stop. "So, I get to spend all day with you and now I get dinner tomorrow? Just the two of us?"

"Yes."

"Fantastic."

Chapter Twenty-three

Ainslon, stop fussing. You look fine." Justin flipped the open sign to closed.

"How can you say that?" Ainslon pulled the hand mirror from behind the counter to check her appearance. Sunday, Lauren had called and had to reschedule their dinner and a movie, explaining she had to deal with a mix up at C and C. Ainslon understood, but had still been disappointed. They had rescheduled for tonight and of course this was the first Monday in weeks they'd been crazy busy. In addition to a movie, they decided on dinner at the Café, a few blocks from C and C.

"It's not your fault we've been swamped all day. Lauren will understand you didn't have time to go home and change."

"Or shower," she mumbled.

He grasped her by the shoulders and turned her around. "Calm down. You've got this." He walked her to the door, opened it, pushed her out, then locked it.

Ainslon took several deep breaths, then headed in the direction of the Café. The cool, crisp night air did nothing to stop her racing heart. She didn't know whether to be happy or disappointed Lauren wasn't there when she walked in. A waitress smiled, then directed her to a seat by the window. Ainslon informed her she would wait for her date before ordering. Even though it was seven-ten she wouldn't freak out. Like herself, Lauren could have been tied up at her store all day.

The realtor still hadn't called and Ainslon tried not to let worry set in. Surely the owner was back from vacation? One good thing that had happened was she and Shelly finally finalized their deal and just in time, considering Colin's birthday was coming up. Justin had taken the book to Lauren on their lunch break today, since she had been tied up with customers.

A few minutes later, she did a double take when she spied Lauren walking down the sidewalk. She hoped she never lost the butterflies in her stomach every time she laid eyes on her.

Lauren breezed in, walked toward their table, leaned down, and kissed her on the cheek before sitting down. "I am sorry I'm late." She pushed hair out of her face. "I can't remember the last time we were so busy."

"We were busy all day also. I didn't go home and change because I didn't want to be late." Ainslon picked at her shirt.

Lauren reached across the table and enfolded her hand. "I haven't been home either. It's not a big deal. We're both here now. That's all that matters."

The waitress arrived and took their orders before Ainslon could comment. After she left, Ainslon said, "I think things are going well for us."

"I think we're doing fine. I know we've talked a lot, but there are a few things I don't know about you."

Ainslon pinched the bridge of her nose while pondering the best way to get and impart information. "How about some standard, dull questions?"

Lauren laughed. "Sounds good. Go."

"Favorite color?"

"Green."

"Blue. Favorite food?"

"Puerto Rican."

"Irish stew. Vacation spot?"

"Disney World."

Ainslon smiled. "Really?"

Lauren looked offended for a moment, then a grin split her face. "Of course. Please don't tell me you've never been."

Ainslon was well and truly charmed by the woman sitting across from her. "When I was younger, my parents didn't have the money to take me, and as I got older and moved in with Nana, life got in the way, but I have always wanted to go. Easton too."

Lauren's eyes lit up. "It's amazing and an experience you won't soon forget. We should go sometime, if only so I can see the look on your face when we walk through the gates. I was never a fan until I took my niece and nephews for the first time and it changed my whole outlook." Lauren let go of her hand when the waitress brought their meals.

Ainslon took a bite of her sandwich. After swallowing, she took a sip of her lemonade. "Favorite book?"

Lauren wiped her mouth. "That's a tough one. My favorite books growing up were fairytales. Now, I can't really say I have a favorite one. Every book is my favorite when I'm reading it."

"That's how I feel. There are too many wonderful books in print for me to pick only one."

"Now it's time for a question of my own."

"Go on."

"If you could go anywhere in the world, and money wasn't a concern, where would you go?"

Ainslon relaxed back into her seat. "At the top of

my bucket list is Greece and from there, everywhere. I haven't had the chance to travel much, so when I do get the chance, I have a whole list. Machu Picchu, Easter Island, anywhere in New Zealand, Maijishan Caves, Masada, Israel."

"Wait." Lauren held up her hand.

Ainslon chuckled. "You did ask."

She grinned. "That's quite the list."

"That's only part of it."

"I see. The last one, Israel. Are you religious, or would you just like to see the country?"

Ainslon took a drink of her lemonade before answering. "I wouldn't call myself religious. I don't believe going to church every week will get you into heaven." She paused for a second. "I believe most religions worship the same God, but that we take different paths to get to him or her." She winked. "A hundred different people can walk a thousand different roads and they will all still make it to the same destination. What that destination is, who knows. But for me, I believe there is a heaven. Whether it's the heaven the Bible speaks of," she shrugged, "I don't know, but I have to believe there is something waiting for me when I die. I can't believe there is nothing."

Lauren nodded and took a moment to answer. "You've really thought about this and you make it all seem so attainable. I have never heard it explained that way. I can't say I am religious at all, but I see your point and where you're coming from. My family is Catholic, but...I don't know. It's never really appealed to me."

"Ladies," the waitress said, clearing the table. "Can I get you anything for dessert?"

Lauren spoke first. "I would love a mini apple pie with a scoop of butter pecan ice cream."

"I would also like the apple pie, but I want vanilla ice cream."

"I will be back shortly with your order."

"See, this hasn't been so bad."

"No, I always enjoy spending time with you." She placed her hand over Lauren's on the table.

"Good." She wiped her brow. "I wasn't sure there for a second." She grew quiet. "I know you're here with me, and like I said, I am having a good time, but it seems like you have something on your mind. Care to share it?" She squeezed her hand.

Ainslon took a deep breath. "It's Nana."

Lauren frowned and slipped her hand under Ainslon's on the table. "Go on."

"I don't know. It feels like she's keeping something from us. Her latest physical exam went well, but…"

"How old is she?"

"Eighty-eight. She'll be eighty-nine at the end of the year." She smiled and moved her hand when the waitress set their dessert down. She fiddled with her spoon before taking a bite. "I know she's getting older. I know that, but I can't grasp it."

"Oh, Ainslon. I know it's tough. I do, but you have her now. I know that sounds so cliché, but it's true. Cherish the time you have with her."

Ainslon wiped her eyes. "Sorry, I've made this sad."

"Don't ever be afraid to talk about something with me. That's what I'm here for. I do believe it's one of the items at the top of this list of being a friend." She gave a gentle smile.

"You're right."

They both finished their dessert in silence, then Lauren insisted on paying. Ainslon stepped outside and waited by the side of the building. She relaxed when Lauren slipped her arm around her waist and pulled her back against her. "I had a good time tonight."

"So did I." Ainslon turned in her arms and readily sunk into Lauren's embrace.

"There's something we haven't talked about. I know we're only friends, but the chatter on the gossip sites is that I'm seeing someone. I wanted to give you a head's up that the more time we spend together, the more likely it is our pictures will start to appear more often."

That didn't scare her as much as it should have. "I hope they get my good side."

Ainslon tightened her arms around Lauren when she chuckled. "I don't think you have a bad side."

"My, my, Ms. Millán. You're smooth."

Lauren stepped back but kept hold of Ainslon's hands and bowed. "It is one of my many wonderful qualities."

"There's a lot."

"You have no idea." She leaned down and for a moment, Ainslon thought for sure she was going to kiss her on the lips but ended up kissing the tip of her nose.

"I can't wait to find out each one."

Chapter Twenty-four

A week and a half after their friend date at the Café found Lauren going over their inventory, but her thoughts strayed to Ainslon and the relationship she kept qualifying as "friendship." It was bullshit, but she would play along as long as it took. She knew Ainslon didn't want to take their relationship to the next level until the business with the building concluded.

Even though the seller acted as if she liked her, Lauren knew she was only waiting around for a better offer. Her intuition leaned toward a better offer from Ainslon. Not that Lauren would fault the seller. After all, this was business and she was partial to Ainslon as well.

She didn't want to bring up her thoughts to Ainslon, because Ainslon had kept mum on the entire subject and Lauren didn't want to push her.

But the fact remained, what she had with Ainslon was a better start than all of her previous relationships except for Gabby, but they started out as friends as well. She checked her watch. Carrie was due to meet with her and discuss her new duties. The last few weeks were rough on the poor girl. A week after their talk, Carrie's mom found out she was pregnant and kicked her out. Thankfully, Ollie quickly found Carrie and her boyfriend a place to live. The apartment was small, only one bedroom, but still thrilled the two teens. They both had broken into tears when Ollie had announced she had paid their first six months of rent and Lauren had taken care of the first six months of their utilities.

Everyone needed a bit of help from time to time. It was exactly the sort of thing her papa would have done. She missed him terribly and would continue to live a life he would be proud of. She glanced down at the small frame on her desk that held the sonogram of Carrie and Larry's baby. It was a sweet gesture on Carrie's part and was a reminder to Lauren that the good things in life would always outweigh the bad.

The expected knock sounded on her door. "Come in."

"Thank you," Carrie said.

"Let's get comfortable, shall we?" She stood and they both settled on the couch. "How are you feeling about working in the distribution center?"

"Oh, it's fun. I enjoy packaging and the other four that work there are really nice. I wasn't sure about Becky, but she's okay."

Lauren chuckled. Becky, at first meet, could come across as cold, but once you got to know her, she was nice. "How are you feeling?"

"A little tired, but my doctor says that's normal. I just…Larry and I are so grateful for everything you've done. He's really excited to start his job next week at Millers."

"I was happy to help him." After her first pick for a job for him fell through, she'd received a lead from her mother about a job notice at Millers grocery store for a bakery position. She sent Larry there with a letter of recommendation. After a week on eggshells, he learned he'd gotten the job. Lauren had practically begged Noe to give Larry a crash course, but he'd given in once he saw how passionate Larry was about being a pastry chef. Lauren had worried, at first, that training with Noe in a private kitchen would deter Larry from working in a grocery store, but it had done the opposite. He was even more excited to start his job.

"He's so excited." She placed her hand over her small bump. "We also visited that used furniture store you told us about and were almost able to furnish our entire apartment. We would like to have you over for dinner once we're settled. Don't expect gourmet."

"I would love to. Would it be all right if I brought a friend?" She had a good feeling Ainslon would accompany her.

"That would be great."

"Did you find anything for the baby at the store?"

"There was a lot of baby furniture, but we decided, since this is our first, we want to get a new crib for the baby. We found the one we want and we're saving the money for it. It's expensive but will change as the baby grows."

"That's great. If you need any help with anything, don't hesitate to ask."

"You've already done so much."

"Nonsense. I'm happy to help." As soon as the words left her lips, her cellphone rang. "Hold that thought." She walked to the desk, then swiped her phone. "Hello." She nodded. "I see. Thank you." She set the phone down and for the first time in a long time it felt like a weight lifted. Finally.

"Carrie, would you mind if we finish this later? There's something I need to do."

"Of course."

"I'll walk you down, then I need to go chocolate

shopping."

⁂

The day had started out slow, but Ainslon wasn't going to complain. She'd finished a ton of work and sold three more books from the ones bought from Shelly. The steady rise of their business bank account was something she would never tire of.

She'd also redesigned both storefront windows and put up all the flyers for their next themed night; talking animals. She knew the kids would get a kick out of dressing up as their favorite animal character and couldn't wait to see their creativity.

After a quick breakfast with Lauren, they'd gone their separate ways, and she hadn't heard from her since. It wasn't odd, but out of the norm. They usually texted on and off all day.

She'd just sat back at her desk when an over-excited Justin ran into her office. He bent over, taking in deep breaths.

"Justin, what's wrong?"

"We...we did it."

"What?" Ainslon got to her feet. "What did we do?"

Justin gripped her shoulders. "We got the building."

Ainslon gasped and felt her heart start to pound. "We got the building?"

"We did. The realtor just called. We got the building." He pulled Ainslon into his arms and held her tight.

"Wow." This was amazing and life changing news.

"Yes, wow." He pulled back, linked their hands,

and pulled her out of the office and toward the store. "This is huge."

Ainslon laid her palms flat on the counter's surface. They got the building. Dozens of ideas flashed in her mind, but one was prominent. They got the building. Lauren didn't. Ainslon looked up when Justin bumped her shoulder and she stared as Lauren walked toward the counter with a small bag in her hand and a smile on her face.

"Ainslon."

"Hi, you." Ainslon walked around the counter, slipped her hand in Lauren's, and tugged her toward the office, shutting the door behind them. Lauren sat in the seat in front of the desk and Ainslon took the seat behind it.

Lauren set the bag on the desk and motioned for Ainslon to open it. With shaky fingers, Ainslon pulled out a small thin, flat box and took the lid off. A bar of chocolate lay atop a bed of tissue paper with the word congratulations written on it. The small box held an origami rose. Ainslon swung her gaze to Lauren.

"I…"

Lauren held up her hand. "I never expected to get the building, but I live on hope, so I tried again. I knew the building was yours the moment we both met with Fredrick. The woman didn't want to sell to me. You gave her another choice, and she took it."

"Wait. You knew?" She stopped herself from getting upset.

Lauren nodded. "Don't be upset. Please. I didn't want to get your hopes up. The seller respects me as a businesswoman, but I don't think she likes me. I wanted the building and was willing to pay over cost for it, then you came along. I didn't know for a fact she would choose you, but I suspected."

"Why didn't you say anything?"

"What would I have said? It was only speculation on my part. Why get your hopes up over a hunch? Would it have made a difference in anything?"

"No," she said softly. Lauren knew she wouldn't get the building and still pursued her. Ainslon smiled as the quiet surrounded them. Lauren drummed her fingers on the desktop. "Lauren?"

"I'm waiting."

Ainslon frowned. "For what?"

Lauren stood and Ainslon followed suit. "I'm waiting for you to ask me out. On a proper date. None of this friends stuff."

"I…" For the second time in Lauren's presence, Ainslon was left speechless.

"I'll make it easy for you. Yes."

"Yes?" Why did her brain decide to go blank?

"Yes. I'll have dinner with you. As in a proper date. I was attracted to you the first time I walked into your store. Also, this whole nonsense with just being friends needs to end. You're only kidding yourself— "

Ainslon lunged across the desk and shut her up with a kiss. Ainslon moaned with the first touch of Lauren's lips on hers, then pulled back to gauge Lauren's reaction. Lauren pulled her back in and deepened the kiss. It was slow, unhurried, and perfect. "Wow."

"I've wanted to do that for weeks."

Ainslon rested her forehead against Lauren's. "You know what I've been wanting to do for weeks?"

"What?"

"This." Ainslon slipped her hands into Lauren's hair and through her curls.

"You like the curls, huh?"

"Yes." She cupped the back of Lauren's head and brought their lips together. "It's even softer than I expected."

Lauren cupped Ainslon's cheek. "Let's do this right."

"I want that more than anything."

"That makes me happy. Dinner Friday at seven? The Café?"

"Yes."

"Perfect." Lauren sighed. "I hate to kiss and run, but I need to get back to the store."

Ainslon masked her disappointment but knew now wasn't the time or place to be exploring this change in their relationship. "Me too. Get back to work, I mean." She smoothed out where her fingers had mussed Lauren's hair.

Lauren pulled her hand down and laced their fingers together. She drew Ainslon into a hug. "I knew your kisses would be as good as your hugs."

Being wrapped in Lauren's arms was perfection. She leaned forward to capture the inviting lips again, when a knock on the door drew them out of their bubble. Ainslon reluctantly pulled away from Lauren and opened it, allowing Justin in.

"Sorry, ladies," Justin said. "Ainslon, the store's getting crowded." He turned to leave.

They both followed him out into a crowded store. "I'll talk to you tonight," Lauren said.

"You will."

Ainslon slipped her hands in her pockets when Lauren walked out the door. She had kissed Lauren Millán, and not just a peck on the lips, but a real, honest to goodness kiss, and Lauren had kissed her back. A good day had turned into a great day.

"Earth to Ainslon." Justin waved his hand in front of her face. "That good, huh?"

"Mind blowing."

"Good for you."

"It really is."

Chapter Twenty-five

Ainslon hummed as she looked over their current sales. Two days had passed since Lauren had asked her out, and their time apart sucked. They'd talked on and off the last few days and texted but hadn't had a chance to see each other. Instead of having dinner at the Café, they'd decided to have dinner at Lauren's house.

Since Ainslon and Justin had all their paperwork in order and the owner of the building wanted to get everything settled, the sale should be completed in a few weeks. Ainslon and Justin were knee-deep in redesigning the building. So much so that their ideas filled an entire notebook. They'd met with Kat, Dylan, Briley, and Leah and had agreed on a sale price for their current building.

A quick glance at the clock told her it was a little after eleven and the morning crowd had dispersed some. She picked up her phone and shot a quick text off. Tonight was their first official date, but she couldn't wait until tonight to talk with Lauren.

Ainslon: I've missed you these last few days. I can't wait for tonight.

Lauren: I'll be at the store until seven, so it will be a late dinner. I'm sorry. I had planned on cooking, but I don't believe that's an option now.

Ainslon: Don't be sorry. Any preference on dinner?

Lauren: Whatever you bring will be fine.

Ainslon: See you tonight.
Lauren: I look forward to it.

"I need only one guess to figure out who put that silly smile on your face," Justin said, laying a folder on the counter.

Ainslon put down her phone. "I'm not going to deny it."

"Bet you're looking forward to tonight."

"You have no idea." She ran her fingers through her hair. "We haven't even known each other long, but..."

"Long enough." He patted her shoulder. "I get it. You're happy. It's nice to see."

"It feels nice."

At one o'clock, Ainslon received another chocolate gift from Lauren and an origami elephant. Today's fare was a set of chocolate truffles. Ainslon looked forward to the origami gifts as much as the chocolate, maybe more. She kept them on a shelf in her office at home. She picked up her phone to continue her text with Lauren.

Ainslon: I'm going to get fat at this rate.
Lauren: Don't be silly. It's only a few chocolates.
A few seconds later.
Lauren: I can quit sending them.
Ainslon: Don't you dare. I'll pick something light for dinner.
Lauren: I knew you would see it my way.

Ainslon chuckled and picked up another piece, took a bite, and moaned. So far, out of everything she tasted, the salted caramel was her favorite.

"Hey, chocolate," Justin said, reaching for one.

Ainslon slapped his hand away. "Not these."

He looked longingly at the box. "That good,

huh?"

"Better."

"Lucky."

"That I am."

The rest of the day passed quickly, and Ainslon swung by the Half Dollar and picked up two orders of their zucchini pasta with grilled chicken for dinner.

At seven-thirty-eight, she knocked on Lauren's door and a few moments later it opened to reveal a smiling Lauren, dressed in a pair of slacks and a sweater.

"Darling, come in." Lauren kissed her lightly on the lips and led the way to the kitchen, where the table was set with two wine glasses and a candle.

Ainslon beamed at the endearment, 'Darling.' Yeah, she could get used to that. "It looks beautiful."

Lauren squeezed her hand. "I'm glad you like it."

Ainslon placed the bag on the table, then grasped Lauren's hand and pulled her into an embrace. "I missed not seeing you for the last few days. I know that's my fault, and I'll try to do better. I promise."

Lauren rested her hands on the small of Ainslon's back. "You don't have anything to be sorry for. This is the next big step for your business and as much as I love spending time with you, this is important for your future. I'm not going anywhere. I went through the same thing you are when I opened my store. Some relationships fell to the wayside, but we're not going to let that happen. We text all the time and we talk every night. Don't worry about us. We're fine."

With each word out of Lauren's mouth, Ainslon's heart beat faster. Could this woman be any more perfect? Ainslon had the overwhelming urge to kiss her, so she did. "Thank you. I needed to hear that."

"Good. Let's eat. It smells amazing."

They worked in tandem, transferring their food from the containers to plates at Lauren's insistence. It was almost eight by the time they sat to eat.

Halfway through the meal, Ainslon brought up her plans for Friday and Saturday. "Justin and I are going to the new building on Friday, but I'm free on Saturday."

"I'm going to spend the day at home. You're welcome to join me."

"How can I say no to that?"

"That's the point." Lauren twirled the zucchini noodles on her fork and took a bite. "Have you decided on the design?"

Ainslon took her napkin and dabbed her lips. "We've got an idea down, but we're going to wait until Friday to finalize everything. We also chose a buyer for our place."

"That's great." Lauren grinned and lifted her wine glass. "Cheers."

Ainslon returned the grin and clinked her glass against Lauren's. "Here's to everything working out."

"I have no doubt." Lauren grew quiet while she looked intently at Ainslon. "I can see a question on your face." She squeezed her hand.

Ainslon thought she had hidden it well, but she couldn't stop thinking about it since Lauren sat. Since the business with the building was over, something else bothered her. "I was wondering about us."

"Yes?"

"Us. You know. As a couple." Ainslon knew she should have kept her mouth shut and enjoyed the evening, but she had to know what Lauren expected out of this. She couldn't start this, whatever this was, blind. She took a deep breath. "What would you like to see come out of this? I need to know. Short term, long term. I know you want more than friendship."

With a nod, Lauren seemed to weigh her response. "That's a fair question. I thought we would get to know each other, then take it from there. I am not going into this expecting to find someone to spend the rest of my life with, but I am not ruling that out either. If the right person comes along, that's fantastic, and if they don't, I will keep looking." She took a sip of her wine. "I've thought a lot about you lately and what exactly it is I am feeling. It's hard to put into words. I know I would like something to come from this. I really like you and, this, whatever this is, I am going to give it my all. We deserve that. Don't you think? We're good together."

Did she? Ainslon would only get one chance at this and she didn't intend to screw it up. If she said something stupid, so be it. "You've got it all wrong." Lauren frowned. "I *am* going into this expecting to find someone to spend the rest of my life with. I can't go into it any other way. If I did, I would only be giving you a part of myself, and for this to work, I have to give you all of me. If I get hurt in the process, then I get hurt." Life really did have a way of sneaking up on you. If she had never run into Justin, she would have never opened the online store, or the storefront, and would have never met Lauren. Edna would say everything happened for a reason and now, she finally understood that. She slipped her hand in Lauren's. "Life is funny. I was going along, minding my own business, then you walked into my store and changed everything. I know my feelings were hard to gauge from the onset. I like you a lot, and since we're doing this, I'm all in. You and me."

"I didn't expect you to say all that."

"I'm not sorry. It's how I feel."

"I'm not upset. On the contrary, I'm happy. We could get hurt, or we could be amazing. I'm going to be an optimist. Will you join me?"

"Yes."

"On that note, I should also make a couple of points. Even though we just started officially dating, my mother wants to have dinner with us next week. I explained to her the change in our relationship status and she wants to get to know you. I can promise you a fantastic meal."

"I would love to have dinner with you and your mom. Nana wants to have dinner with the two of us."

"I would love to have dinner with you and Edna." Lauren took a sip of her wine. "We will be monogamous, of course."

"Of course. I don't like to share."

"Nor I."

"There's also the matter of sex."

Lauren's eyes widened for a moment. "Hitting all the questions hard tonight."

"I...I just—"

"I'm only teasing. Go on." Lauren slipped her hand under Ainslon's on the table and squeezed.

"I'm not a hop into bed kind of girl. I don't want you to be offended if it doesn't happen right away." She didn't see the problem with getting to know someone first and hoped Lauren agreed.

"Ainslon, I'm only going to say this once. Sex is an important part of any relationship as long as both parties agree. I would never force you to do something that makes you uncomfortable. No matter what that something is. If I do, tell me. Intimacy does not equate sex. When we're both ready, it will happen. Also, I keep in shape but I'm not in my twenties anymore."

Ainslon rolled her eyes. "Lauren, all you have to do is walk in a room, and I get weak. You're gorgeous and the sexiest woman I've ever seen. No worries in that department. You need to tell me if I do anything that makes you uncomfortable. We both agreed to start out on the right foot, and that's what I want to do. We have something special."

"We do."

Ainslon gave her a knowing smile. "So, do I make you weak?"

"Are you kidding? It takes all the restraint I have not to rip those ten-year-old jeans and t-shirt off you every time I see you."

Ainslon's grin turned into a frown and she leaned forward on the table. "Are you making fun of my clothes?"

Lauren waited a beat before answering. "No." Lauren leaned forward. "Would I do that?"

"Not all of us can dress like a fashion goddess, now can we?" Ainslon ghosted her fingers across Lauren's arm.

"No, we cannot." Lauren closed the distance between them and pecked Ainslon on the lips. "All kidding aside, I hope you know, even though I find your choice in clothing…unique most days, it has never been an issue with me."

"Unique, huh? How diplomatic of you."

"I do what I can."

"I bet you do."

Lauren chuckled and finished her wine before diving into the dessert. "Any other hard-hitting topics we need to discuss?"

"Actually, yes. Kids."

Lauren's eyes widened in surprise. "Kids?"

"Do you want them?" She'd always wanted kids and it could be a deal-breaker if Lauren didn't. Best to get that out of the way now, instead of it coming up down the line and derailing their relationship.

"Do you?"

"I do."

Lauren nodded and took a sip of her wine. "When I was younger, I didn't want children. As I grew older, the yearning for one or two made itself known, but in the last few years that dream waned some." She swirled the wine in her glass. "You don't think I'm too old for them?"

Ainslon wracked her brain for how old Lauren was. Forty-four. "I don't think you're too old to be a mother; however, between the two of us, I would be the one to carry a child. In fact, I would insist. There are a lot of medical advances, but I would feel more comfortable if it was me." Ainslon tilted her head. "Do you think you're too old?"

"In some ways I do, but in others I don't. I think I would make a fantastic mother, but I've never had the desire to birth one. Adoption is always an option, but I have to be honest with you. If I we're going to have children, it would have to be in the next couple of years. I don't want to be an old woman when my children are in college."

"So, you would want kids with me?"

Lauren leaned across the table. "I do believe we were talking about taking chances." She slipped her hand in Ainslon's. "So, yes, that's what I'm talking about. Taking chances, remember? Does that answer your question?" Ainslon nodded. "Would you want to have children with me?"

"I wouldn't mind it." Ainslon feigned nonchalance. "You're gorgeous. Have a successful business." She grinned. "Not to mention I'm crazy about you. I think you would make a wonderful mom."

Lauren held up her glass. Ainslon did the same and they clinked their glasses together. "To our future."

"To us."

After they drained their glasses, Lauren asked if there was anything else she wanted to discuss.

Ainslon searched her brain but couldn't come up with something else. "I want to move forward with the understanding that this could turn into a lifetime of firsts for us."

As the silence stretched on, Ainslon feared she'd said the wrong thing.

"That's sounds wonderful."

"I'm glad." They finished their dessert in silence.

After cleaning up, they retreated to the living room. Ainslon lay back on the couch and let out a contented hum when Lauren curled up by her side.

"Dinner was lovely."

Ainslon wrapped both arms around her and kissed her cheek. "I'm glad you liked it. I like this. Just relaxing with you. Having you in my arms."

"It's a wonderful ending to a taxing day."

"I'm all ears."

"From the vendors sending the wrong chocolate to a two-year-old throwing a temper tantrum in the middle of the store, it seemed like everything that could go wrong today did. On top of all that, a shipment of chocolate I ordered from Italy was delayed."

"That qualifies as a shitty day. I've had plenty of

those." Ainslon absentmindedly stroked her hand up and down Lauren's arm. "Tomorrow's another day."

"That's one vendor I won't be worrying about anymore, considering I dropped the contract and went with another one."

"Even better."

Lauren chuckled, turned to Ainslon, and ran her fingers down Ainslon's cheek. "I'm so happy I walked into your store."

"I am too." Ainslon rested their foreheads together before kissing her. "So, so glad." Lauren turned and settled back against Ainslon's side.

"I'm finding myself feeling things for you that even surprise me in the short amount of time we've known each other."

"I feel the same way."

"Let's pick something to watch and relax."

Ainslon held Lauren as the movie played, marveling at the fact she got to hold this amazing woman in her arms. Nothing else mattered but this moment.

Chapter Twenty-six

That following Friday, as Ainslon and Justin stepped into their newly acquired building, Ainslon's heart raced. This was it. What they'd been building up to and it felt amazing.

Justin squeezed her shoulder. "Feels good, doesn't it?"

"Feels amazing." She took a deep breath. "We have work to do."

"That we do."

Ainslon had woken early with a text from Lauren wishing her a good morning and good luck for the day. It was a nice start after her fitful night. After having breakfast with Easton, she'd met Justin at the store at eight thirty. They'd left Turn the Page in the capable hands of Sarah and Bradley, their employees. Easton was going to meet them later to help figure out the layout for the building. The contractor they'd hired would meet them around two to finalize the plan. Everything had moved fast but that was the way Ainslon liked to work.

Three hours later, Ainslon, Justin, and Easton lay on their backs on the second floor, staring up at the tall ceiling.

An idea popped into Ainslon's head as she gazed up at the ceiling. "We should plan a space scene, then have the cardboard spaceships we already have hanging from the ceiling. With this space we can easily add half a dozen more and the space wouldn't be crowded."

"I like that idea," Justin threw in.

"I do, too. In that corner over there," Easton motioned with her head. "You can set up your Hippogriff/Harry Potter section."

"And over there." Justin grew excited. "We can set up our gaming center."

"Place all our life-size superhero cutouts all over the space," Ainslon chimed in. "This is going to be awesome." They all high-fived. "We can put up a half-wall to separate the gaming area from the actual store. The outside door will be locked until game nights."

"Ainslon," a voice called from downstairs.

Ainslon perked up. "That's Lauren." Ainslon jumped up. "I'll be back, guys."

"Take your time," Easton said.

"We'll still be here when you get back," Justin said.

Ainslon bounded down the stairs and stopped at the bottom, taking in the vision before her. Lauren wore a black pencil skirt and a white wrap around blouse. Good grief, Lauren took her breath away.

Lauren greeted her with a cheeky grin. "Well, I don't need to interpret that look."

Ainslon couldn't suppress her wide smile as she walked across the large space. "In my defense, you look beautiful today."

"I always love a good compliment, and when it comes from your lips, even better." They shared a quick kiss, then Ainslon let her fingers trail down Lauren's arm and grasped her hand.

"What brings you by?"

"I wanted to see you."

Ainslon's heart skipped a beat and she pulled Lauren into her arms. "That's so sweet."

Lauren rolled her eyes but didn't let her go. "And I wanted to check on your progress."

"It's going good. The contractor is supposed to be by around two. We've already discussed most of what we want done and the papers have been drawn up, but he wanted to go back over it with us. It's all coming together."

"I never doubted you for a second."

"Would you like to hear what we're going to do down here?"

"I would love to."

For the next twenty minutes, Ainslon walked Lauren through the things they wanted to implement and wrote down a few of Lauren's suggestions that neither Ainslon nor Justin had thought about.

"I need to get back to the store so I can finish up a few things before going to Colin's birthday party. I know I've said it before but I'm so glad you found the book."

"It's all in a day's work ma'am."

Lauren kissed Ainslon's lips, then stroked her fingers down Ainslon's chin. "I'll call you tonight."

"I can't wait." A knock on the door grabbed their attention.

"That would be lunch," Lauren said. "I wanted to make sure you three were fed."

"You bought us lunch?" Ainslon grinned.

"Of course I did." Lauren opened the door, then directed the man to place the bags on the table by the wall. The movement drew Ainslon's eyes to the three small C and C gift bags on the table. As soon as the man walked out, Ainslon dragged Lauren to the small office, pushed her up against the wall, and kissed her like she'd wanted to do for days. The feel of Lauren in her arms drove her crazy. They were both panting when the kiss ended.

"Not that I'm complaining, but what brought that on?" Lauren asked, relaxing into Ainslon's arms.

"You. You're amazing." Ainslon leaned forward, but stopped a breath away from Lauren's lips, and looked into her eyes. "I'm going to kiss you again."

Lauren arched a brow and closed the distance between them. Ainslon ran her hands up Lauren's sides and gripped her waist. She pulled back when she heard footsteps on the stairs. Before Ainslon could kiss her again, Lauren pushed her away with a hand on the center of her chest.

"If you do that again, I believe your friends are going to get more than they bargained for."

"You're right. I…" Ainslon blushed. "Too much?"

"No, but I do need to get back." Lauren kissed her cheek. "How do I look?"

Ainslon fixed Lauren's hair. "Enchanting."

"You're cheeky."

"Only for you. I'll call you tonight?"

"Since it's become our nightly ritual, you better." Lauren pulled her along. "Justin, Easton, I'll see you both later. Ainslon."

The smile never left Ainslon's face even when the door closed behind Lauren.

"I'm pretty sure you didn't have that shade of lipstick on a half hour ago," Easton threw out before picking up her sandwich and taking a bite.

"Your point?" Ainslon said, wiping her lips. She pulled her small gift bag near, then accepted the sandwich Justin handed her.

"No point. Just saying. I'm happy you're happy."

Ainslon sipped her water. "It's your turn to pick up dinner for Nana tonight, isn't it?"

Easton nodded. "Yep. She said she wanted Chinese. So, we're having Chinese."

Thirty minutes later, as Justin cleared off the table, the contractor arrived, and they got down to business. For the next few hours they discussed what changes needed to be made and by six o'clock, Ainslon was on her way home. She thought for a minute about stopping in to see Lauren but knew she didn't have the time if she was going to get to dinner with her sister and Edna.

By the time Ainslon pulled into Edna's driveway, she was beat. The shower she had before leaving didn't do much to wash the fatigue away, but she would never miss one of these dinners if it was at all possible. Easton hadn't arrived yet, so Ainslon joined Edna in the living room on the couch, but not before giving her a hug.

"You look dead on your feet."

Ainslon sighed. "It was a long, but productive day. We have a plan and it's going to look great, Nana."

"I always knew you girls would do great things."

"Thanks, but we're only so well adjusted because of you."

Edna chuckled. "I have no problem taking credit for it. In fact, I insist. Now," she patted Ainslon's leg. "How are things going with Lauren?"

"Great." Ainslon sat up and turned to give Edna her full attention. "Really great. I'm going to spend the day with her tomorrow."

"You'll be fine."

"I hope so. I want this to work."

"And it will. Lauren is a smart woman. She knows what she's doing. I can't see her doing anything she didn't want to. You're in her life for a reason. Simply, because she wants you there."

"You always know the right thing to say."

"And don't you forget it." Edna pushed herself up and off the couch when the backdoor opened and Easton walked in. "I'm hungry. Let's eat."

Later, after they demolished the food, and bid their goodnights to Edna, Ainslon and Easton stood beside their cars.

"She looks tired," Ainslon said, staring into space.

"More so than usual."

"You went to her last doctor visit with her. You said everything was okay."

Easton leaned back against the car beside Ainslon. "He said for someone her age she was in good health." Easton clasped their hands together. "We have to face the fact that she's getting older."

"That's easier said than done."

"Don't I know it. I don't even want to imagine the day we have to say goodbye to her. If it wasn't for her taking me in when my parents died, I don't know where I would be right now."

Ainslon choked back a sob and shook her head. "I can't think about that day. I don't know what I would do."

"Me either, but she's seems more tired lately. I hate to see her struggling so much."

"Maybe we should talk to her about moving out of this place and into a retirement home."

Easton snorted. "There is no way she would move into a place like that. Do you remember the last time we brought it up?"

"She didn't talk to us for three days." Losing Edna wasn't something Ainslon ever thought about because it would be like losing a part of herself. Edna had always been there for her, and to think there would be a day when she wouldn't didn't sit right. That day was coming, Ainslon knew, but she couldn't acknowledge it, not yet. "What do we do?"

Easton pulled Ainslon into a bone crushing hug. "Sis, I don't think there is anything we can do. We visit with her a few days a week and talk with her every day. She has Shelly. I know for a fact they see each other every day. We're doing everything we can. You know she wouldn't let either one of us move in with her, and she wouldn't move in with us."

"I know." Ainslon pulled back and wiped her eyes. "I know."

"Now, it's getting late and you have a busy day with your girlfriend tomorrow and I have a full day of baking ahead of me. I'm working on a few new recipes."

"Good luck." Ainslon kissed Easton on the cheek, bid her goodnight, then strapped herself into her car and headed home. The one thing that would help right now would be to hear Lauren's voice, and as soon as she made it home, she would call her.

Chapter Twenty-seven

The day flew by and even though Ainslon had spent the previous evening with Edna, she looked forward to lunch with her today. Edna had called that morning and asked if she and Lauren would be available for lunch. It wasn't an unwelcome request but still odd. Usually Edna was content with their weekly meet-ups. However as much she knew Edna liked Lauren, it was still scary. Ainslon pulled into Edna's driveway, put the car in park, then turned to Lauren. "Still doing okay?"

"Edna and I get along fine. I'm not worried. Why are you?"

"You've never been here before."

"It's just lunch. What's really bothering you?"

Ainslon sighed and pulled the key out of the ignition. "Nana hasn't been feeling well lately and I'm worried about her."

"I thought you said her check-up went well."

"It did, but she's old."

"Darling."

Ainslon wiped her eyes. "I don't know what I'll do if something happens to her. She's been my rock since I came to live with her. I can't lose her."

Lauren took her into her arms. "We can't escape death, but what we can do is not let the notion of someone dying taint our view of them. It's okay to be sad, but she's not gone yet. She's inside the house you and Easton grew up in and waiting for us to have lunch with her." Lauren cradled Ainslon's face. "I don't know Edna well, but what I do know of her, would she really want you out here crying over her?"

"No." Ainslon pecked Lauren on the lips. "No, she wouldn't. Can we talk about this later?"

"Of course we can. We can talk about anything."

Ainslon took a deep breath and blew her nose after accepting the Kleenex from Lauren. "You ready?"

"When you are."

Ainslon opened the backdoor and held it open for Lauren to walk through.

"Nana," Ainslon hollered.

"In the living room. Be a dear and bring me a cup of tea."

"Sure." Ainslon and Lauren worked silently side-by-side, getting the three cups of tea ready, then carried them into the living room. Edna was on the couch surrounded by photo albums. Ainslon got a sinking feeling. "Nana."

"Ainslon, you sit in the recliner. And Lauren, you can sit here." Edna patted the spot beside her on the couch.

"Do you happen to have any naked baby photos?" Lauren asked, smiling at Ainslon's glare.

Edna patted Lauren's knee. "That and then some."

"Really, Nana?" Ainslon grew still the longer Edna stared at her. "You okay?" Edna nodded, then turned back to Lauren and pointed to a photo album on the far side of the coffee table.

"Why not start at the beginning?"

Ainslon sat quietly while Edna showed Lauren dozens of photos and told countless stories of Ainslon and Easton. She only corrected her a time or two when she got them mixed up in their later teenage years. Ainslon couldn't remember the last time she'd laughed so much or seen Lauren smile so much.

After Edna closed the last photo album, she asked Lauren to switch places with Ainslon.

"Nana." Ainslon got a sinking feeling in the pit of her stomach.

Edna held Ainslon's hand in-between hers. "I got an unexpected phone call last night."

"Really?"

"Yes. I will never forgive them for what they did to you, Ainslon, but I won't lie and say it wasn't nice to hear their voices."

She hadn't talked to her parents in years. "What did they have to say?"

"Asked how I was doing, then asked about you."

Ainslon laughed but it was hollow. "Why after all this time? This is the first time they've called, isn't it?"

"It is, and why, they just wanted to talk. It's been a long time."

"I don't know if I'll ever be able to forgive them," Ainslon said.

"And that's your right, but forgiveness isn't about them, dear, it's about you. It's okay to forgive them, but it's not something you will ever forget. Your mother mentioned something about visiting."

Ainslon closed her eyes and tried to breathe evenly but her breaths were coming quicker than she could keep up.

"Ainslon."

She felt hands cup her face.

"Listen to my voice, darling. Breathe. In and out. In and out. That's it. Take a deep, steady breath."

After what felt like a lifetime, Ainslon slowly

opened her eyes and came face to face with a kneeling Lauren. She rested her forehead against Lauren's. "I can't see them."

"Then you don't have to," Lauren said, rubbing her hands up and down Ainslon's arms.

Edna agreed. "Oh, Ainslon, I told her I wasn't sure it was a good idea."

"No, Nana. If you want to see them, you should. I would never hold that against you, and I love you no matter what. Don't make the decision for them to stay away because of me."

"I would like to see them," Edna said.

Ainslon would forever feel guilty if Edna made the decision not to see them because of her. To her, it felt like only yesterday they'd turned their back on her, and she wasn't sure if those old feelings would ever go away. Her trust in her parents would forever be broken.

"I have something for you," Edna said, then stood and walked out of the room. Lauren sat beside Ainslon, pulled her into an embrace, and kissed her forehead.

"This sure isn't the lunch I had expected," Ainslon said.

"It's fine. I wish you weren't hurting."

"I think I'll always hurt a little bit because of them." Lauren made to stand when Edna walked in, but she waved her off and sat on the other side of Ainslon.

Ainslon's eyes widened and her fingers trembled when she took the small wooden box into her hands. For as long as she could remember, the plain wooden box had always sat on Edna's dresser. Ainslon knew the two items inside by heart; a cameo brooch and her grandpa's Hamilton Pocket watch. "Nana, not yet."

"I'm not getting any younger and I want to give you these items now. I gave Easton her items yesterday. I need to do this."

Ainslon swallowed the lump in her throat. "Okay."

"Easton got my recipe books and my pearl necklace, but that box and what's in it has always fascinated you, even before you could walk. Your eyes would stay glued to it. You may never wear them, but I know you'll take good care of them. When something happens to me, you can do whatever you want with the items in the house. Please don't keep all this stuff. I don't want you two weighed down by it all. I'm giving my permission now to sell whatever you two don't want. You and Easton can split the pictures and of course, you two can keep whatever you want. I'm not going to haunt you for selling Great Aunt Martha's dresser."

Ainslon tightened her hold on Lauren's hand to ground herself. "Anything else?"

"Dear, I know this is hard for you, but it needs to be said. I've already handled all my funeral arrangements. The house will go to you and Easton. Do with it what you will. Keep it or sell it. All my other assets will be divided between you two." Edna pointed to a filing cabinet in the corner of the room. "All my papers are in there."

"Okay."

"Lauren," Edna said.

"Yes."

"You're good for Ainslon. Don't hurt her."

"Never intentionally."

"That's what I want to hear."

Edna stood and cupped Ainslon's cheeks. "No

tears, dear. I'm not dead yet, but it was time I told you girls my plans. It's always better to be prepared. Now, I have some pie left. While I'm slicing us up some, it will give you two a few minutes alone."

Once Edna was out of the room, Ainslon turned to Lauren. "I was not ready for that."

"No, we never are. My mother sat us down a few years ago and walked us through her desires. She's right, though. She's not gone yet, Ainslon, and getting all this out in the open isn't her giving up. She doesn't want you or Easton to be blindsided."

Ainslon wiped her eyes. "Do you think I can come over tonight and hang with you?"

"You're always welcome in my home, darling. I would love to have you."

"I wish Easton would have said something to me."

"Maybe she wasn't ready. Edna did want to talk to you both separately."

Ainslon handed the box to Lauren and stood to take the tray from Edna when she walked back in. They all settled down on the couch and enjoyed their apple tart. They stayed for another hour, then Edna shooed them out with a box of photographs for Ainslon and the rest of the pie for Lauren.

Back in the car, Ainslon rested her head on the steering wheel and relaxed a little when Lauren rubbed her back.

"After you take me home, you should talk to your sister, then come by later for dinner and games."

Ainslon raised her head, clasped Lauren's hand, and kissed the palm. "You're too good to me."

"Don't be ridiculous. I care about you. Of course I want to take care of you."

I love you. The words lay on the tip of her tongue, but she knew it was way too soon to say them. "I care about you too."

⁂

At half past six, Lauren ushered Ainslon into her condo. Lauren opened her arms wide and held Ainslon tight when she relaxed into her embrace.

The only thing Lauren could do was be there for Ainslon. Though her parents voiced their concerns when she came out, it didn't take them long to put their doubts aside and embrace the fact that she was a lesbian. She didn't dare assume what Ainslon was feeling.

In Ainslon's shoes, she wasn't sure if she would want to see her parents or not. It was a touchy situation either way.

"How are you feeling?" Lauren raised her hands and cradled Ainslon's face.

"Tired."

Lauren slid her hand down Ainslon's arm, grasped her hand, and led her toward the couch, where they both sat. "Do you want to talk about it?"

"We talked. A lot. Cried. Laughed. Easton was sympathetic about my parents, but she could understand Nana's point of view. I understand it too. It's just a lot."

"I've never been in your shoes, and I don't want to assume what you're going through, so you'll have to tell me."

"Why after all this time? Why now? I don't understand, and on top of that, Nana. It's everything at once."

Lauren lay back and opened her arms. "Come here." The moment Ainslon was in her arms, the worries of the day slowly melted away. "Do you want to talk about what happened with Edna tonight?"

"Honestly, tonight, I just want to be with you. I'll deal with everything tomorrow." She squeezed Lauren's arms around her waist. "I believe you promised me dinner and games."

"That I did." After a moment of silence, "So, I was thinking."

Ainslon turned in her arms. "What has you nervous?"

Lauren gulped. "Uh…If you wanted, I wouldn't mind if you stayed tonight."

"You're asking me to spend the night?"

"Yes, but only for sleeping. You've had a big day."

"That would be wonderful. I stopped by my apartment before coming here and spent some time with Shady. But I don't have anything to wear."

Lauren slipped her arms around Ainslon and pulled until they were nose to nose. "I do believe I can remedy that." Ainslon lay her head on Lauren's chest. Lauren placed a tender kiss on top of Ainslon's head. "But, first let's lie here for a few more minutes before we start dinner."

"Sounds heavenly."

"Then, I'm going to test your money skills in Monopoly."

Ainslon chuckled. "You're not going to know what hit you."

"I'm willing to take my chances."

Chapter Twenty-eight

The next morning, Ainslon woke first and it took her a few minutes to get her bearings. When Lauren sighed next to her, Ainslon tightened her hold around Lauren and closed her eyes. The day before had been a whirlwind of emotions and she didn't know what she would have done if not for Lauren.

The previous night, Lauren had promised today would be filled with food and relaxing. Something Ainslon badly needed. Ainslon vowed to try and redeem herself from the previous night where she lost spectacularly at Monopoly. Ainslon knew she needed to enjoy this weekend because the following week, renovations on the new building were set to begin. The fact that she could have lunch every day with Lauren was an added bonus.

"I can hear you thinking," Lauren mumbled.

Ainslon held her tighter, moved the hair away from her neck, and kissed the spot below Lauren's ear. "Not bad things."

Lauren turned in Ainslon's embrace. "I would hope not, considering you're in bed with me."

"You're beautiful," Ainslon blurted out and smiled when Lauren's cheeks flushed.

"I feel beautiful when I'm with you."

"I don't want you to ever feel anything less than beautiful when I'm around." Ainslon ran her finger down Lauren's cheek.

Lauren caught the roaming finger and kissed its tip. "You're the beautiful one."

Ainslon leaned forward and pulled Lauren into a full body embrace, burying her face in Lauren's neck. "I really like waking up with you." She pulled back and rested their foreheads together. "It doesn't hurt that the gods themselves made your mattress."

Lauren chuckled and pulled away from Ainslon and slipped out of bed.

"Where are you going? It's Sunday. We're allowed to sleep in."

"I never sleep in on Sundays." Lauren stopped at the door to the bathroom and hesitated. "I'm going to take a shower. You're welcome to join me if you wish."

Ainslon's eyes widened and her heart pounded in her chest.

"Or not."

Lauren looked so unsure, Ainslon did the only thing she could and hopped out of bed and approached her. "Really?"

"Really. No funny business, though." She gave a slight smirk. "I figured we'd see each other naked sooner or later and I want us to be comfortable with each other's bodies when we finally make love."

Ainslon pinned Lauren to the wall next to the bathroom door. "If you're sure?"

"When have you known me to be indecisive?"

"Good point." Ainslon bit her lip. "I am going to shower with you, but be forewarned my eyes will wander."

Lauren slipped her arms around Ainslon's neck. "I can handle wandering eyes. The wandering hands can come later."

"Definitely."

Forty-five minutes later, they were both dressed and downstairs. Showering with Lauren, while an amazing experience, would be on Ainslon's mind for hours, but Lauren was right; there was no need to be unsure around each other. It also allowed Ainslon to see a birthmark to the right of Lauren's navel she couldn't wait to get her lips on.

"You're staring."

Ainslon's eyes jerked up from said navel level into the laughing eyes of Lauren. "Sorry."

"It's fine. I like being looked at."

Ainslon approached her, took the cup out of her hands, and set it on the counter, then pulled a willing Lauren into her arms and kissed her. When Lauren deepened the kiss, it took all of Ainslon's willpower not to let her hands stray from around Lauren's waist.

When Lauren pulled back, Ainslon looked unsure.

"Later," Lauren said.

"Later."

"What would you like for breakfast?" Lauren asked.

"Anything?"

"Food wise."

"French toast."

After breakfast, they settled down on the couch.

"Now that you have me here, what are you going to do with me?"

"Talk."

"Talking I can do." Ainslon slipped her hand into Lauren's. "Was there something specific you wanted to talk about?"

"Actually, yes. As you know, C and C has been named in the top ten businesses of the year for the past ten years."

"I would have to live under a rock not to."

Lauren rolled her eyes. "The mayor's annual dinner and dance are next week, and I can bring a plus one." Lauren looked at her expectantly.

"You want to take me?"

"I do." Lauren played with Ainslon's fingers.

"I would love to go with you. I wasn't sure you wanted to go public yet. The gossip sites don't count."

"Don't be ridiculous, Ainslon, I'm not ashamed of us and I care about you. There is no one else I want to go with me. And besides, people have already seen us together and the gossip site *has* been awash with speculation lately. Now it will just be official."

"How can a girl say no?"

"She can't. That's the point."

"Okay. This thing is fancy, isn't it?"

"Formal, yes. Is that a problem?"

"Of course not. Easton and I will have to go shopping." Ainslon slid closer to Lauren and wrapped her arms around her waist. "This is like our coming out."

Lauren laughed, but still hugged Ainslon tight. "In a way, I guess it is."

"Nice." Their lips were only an inch apart when the phone rang.

Lauren pulled back. "That's my momma."

Ainslon sat back when Lauren stood to answer the call. The Mayor's Ball was one of the biggest events of the season and it thrilled and scared her that Lauren wanted to take her. Though, she could do without being in the mayor's presence.

"Sorry about that. Momma was confirming our dinner plans for Thursday night."

"I wouldn't miss it. Now come snuggle with me."

Lauren chuckled, then lay down on the couch and into Ainslon's arms.

An hour later, Lauren was asleep in Ainslon's arms. Ainslon rested her cheek on top of Lauren's head, relaxed into the couch, and closed her eyes.

Chapter Twenty-nine

Ainslon sighed and took a deep breath, ignoring the glares Easton kept throwing in her direction. This was taking forever.

"Sis, you're the one that needs an outfit. I just came along for moral support."

"I know." Ainslon hadn't expected it to be this hard to find a dress for the Mayor's Ball, but there was so much at stake. Even though she was an accomplished businesswoman in her own right, she hadn't garnered the kind of attention Lauren had. Only the most elite received invitations to the ball.

"You're thinking about this too much. You've looked fabulous in all of the dresses you have tried on."

"I don't want to embarrass her."

Easton rolled her eyes. "Stop being so stupid. That's not going to happen."

"Okay. Okay." She decided on the first dress she'd tried on. An hour later, they were sitting down to eat, and Ainslon's new dress was tucked away in her Jeep.

"Still nervous about the event?" Easton asked.

Ainslon took a sip of her iced tea. "Yes. This is big."

"Is it because this is showing you she cares as much about you as you do for her?"

"Yes. I knew she liked me before but now, she's

going to be telling the whole city she cares about me. It's a little overwhelming."

"I can appreciate that. You deserve this. You deserve to be wined and dined. To have a woman want to introduce you to her inner circle. To show you off." Easton scrunched her nose. "Not as a possession."

Being with Lauren was so easy. She didn't know why she was making such a big deal out of this.

"Listen, Ainslon," Easton said. "This is what you wanted. You wanted a shot at a future with her. Don't freak out too much about this."

What Ainslon needed was to relax. "I feel so comfortable with her."

"I'm so happy for you, Ainslon, but your swooning over your lady love is nauseating."

Ainslon chuckled and tossed her napkin on the table. "You wish you had what I do."

"All in good time. All in good time." Easton took a sip of her iced tea. "What do you want to do next?"

Ainslon was about to answer when her phone rang. She didn't even try to mask the smile on her face when she answered. "Hello, Lauren."

"Are you busy?"

Ainslon looked at Easton but she mouthed for her to go. "Nope. What do you need?"

"You."

"Really?"

Lauren laughed. "That's not what I was talking about, but soon."

"Soon, huh? I can live with that."

"Good. Now the reason for my call is I was wondering if you would like to spend some time with me?"

"I would love to. Give me an hour and I'll be by.

Do I need to bring anything?"

"Actually, yes. I was planning on making a cheesecake, but I need some graham crackers."

"I'll see you in a bit."

"I look forward to it."

"You ditching me?" Easton asked.

Ainslon stood. "You bet."

"Take me home, dork, then have a good rest of the day with Lauren."

Fifty-two minutes later, Ainslon walked through Lauren's front door. Lauren had texted her that she had some work to do, but her front door would be unlocked. She dropped her grocery bag on the kitchen counter, then went in search of Lauren. She found her seated at the desk in the study with the phone pressed against her ear. Ainslon moved to leave, but Lauren motioned for her to come in.

Ainslon relaxed back on the couch as Lauren continued with her phone call. The study, one of Ainslon's favorite rooms in Lauren's condo, was also one of the biggest. The light blue color on the walls filled the space with warmth and the three windows behind the desk let in a ton of natural light. A shelf to the right of the desk held all of Lauren's awards and certificates. Besides the couch and desk, there was a fireplace, and floor to ceiling bookshelves made up the rest of the space. A few minutes later, she heard Lauren set the phone back in its cradle, but she kept her eyes closed even as the couch dipped beside her and a finger trailed up her neck.

"How long do you think you can ignore me?"

"Oh, I'm not ignoring you. I'm playing hard to get." Ainslon opened her eyes. Before she could blink, Lauren leaned forward and captured her lips. Ainslon cupped the back of Lauren's head and pulled her even closer. "Wow."

"Wow indeed."

Before Lauren could move away, Ainslon pulled her into her lap and kissed her neck.

Lauren relaxed and wrapped her arms around Ainslon's neck. "If someone would have told me I would be in a relationship six months ago, I would have laughed in their face."

"I agree." Ainslon ran her hand up and down Lauren's side. "It feels good though, doesn't it?"

"Yes, it does."

They spent the next few minutes holding each other. Ainslon loved going out with Lauren, but this is what she lived for. She rested her forehead against Lauren's. "I would love nothing more than to sit here and hold you, but did you have anything else in mind?"

"Besides the cheesecake?"

Ainslon leaned back. "Yes, besides that."

"Just a quiet night in. Later we can order dinner. Maybe watch a movie."

"Dinner and a movie. How old fashioned of you."

Lauren kissed Ainslon's forehead, then stood and straightened her blouse. "I dare say, you're going to come up against more of that behavior in the future."

Ainslon jumped up, grabbed Lauren's hand, and pulled her toward the kitchen. "I look forward to it, but now I believe someone promised me cheesecake."

Lauren already had the rest of the ingredients laid out and Ainslon got to work on the crust, per Lauren's directions. "So, what can I expect from the Mayor's Ball?"

"We'll arrive by car at seven. There will be some press and we'll have our picture taken, then we'll enter, where they'll announce our names and we can mingle until dinner." Lauren took the crust from Ainslon and poured the filling in, then popped it in the oven. Lauren leaned back against the counter. "After dinner, there'll be more mingling, then at the stroke of midnight everyone will be expected to give a blood sacrifice, binding them to the city and the mayor in turn." Ainslon chuckled, but relaxed when Lauren pulled her into an embrace. "You looked so worried. If you don't want to accompany me, you don't have to."

"Don't be silly. I do, but this is a big deal."

"It is."

"You agree?" That put some of Ainslon's fears to rest.

"I'm introducing you to the town as my girlfriend. It is a big deal. I've been single for a long time. I'll have you know I've made the list as the most eligible bachelorette for three of the past six years."

"Wow." Ainslon leaned forward and whispered in Lauren's ear. "You mean to tell me I'm dating someone famous?"

"Come now. Was there really any doubt?"

Ainslon threw her head back and laughed. The laugh quickly turned into a moan when Lauren kissed up her neck. "You didn't have to stop."

"I know. You're the first person I've ever felt like this with."

"Like what?"

"Like you won't run if I'm not perfect."

"I don't have any intention of running, Lauren, and nobody's perfect." Ainslon kissed Lauren on the cheek. She wanted to take it slow and Ainslon would honor that. "What are we having for dinner?"

"Whatever you want." Lauren tapped Ainslon on

the nose.

"I like the sound of that."

They'd ended up ordering a pizza for dinner and the comedy they'd watched helped relax them both even more. Ainslon lay back on the couch, taking Lauren with her. Lauren felt so right wrapped in her arms. She fit perfectly in Ainslon's embrace.

"Will you stay?" Lauren asked. "I would love for you to hold me."

"I would like that too." They stayed on the couch for another hour before turning in. Now that she knew what it felt like to fall asleep with Lauren, she couldn't wait for all the rest of the firsts they would experience together.

Chapter Thirty

Five o'clock the next day, Ainslon followed Lauren up the stairs in her two-story condo to get ready for the Mayor's Ball. Easton and Callie had come by earlier in the day to spend some time with them before the event. While Lauren got ready in her bedroom, Ainslon went to the guest room. After a ten-minute pep talk and a text from Easton, Ainslon calmed down and started getting ready. It wasn't until she had the dress on that the doubts surfaced.

She glanced in the bedroom mirror and smoothed the fabric over her stomach. Instead of going with something elaborate she'd chosen a simple knee-length black sleeveless dress with a high neckline and paired it with a pair of black heels. She'd opted to put her hair up, but a glance in the mirror had her second guessing her decision. Was it too simple?

She didn't know what clothes Lauren had chosen, only that she had opted to wear ivory. It didn't matter. Lauren could rock anything she wore. Ainslon, on the other hand, wasn't so sure now. Lauren was choosing to introduce her to the city as her girlfriend and this is what she chose to wear?

As soon as her doubts picked up force, a knock sounded at her door.

"Come in."

When the door opened, Easton and Callie walked in.

Ainslon held her hands up. "How do I look?"

"You look beautiful," Callie said. "Lauren is going to be awestruck."

Ainslon glanced back at the mirror. "You don't think it's too simple? Zip me."

"Nope." Easton pulled her away from the mirror and zipped up the back of the dress. "You're beautiful."

Some day she would kick her overthinking mind in its ass, but today was not that day. A glance at the clock told her it was too late to turn back anyway.

Once downstairs, Ainslon turned toward the kitchen but stopped in her tracks. Lauren stood at the counter, looking at her phone. Beautiful didn't begin to describe how she looked, in a tailored ivory tuxedo, complete with cummerbund. The white shirt underneath had a plunging neckline and the silver heels only made her look twice as enticing. A throat clearing had her looking up. Straight into the amused eyes of Lauren.

"Too much?"

"No. Just right." Ainslon's gaze traveled down Lauren's body. "You look amazing." The smoky eyeshadow Lauren had decided to go with made her eyes pop. Not to mention how enticing the red lipstick was, and she'd kept her hair curly. Ainslon loved what Lauren usually wore, but she could get used to this look.

"As do you. I've always enjoyed the little black dress, and on you, it looks fetching."

"We should get going."

"I'm ready."

"Wait," Easton said. "We want pictures first."

Ainslon couldn't keep the smile off her face even as Lauren rolled her eyes as they posed for several photos.

Tonight, Ainslon knew, would be one for the record books.

❧❧❧❧

The hired luxury sedan ride to the venue was mostly in silence with Lauren's hand firmly clasped with Ainslon's. Her nerves seemed to rise ten-fold the closer they got to the event and when Ainslon finally got a glimpse of the waiting cars, and the camera flashes going off, her gut churned. Watching clips of this event on the news didn't compare to being amid the bustle. She tightened her hold on Lauren's hand and turned to Lauren when she tugged her hand.

"Remember, darling, they are here to see us, not the other way around and you don't owe them anything. The papers make this event out to be bigger than it is. At the heart of the ball, it's the mayor showing off his wealth, and bragging about his position to everyone in attendance."

"Then why do you come?"

"Because I was invited, and it's good business sense to go. I might not like these people, but if you can ignore them, and enjoy the food, and the dancing, I believe we will have a pleasant evening."

"It's always a pleasant evening when I'm with you."

A smile graced Lauren's face. "Charmer."

"Only for you, sweetheart. Only for you."

"Darling, look at me. People will be interested in us because I haven't brought a date to this event in years, but I would never allow anyone to disrespect you or us. I may not have the money that some of these people do, but I have a few connections that could paint some of these people in a bad light."

Ainslon liked seeing this new side of Lauren and she couldn't help the flutter in her stomach at each word out of Lauren's mouth. It made Lauren even more desirable. "That's sexy."

Lauren huffed, but lifted Ainslon's hand and kissed the knuckles. "Are you ready?"

"With you? Always."

The sedan pulled to a stop, where an attendant waited to open the door.

Lauren knocked on the divider between the seats to alert the driver, and a few seconds later, the door unlocked. The attendant extended his hand to Lauren and assisted her out of the sedan. Lauren then held her hand out for Ainslon amid the cameras going off. Ainslon took a deep breath, clasped Lauren's hand, and slipped out of the car. She didn't even have time to worry about the photographers, because by the time she got her bearings, they were already inside the building. At the top of the landing, Lauren turned to her and winked before a steward announced them to the crowd below.

It was such a surreal moment, Ainslon wasn't even sure it *was* real.

"Introducing Lauren Millán and Ainslon O'Neil."

Almost everyone in attendance stared at them as they descended the stairs, but Ainslon couldn't have cared less in that moment, because she was right where she belonged. On Lauren's arm. When they reached the floor below and Ainslon finally tore her eyes away from Lauren, she noticed the envious looks in a number of men's and women's eyes.

"It's all for you, darling," Lauren whispered

in her ear. "They are all wondering how I snagged a woman like you."

"Well, I, for one, will agree to disagree. That suit fits you like a glove. I can't keep my eyes off you."

Lauren chuckled, then led the way toward the bar, where a half dozen people stopped them to talk and meet Ainslon. By the time they made it to the bar and retrieved their drinks, the venue was filling up fast.

"How many people are here?" Ainslon asked.

"Last year there were four hundred. Looks to be the same this year."

"That's more than I expected."

"Most of the people in attendance are here for the same reason I am. To be seen. This may come as a surprise to you but most of these people don't like me." Lauren arched her brow and took a sip of her champagne.

"Honestly, I find that hard to believe. You've been nothing but nice to me."

Lauren placed her empty glass on the tray nearest her, then turned to fully face Ainslon. "You, my dear, have always been the exception. I've never really fit into the high society life, but I can play my part and I love clothes and expensive shoes." Lauren traced Ainslon's jawline with the tip of her finger. "From the start, there was something about you that spoke to me and I would have been a fool to say no. I love my friends and my family, but at the heart of everything, I am a businesswoman and will do almost anything to make sure it succeeds. I've had to step on some toes for that to happen and I will not apologize for it. However, here lately, I would rather spend a day with you than at work. It's a feeling I'm getting used to. You bring out the best in me."

Ainslon slipped her arms around Lauren's waist and rested both hands on the small of Lauren's back before pulling a willing Lauren closer. Lauren rested her hands on either side of Ainslon's neck. "I like all of you and I would never ask you to apologize for what you've had to do to succeed. Seeing you with your family sends a warm feeling through me but seeing you in this type of setting turns me on to the point of combusting." Ainslon swooned when Lauren tightened her hold.

"Now, you're playing a dangerous game."

"I'm good at games."

"You will never win against me."

Ainslon smirked. "Who said I wanted to win?"

Lauren loosened her hold and chuckled. "My, my, you're being feisty tonight."

"I…"

"That wasn't a question, and I like it."

Ainslon stopped a passing waiter with a tray of drinks, grabbed a full glass of champagne and downed it, then set the empty glass back on the tray. She slightly bowed to Lauren, holding out her hand. "Dance with me."

"I would love to."

Maybe Ainslon shouldn't have had that second glass of champagne, but she was having so much fun, she wasn't sure she wanted the night to end. Even some of the glares directed at them didn't bother her. As she held Lauren close and inhaled a scent unmistakably Lauren, she felt so at peace it almost brought her to her knees.

"You're a bit tipsy," Lauren whispered in her ear.

"A little, but no worries, I would never do

anything to tarnish your image."

Lauren lightly laughed. "Just having you here tonight has irrevocably changed my image. I can't seem to keep my hands off you and I don't care who knows that. These people aren't used to seeing me like this."

"I'm sorry."

"Don't be. I'm not."

Ainslon was about to say something when the announcement for dinner came over the loudspeakers.

"Whatever you were about to say can wait," Lauren said. "After dinner, if you want, we can dance some more, then go back to the condo."

"That sounds like the best idea I've ever heard."

"I had a feeling you would say that." Lauren intertwined their fingers and Ainslon held tightly to her as they made their way into the dining hall and quickly found their seats. To Ainslon's surprise, Lauren's table was at the front of the hall. Ainslon's eyes widened when the other occupants of the table arrived—The mayor and his wife, along with a man and woman Ainslon vaguely recognized.

The smirk Lauren sent her way told her she knew who their table companions would be. Ainslon wasn't sure how to feel about this revelation, considering she didn't even vote for the man. He had only won by a small margin and a few people still believed he'd rigged the election. She'd never asked Lauren her political affiliations, but she hoped she hadn't voted for him either. Ainslon acted appropriately when she was introduced to Dennis Rodgers, the mayor of Garriety, and his wife Lynette, even though she disliked the man. Marcus and Sharon Holcomb, the owners of Garriety's lumber mill, filled the other two seats of their table.

Dinner went by quickly, but as soon as the mayor

opened his mouth, Ainslon had to hold back her tongue after their plates were cleared. He was just as pompous sitting in front of her as he was on television. When he addressed her, she cringed inwardly.

"So, Ms. O'Neil, is it?" The mayor said.

"Ainslon."

The mayor frowned. "Ainslon. What is it that you do?"

"I own a children's and comic bookstore."

The mayor laughed. "Comic books. That seems a bit childish." He waved his hand dismissively.

The sneer on his face put Ainslon on edge and she gripped her glass almost to the point of breaking. "Well, considering I'm the one that opened the store and not you, I don't see how it's really any of your business." Maybe she shouldn't have had that glass of wine on top of the champagne.

Everyone at the table looked shocked at her outburst. The vein on the mayor's forehead popped out.

"Young lady, I will not have anyone speak to me that way."

"I am a woman and my name is Ainslon, not young lady." Not even Lauren's hand squeezing her leg could curtail her anger. She'd dealt with men like this her entire life.

"You have some nerve—"

"Now, Dennis," Lauren said, addressing the mayor. "The least you can do is address Ainslon by her name and not some nickname you've deemed appropriate for her. This city is made up of all types of businesses and one could say mine is also childish, but we both know it is in the top three businesses this year." Lauren took a sip of her wine. "I have had a lovely evening and I won't have it ruined by your outdated views on women and what you think acceptable for this city. We both know I didn't vote for you. We both also know a couple of years—"

"All right," Dennis quickly got up and loosened his tie. "Lauren, you're right. Ainslon, if your business is up to code, we won't have any issues. If you'll excuse us." Dennis and Lynette quickly left, followed by Marcus and Sharon.

Ainslon squirmed in her seat before turning and facing Lauren. "I'm sor—" Lauren cut her off with a quick but efficient kiss.

"Don't be sorry. He's an asshole and thinks he has more power in this city than he does. I have something on him that he doesn't wish to be made public. I have never blackmailed someone, but I can't say I wouldn't."

"God, you're hot," Ainslon blurted out. "But you don't have to use your leverage for me. I suppose I should have kept my mouth shut."

"You should always stand up for yourself, but in the future, you could use a little more tact. A well-placed word said calmly will do more than words said in anger."

"I'll heed your advice."

"As you should." Lauren finished her wine. "Let's get out of here."

"What about dessert?" Ainslon asked.

"Trust me," Lauren said. "I haven't forgotten about dessert."

⁂

The ride back to Lauren's condo dragged on.

All Ainslon wanted was to trace her fingers down the exposed skin of Lauren's chest. That tuxedo was what dreams were made of, and the woman wearing it was a dream come true. Once inside, Ainslon pushed Lauren back against the closed door and placed kisses all along her collar bone, then along the exposed skin before working her way back up and nipping Lauren's jaw.

"I've wanted to do that all night."

Lauren lay her head back against the wall. "And I've wanted you too."

Ainslon took in Lauren's ragged breathing, then ran her tongue along the exposed skin of Lauren's neck, before whispering in her ear, "I hope this is the dessert you were talking about because you look good enough to eat, and I intend to do just that." Lauren's laugh sent shivers down her spine.

"Well." Lauren gripped Ainslon's wandering hands and pulled their bodies flush together, before pushing her up against the wall. "I had intended for you to be dessert, but I'm more than willing to allow you a bite." Lauren lifted Ainslon's hand and bit the tip of her finger. "You've already had your lick." She licked Ainslon's finger. "But I've thought of nothing but getting you out of this dress all night, and I hope you'll do me the courtesy of getting out of it slowly."

"Slowly, huh?" Ainslon wiggled out of Lauren's embrace, turned, and took a few steps back to stand beside the couch. "Take your jacket off."

Ainslon watched with pleasure as Lauren stepped forward, slid the jacket off, and draped it over the chair, slipping the cummerbund off to join the jacket. Ainslon watched with rapt attention as Lauren lifted her shirt out of her pants. She did like a woman who knew how to follow directions. "Now the shirt."

With eager anticipation and rising excitement, Ainslon watched as, with deliberate slowness, Lauren unbuttoned her shirt to expose the lacy ivory bra, with its front clasp, covering the swell of breasts. It was all Ainslon could do to restrain herself from tearing off the offending fabric and fill her hands with the warm softness it covered.

Lauren draped the shirt over the jacket, a small smile playing on her lips. "Anything else you want me to remove?"

Ainslon wet her lips, a flood of desire warming her. She moved her eyes up to Lauren's face. "May I?" Then glanced down at Lauren's breasts.

"Yes, you may."

With shaky hands, Ainslon reached out and unclasped the bra, sliding it off Lauren's shoulders to fall onto the floor. God, Lauren was beautiful. She ran her hands over Lauren's breasts, then filled her palms with soft firmness to gently squeeze, eliciting a small moan from Lauren.

"You like to tease me, huh?" Lauren said almost in a growl.

"God, yes." Ainslon leaned forward and ran her tongue along Lauren's collar bone, before biting down on her left shoulder, bringing forth an almost breathless moan from Lauren. "How much?" Ainslon raised her head and took a step back. "How much do you want me?" She ran her fingertip along Lauren's nipple. "I'm waiting." The rise and fall of Lauren's chest urged Ainslon on. "I don't like repeating myself."

Lauren smirked. "Are you sure you want to play this game?" She took a step forward.

"Yes." Ainslon took another step back. "If you can catch me, you can have me." She'd just stepped onto the second-floor landing when Lauren wrapped her arms around her and pushed her up against the wall.

"So, it's games you want to play?" Lauren ran her hands down Ainslon's back, then around her waist and cupped Ainslon's breasts. "You are so sexy," Lauren whispered in Ainslon's ear. "Tell me something?"

"Anything." There wasn't anything she wouldn't give her.

"Is this a game you think you can win?"

Ainslon pressed onto the wall when Lauren placed kisses on her neck. "I don't think I want to win." The pounding of Ainslon's heart slowed when Lauren chuckled against her skin. While Lauren was distracted, Ainslon turned and wrapped her arms around Lauren's neck. "I think you're going to have to teach me the rules."

"That could take all night."

"I'm counting on it." Ainslon lowered her hand and unbuttoned Lauren's pants before pushing them down her hips and cupping her ass. "Are you going to make me do all the work?" Ainslon squeaked when Lauren lifted her and threw her over her shoulder. Good grief, this woman was amazing.

"Your smart mouth is going to get you into trouble, Ainslon."

"Promise?"

Lauren slapped Ainslon's butt, then laughed. "I promise. But first, I want to get you out of that dress… and what's underneath it."

Chapter Thirty-one

Ainslon slowly became aware of her surroundings, a smile making its way onto her face. She kept her eyes closed but wrapped her arms more securely around Lauren's waist and placed a kiss on her neck. As her hand traced circles on Lauren's bare stomach, Ainslon trailed kisses from Lauren's neck to her shoulder before biting, then licking it. What a way to wake up.

"If you keep doing that, we'll never get up," Lauren mumbled.

"Is that a challenge?" Ainslon ran her fingertips along Lauren's bare stomach, down her waist and settled on her thigh. "I do love a good challenge." She scraped her fingernails along the skin.

Lauren stilled Ainslon's hand from going any further and twined their fingers. "As much as I would love to continue this, we should get up soon."

Ainslon kissed Lauren's shoulder, then pulled her snug against her. "I hope making love with you always feels like last night did." Ainslon let a memory from the previous night invade her thoughts.

Ainslon melted immediately into the kiss. She grasped onto Lauren's hips, her insides melting with the ghost of Lauren's fingers along her spine. Lauren barely gave her a second to breathe before pulling her down onto the bed and flush against her. Just the feel of those soft, warm breasts against hers sent Ainslon's mind into overdrive. Lauren's touch sent chills along her body.

"You're stunning," Lauren managed to say between heated kisses.

Ainslon kissed her way down Lauren's chest and closed her mouth around a nipple, sucking lightly.

"Yes, darling."

Lauren turned in Ainslon's arms, the morning light shining on her face. "That can be arranged. I would love nothing more than to stay in bed with you, but the day awaits us. We can spend the day here, then tonight, dinner with my family."

"I know." Ainslon kissed her cheek.

"Darling, I want you to understand something."

She sounded so serious Ainslon stopped her exploration of Lauren's body and paid attention.

"Last night surprised me. I hadn't expected we would be here yet."

"Do you regret it?"

"No." Lauren pulled her close. "Never, and I hope you don't either."

"Not a chance. We're good together. So good. Last night was amazing and I can't wait to do it again. We're doing a good job of balancing our relationship. Last night was a new first step."

"It was a good one." Lauren pecked Ainslon's lips, then slowly got out of bed. Ainslon gulped when the sheet fell away, exposing every bit of Lauren to her.

"You're a goddess."

Lauren threw a wink over her shoulder. "If you ask nicely, this goddess will allow you to shower with her."

Ainslon didn't have to be told twice and scrambled up off the bed.

The shower was over far sooner than Ainslon wanted. After breakfast, Ainslon stood and helped Lauren with the dishes. Last night was perfect and despite feeling terrified, Ainslon had known it was the right time.

She slipped her arms around Lauren's waist, moved the hair from her neck, then placed a kiss on her nape. "I love you." Lauren stiffened but only for a moment, then grasped the hands around her waist. "Every part of you, and I can't wait to see what the future holds for us. It's going to be a wonderful adventure." Ainslon went to move her arms, but Lauren's soapy ones clung to her.

Lauren turned slightly so she could see Ainslon but kept their arms held tight. "I love you too. You've taken my life by storm and I've enjoyed every minute of it."

"I can handle you. We'll have ups and downs but at the end of the day, I'll still be able to call you mine."

Lauren grinned. "What am I going to do with you?"

"Whatever you want." Before Ainslon could connect their lips, her cellphone rang. Edna's ringtone. "That's Nana." Lauren let her go and Ainslon retrieved the cellphone from the kitchen counter. "Nana." It was a bit odd for her to be calling so early.

"I was wondering if you had the time to stop by today? There is something I wanted to talk to you about."

"Of course. When do you want me?" Something didn't feel right, but Ainslon would never tell Edna no.

"I know you are having dinner with Lauren's family tonight, so how about lunch with me?"

"Is it all right if I bring Lauren?"

"I insist."

"Okay. I'll see you in a few hours. I love you."

"I love you too."

After the call, Ainslon placed her phone back on the counter.

"Ainslon?"

"I should have asked you, but Nana wanted to have lunch with us. She said she needed to talk with me about something."

"You look worried."

"I...I feel like something's wrong." Ainslon relaxed into Lauren's warm embrace.

"Whatever it is, I'll be here, and we'll deal with it together."

"Together. I like the sound of that."

⁂

As they pulled up to Edna's house, Ainslon's stomach flipped. Earlier, she'd called Easton about this meeting, but she didn't know what was going on. She stressed that Edna hadn't mentioned anything when they last talked.

Lauren placed her hand on Ainslon's shoulder and gave a comforting squeeze. "Let's go in."

"I suppose you're right." Ainslon held the kitchen door open for Lauren, then walked in behind her. Edna was standing at the counter. "Nana."

"Just a moment, dear. Help me with the tea."

In the living room, Edna spoke up. "I can see the worry on your face. You never could hide your feelings well."

"I'm just..." She sighed. "Nana, what is it?"

"I talked to your father yesterday."

This being about her parents never crossed her mind. "You're not dying?"

"We all are, but not yet, dear. Not yet. I'm sorry I worried you."

"No. It's fine." She slipped her hand under Edna's. "Go on." She relaxed even more when Lauren rested her arm on the back of Ainslon's chair and caressed her shoulder.

"They've decided to come for a visit." Edna squeezed Ainslon's hand.

"Okay. I kind of figured they would after our last talk. When are they coming?"

"In three and a half weeks and they'll be staying a week."

"Less than a month away. That's the food festival." Of course, they would have to mess up that time for her. Edna had already agreed to read a traditional Irish children's story at their booth.

"It is and I've already told them not to bother you and that me, you, and Easton have our weekly dinners. They will not be invited. Yes, I want to see them, but you are my priority. Tell me if any of this bothers you."

"All of it does, but I understand your need to see them. I don't, and I can't stress this enough, I don't want to see them."

"They know."

Ainslon laughed. "It's not like they want to see me."

Edna pursed her lips. "They do. I don't agree with the way they treated you, but I will forever be grateful I had the opportunity to raise you. You and Easton have done my heart good. You girls are my greatest legacy."

Ainslon held back her tears. She'd be lying if she hadn't wondered what they'd been up to all these years, but she never let it overwhelm her. Now, they were coming to Garriety. "I'm still not going to meet them."

"I didn't expect you too." Edna took both of Ainslon's hands in hers. "Grá gheal mo chroí thú."

"I love you, Nana."

"Now, I made a nice chicken salad for lunch. I'm going to go get everything ready and give you two a minute."

Ainslon didn't object when Edna walked out of the living room. She welcomed Lauren's arms when she sat beside her on the couch.

"You seem conflicted."

"I am. They refused to accept me when I came out. After they caught me and my best friend Deirdre making out, they were furious. They grounded me for weeks and forbade me from seeing her. I was miserable, then one day Nana showed up. She was there for two weeks." She turned to Lauren and traced her jawline with her hand. "They gave Nana guardianship of me. Signed me over for being a lesbian. I know a lot of gay kids had it a lot worse than me. They never abused me, physically or verbally, but they let me know being gay wasn't something they would accept. It wasn't normal. I wasn't normal." Ainslon chuckled. "Every hour of the plane ride home, Nana would tell me something she loved about me and there was nothing wrong with me liking girls. It was normal and I was normal. I've never felt anything but loved with her."

"And that means everything. When I first came out to my parents, they didn't understand it, but over time they made it clear they loved me no matter what.

They apologized for their initial reaction and we've been good ever since. Have they never tried to contact you?"

"Me? No. It's been almost twenty years. They'd be in their late fifties now. Everyone always said I was the spitting image of my mom. I don't know." Ainslon stood abruptly, then held out her hand for Lauren. The warm fingers wrapped around hers, grounded her. "We can talk about this later. Right now, we have lunch with Nana, then dinner tonight with your family."

Lauren wrapped her arms around Ainslon and pulled her close. "I love you."

"I love you too."

Chapter Thirty-two

Lauren slipped the black sleeveless turtleneck on, then stepped into and pulled on her black slacks. After a quick glance in the bedroom mirror, she declared herself ready. At the door to her bedroom, she slipped her feet into a pair of black heels.

When they'd left Edna's, Ainslon had asked to go to the park and they'd sat quietly and watched the water for an hour. She couldn't imagine what Ainslon had gone through with her family, but she vowed to make sure their visit had the least amount of impact on Ainslon. No matter what she had to do to accomplish that.

She snatched her black leather jacket off the hook in the hallway and made her way down the stairs where Ainslon was waiting. At the bottom of the stairs, Lauren drew in her breath at the vision in front of her. Ainslon had opted for a long sleeved, knee length black dress. Her hair flowed down her back, and a pair of glasses added to her appeal.

"Wow. Love the sexy librarian look."

Ainslon grinned. "Not wow. Since my eyes were bothering me, I opted for my glasses instead of the contacts I normally wear." She scrunched her nose up. "You haven't seen me in my glasses, have you?"

Lauren looked sheepish. "Just once when I googled you." She drew Ainslon into her arms. "I wouldn't mind seeing you in them more often."

"Do you have a glasses fetish?"

"I have an Ainslon fetish." Ainslon's laugh warmed Lauren to her core. She hated seeing her sad. "Are you ready?" Lauren slipped her jacket on, then helped Ainslon with her cardigan.

"My, you look good." Ainslon ran her hands down the jacket's zipper. "Black is your color."

Lauren held her arms out wide. "You think so?"

"We both know it is."

"True, but, so you know, your accent is so hot I'd want you in anything you dress in."

"So, you let my unique clothing pass because of my accent."

Lauren swooned at the more pronounced accent. "Be still my heart."

"Come on, dork." At the car, Ainslon pulled Lauren to a stop. "Thank you for today."

"No thanks necessary." Lauren kissed her lips lightly. "How would you like to taste the best Puerto Rican food ever? My family and I wanted to give you a taste of my heritage and they love going all out."

"I can't wait."

"Good, because my mother and sister have gone a bit overboard for today. They made pernil. Trust me, you'll love it. If you've never tasted heaven on Earth, you're about to. It's so good." Lauren put the car into drive and pulled out onto the road.

"What is it?"

"It's a slow-roasted marinated pork shoulder. My sister made arroz con gandules."

"I've had that."

"Jeffrey made pastelon. It's his specialty. He's been perfecting it since he and Callie got married."

"That's made with plantains, isn't it?"

"Yep. They're mashed and layered with ground beef, like a lasagna."

"I can't wait."

"They want you to feel welcome and what better way than food." Lauren flipped the blinker, then drove a few blocks before pulling up to an average looking house. Lauren took off her seat belt and turned to Ainslon. "Now, it's fine to be nervous, but no need to be scared. They like you. I promise."

Ainslon cupped Lauren's cheeks and kissed her. "Let's go."

Lauren held tightly to Ainslon's hand as they entered the house.

"Lauri, we're in the kitchen," Callie called out.

"Let me take your cardigan." Lauren hung it up along with her jacket. She held tight to Ainslon's hand and led her into the kitchen.

Patricia stood at the stove, stirring something in a pot, and Callie lifted a pot and carried it past them into the dining room.

"Where's Jeffrey and Charlie?" Lauren accepted a kiss from her mother.

"Setting the table." Patricia wiped her hands, then drew Ainslon to her. "It's good to see you again, Ainslon."

"You as well."

Patricia patted her cheek before going back to the stove. "I hope you like what we've prepared tonight."

"I'm sure I will. It smells delicious."

"Thank you. It should taste as good as it smells."

"What can we do?"

Patricia looked scandalized. "You will do nothing. Dinner is almost ready." Her attention turned to her daughter. "Lauren, help your sister."

After the table was set, everyone took a seat. Food littered almost all the available surface. They really had gone all out.

"Dig in," Patricia said.

Lauren explained the items of food as she put a little of each on Ainslon's plate. At the first bite of the pernil, she knew it was time for her to start cooking more. The pork melted in her mouth. "Momma, you've outdone yourself."

"Don't be silly. It's just dinner." She might have been trying to come across as modest, but Lauren could tell she was pleased.

"Lauren's right," Ainslon said. "You've all outdone yourself. It's delicious."

"Ainslon," Patricia said, "Do you cook many traditional Irish dishes?"

"Not nearly as much as Nana would like me to."

"It's important to keep our legacies alive," Callie said.

"It is. My sister owns Brew and Bake, and she sells a handful of Irish desserts Nana has passed down to us. Easton has never visited Ireland but we both know how important it is to Nana to keep those traditions going."

"Aunt Lauren said you have competitive game nights at your store?" Charlie asked.

"We do. Twice a month. You should come sometime. There's no cover charge and prizes are given away."

"Is it only video games or board games too?"

"Both. We alternate. Next month we're having a classic board game tournament."

"Is there an age limit?" Jeffrey asked.

"We cap at eighteen, but once we're in our new

store, we're thinking of having an adult's game night." Ainslon took a sip of her wine.

"Really?" Lauren reclined back in her seat. "That would be great."

"I could kick your ass," Jeffrey threw out.

Lauren arched her brow. "You wish. I believe it was this woman," she touched her chest, "That kicked your ass at Monopoly last month."

"That was a fluke." He downed his wine.

Lauren sat back as Jeffrey and Charlie talked about the latest video games. Patricia, Callie, and Ainslon talked about the food festival.

"Lauren," Patricia said. "Do you have everything settled for the festival?"

"I do. Noe has the menu planned and I've got our booth squared away. Ainslon also has a booth."

"Do go on," Patricia encouraged.

"We're having children's story hour. Every two hours, someone will read a new story. Nana is going to read a story, and I've got people settled to read other books." Ainslon nudged Lauren. "Give me another tostone, please."

"Addictive, right?"

"Yes."

After dinner, Lauren helped her mother with the dishes while everyone else retired to the living room.

"You love her," Patricia said.

Lauren's soapy hands slipped on the plate, but she quickly got her bearings. "Yes."

"We may not have understood when you told us you were gay, but I hope you know how proud of you I am, and your papa was as well. All we've ever wanted was for you to be happy."

"I know, Momma. We've made our peace. Papa

never let a day go that he didn't tell me he loved me." No matter what she was doing, if her papa called, Lauren would always answer the phone. After his death from a heart attack, Lauren would sit in her house with a glass of wine, staring at her phone, waiting for a phone call that would never come. It took her waking up to a wine-soaked shirt to conclude something had to change, and she began to spend more time with her family.

"Good. Now that you've found someone, there is no reason not to give me my next grandchild."

"Momma." Lauren laughed along with Patricia. "I believe you said something about dessert."

"For you, little duck, only for you."

"As it should be, Momma. As it should be."

Chapter Thirty-three

So, I was thinking about something," Lauren said, over lunch Tuesday.

Ainslon had just bitten into her sandwich, so she chewed slowly, then wiped her mouth. "Oh, about what?"

"Us."

"Go on."

"Besides the axe throwing and water balloon fight in the park, we haven't really done anything besides dinner, movies, and hanging out. How about we each plan a date? What each of us would consider a perfect date."

"That sounds wonderful. Though, I'm not sure you'll be able to survive my perfect date."

Lauren smirked. "I'm tougher than I look."

"Maybe." Ainslon leaned across the table and kissed her on the lips. "Saturday, me and you. I'm going to blow you away."

"We'll see. We'll see."

"I'm telling you; this woman knows how to plan dates."

"I've been known to plan the perfect date as well. Also," Lauren said, pushing her plate away, "I thought it would be nice to pick some fun activities for the two of us and our families and throw them into a jar. We could pick one out once a month and do them together."

How could this woman get any more perfect? "Sounds wonderful."

Forty minutes later, Ainslon rushed into Turn the Page.

"Where's the fire?" Justin proclaimed.

"Lauren had this bright idea that we should each plan out a perfect date."

"And what's the problem? That sounds nice. I'll have to say something to Brandy."

"Not really a problem, but we've already had our perfect date."

"You have?"

"Us spending time together. That's all I need."

"Well then. There's your answer."

She wracked her mind all day to come up with the perfect date, even searching Pinterest. It wasn't until she dusted a picture book with a cabin on the front cover in one of the display windows that she got the idea for the perfect date.

❧ ❧ ❧ ❧

Saturday morning, Lauren took one last look in the living room mirror, then headed out of her condo and down the elevator to join Ainslon. She couldn't wait to see what Ainslon had planned. Ainslon had stayed mum on her plans all week.

Lauren hoped this had taken Ainslon's mind off her parents. She'd made it clear she didn't want to see them; however, Lauren knew, the thought of them being in the same town put Ainslon on edge. Lauren would do whatever it took to make sure Ainslon didn't get too stressed out this week.

When Ainslon's Jeep pulled up, Lauren climbed

inside.

"Does my attire suit you?" When Ainslon had told her to wear jeans, a t-shirt, and sneakers, she had been skeptical, but went with it. She knew Ainslon wouldn't steer her wrong.

"Beautiful. Now, we have our whole day ahead of us. Are you ready?"

"Take me away."

Three hours later, Lauren slid her knees up and hugged them to her chest, resting her chin atop of them. Rolling hills spread out in front of them as far as the eye could see. A lake was to the right of their location and a small, rustic cabin to the left. Ainslon sat beside her and mimicked her position. Lauren wasn't aware a place like this existed so close to Garriety.

"How did you find this place?" They'd driven for an hour and a half before Ainslon had pulled off onto a dirt road. Forty minutes later, Lauren was in awe as their destination came into view.

Ainslon picked at the grass. "I own it."

Lauren turned to look at her. That she hadn't expected. "It's beautiful."

"Thank you. When I turned twenty, I used to help the owner. When he got sick, I was the first one he asked if I wanted to buy it. He was amazing and I got a steal. He wanted someone he knew would take care of it. I pay my neighbor, Brian, to come out and check on it every few days. In return, I allow him and his kids to fish in the lake along the land I own and to camp. I own ten acres." Ainslon leaned back on her hands. "It reminds me a little of Ireland. My own little piece of heaven. I try to come out here a few times a year to relax. Sometimes Nana or Easton will come with me. Most of the time I'm by myself. Not many people know I own this land."

"Thank you for telling me. It's relaxing here." It was what she would have bought herself for a getaway property. The landscape could use a few more flowers but for the most part it was perfect.

"It is. This is my perfect date. Just spending time with you in a place that takes all my stress away."

Lauren turned quickly, easily pushed Ainslon to the ground, and rested atop her. "I love you and this is perfect. I bet it's beautiful in the winter."

"It is." Ainslon wrapped her arms around Lauren and pulled her close, nuzzling her neck. "It's funny. Where Garriety hardly gets any snow, last winter, this place got close to two feet the two weeks Nana and I stayed."

"We'll have to come some winter and see." Lauren rested her head on Ainslon's chest and enjoyed the moment. When the air chilled, Lauren stood up. "While I am enjoying this, I would love to see the inside of the cabin."

"Let's go."

Lauren stood and clasped Ainslon's hand. The cabin, on closer inspection, wasn't as small as she'd first thought. It looked to be well built and well-maintained. Two rocking chairs sat on one end of the porch and a red porch swing on the other end. "How big is the cabin?"

"Sixteen feet wide by twenty feet long."

Once inside, Lauren stood in awe. This wasn't what she expected. The walls were lined with wood planks and gray slate tiles covered the entire floor. Directly to the right of the door was a small kitchen, complete with sink, stove, fridge, and pantry. A moderate sized wood stove was to the left of the kitchen.

A couch and a large bookcase took up the middle half of the cabin and from an open door, she could see the bathroom at the back of the cabin. Two large area rugs and a handful of pictures completed the look. "This is amazing."

"Easton helped me redo the inside. It took us close to a year."

"You are full of surprises." Lauren drew Ainslon into her arms. "You did a good job." She took a step back, taking Ainslon with her. "The bed looks comfortable."

"Oh, it is." Ainslon wiggled out of Lauren's arms and walked to the bed, leaving a trail of clothes in her wake. "I had Brian, the guy who checks on my place, change the sheets a couple of days ago. Care to join me?"

The sight of Ainslon naked, beckoning her was not something Lauren would ever take for granted. "You don't have to ask me twice."

Lauren followed Ainslon's lead and undressed before joining her on the bed. She kissed her ankle, then placed feather light kisses on Ainslon's calf before she straddled her lap. Lauren shivered when Ainslon slipped both arms around her, then ran both hands up and down her back in slow motion. "Are you trying to kill me?"

Ainslon laughed. "No, I'm trying to love you."

When Ainslon rose and flipped their positions, Lauren easily rolled with her, pulling her down and kissing her deep and slow. When Lauren pulled back, Ainslon's eyes stayed closed. She took the opportunity and ran her tongue along her jawline before reconnecting their lips. "You drive me crazy." She hissed when Ainslon cupped her breasts. "Absolutely crazy."

"You love it."

Ainslon trailed kisses down Lauren's throat before latching onto a nipple to stroke it with her tongue, then suck.

"That…don't stop." Lauren pushed her chest upward, a hand at Ainslon's nape, small sounds of pleasure sounding in her throat.

Ainslon released the taut nipple to run her tongue down the slope of breast to kiss Lauren's abs. "I have no intention of stopping."

A few hours later, Ainslon lay in Lauren's arms after making love and a short nap. "How long can we stay?"

Ainslon ran her fingers along Lauren's arm. "Maybe another hour. There's a diner in town we can eat dinner at before we head back."

Lauren traced circles on Ainslon's stomach. "Sounds wonderful. Can you spend the night with me?"

"Like you would even have to ask. My perfect date night ends with us in bed together."

"Good, then we can get an early start on my perfect date."

Ainslon turned in Lauren's arms. "I'm sure whatever it is you have planned, I'll enjoy."

"I hope you will." It was too late to second guess her choices now. She only hoped Ainslon would enjoy it.

❦ ❦ ❦ ❦

Sunday dawned bright and early. After a leisurely shower and a wonderful breakfast, Ainslon and Lauren relaxed on the living room couch.

Ainslon took a sip of her tea. "What have you got planned for today?"

"Well." Lauren set her cup of coffee on the coffee table. "I hope you won't be disappointed." She ran her fingers along the back of the couch. "But I've already had my perfect date with you. Like you said, I enjoy being with you, so for today I took the liberty to pull an activity out of the jar."

"Okay." That wasn't what Ainslon expected but it didn't make her angry. "Go on."

"As you know, I like to have fun and I've arranged something for us. In any relationship, you have to keep each other on your toes."

Ainslon had known Lauren long enough to know that the way her forehead scrunched was a sure sign she was nervous. Ainslon finished her tea, set her cup beside Lauren's, then took both her hands. "I'll enjoy anything you planned."

"Softball isn't the only thing my sister roped me into."

"Oh." Ainslon rose up and straddled Lauren's lap. She would never get tired of the feel of Lauren's arms around her. "What is it? It can't be that bad."

Lauren quirked up her brow. "Paintball."

Ainslon blinked. That…wasn't what she had expected. "Paintball?" Now she was sorry she'd never gone with Easton when she'd tried to drag her along with her.

"It'll be great. Us bonding over something with our family and friends. I haven't had a chance to try out your planning and attack strategies yet. I think for a relationship to work, sometimes we have to get down and dirty."

"I can do dirty."

Lauren turned and guided Ainslon to recline back on the couch, then the tickling commenced. Ainslon squealed and tried to get away but Lauren kept a firm grip. "Do you give?"

"I give. I give," Ainslon said between laughs. Lauren raised Ainslon's arms above her head and leaned down to place a kiss on the tip of Ainslon's nose before settling in beside her and holding her tight.

Ainslon relaxed into Lauren's embrace, tracing shapes on Lauren's t-shirt clothed stomach.

Lauren rose up. "I would love to take you right now on this couch, but we have to meet everyone in an hour and a half." Lauren hopped up off the couch.

"Wait. Everyone? How many people are going to be there?"

A mischievous smile turned up the corners of Lauren's mouth.

Chapter Thirty-four

Two hours into the paintball game, Ainslon feared she had made a terrible mistake, agreeing to this madness. One of the opposing teams lost Charlie first, along with Jeffrey, leaving Callie on her own. Surely, she would be easy to take out. When the teams were divided that morning, Ainslon had naturally been paired with Lauren. Brandy and Justin were paired together. Paintballs whizzing by her wasn't as fun as Ainslon hoped it would be.

More than once, Lauren sent her hand signals, but Ainslon didn't know what the hell she was going on about. For a good twenty minutes, she huddled behind this outbuilding, trying to steer clear of the multiple teams on the field. Per the leaflet, at any given moment, there could be up to twenty-five teams in play.

She jerked her head around and came eye to eye with Justin. The look of shock on his face mirrored her own. She'd been surprised, but happy Lauren had invited Justin and Brandy along today. Easton would have joined them but it was a rare Sunday that she had to work. Justin's blue vest was paint splattered, but not with the green color paintball they were designated at the beginning. Ainslon's pink vest was spotless and from time to time she would see the orange of Callie's but never worked up the nerve to shoot her.

The instructor had stated it was up to the group

how they wanted to be split up and how their game would play out, but it was illegal to shoot another group for the hell of it. It looked like whoever shot Justin didn't take those rules into account. They'd decided on green paintballs and one hit would take you out of the game.

"So, this is where you've been hiding," Justin said, his gun aimed at her chest, voice muffled a bit by his face shield.

"Better here than out there." Ainslon raised her gun. It wasn't a hot day but with all the layers she had on, she was already worn out. Maybe she should consider exercising more.

"I don't want to do this anymore," Justin said. "They're psychos."

"I don't either. Lauren is crazy." Lauren had a desire to win and on one hand, it was hot and the other, she was scary.

Justin nodded. "She's not the only one; so is Brandy. I didn't know she was such a beast. So, how about on the count of three we shoot each other and go join Jeffrey and Charlie with the pizza?"

"They're eating pizza?" She could go for pizza right now. Hell, anything to get out of this horrible situation. She couldn't believe Lauren had picked this for their date.

He nodded. "Yes."

Ainslon had no problem going out like this. "We can say we ambushed each other."

"Sounds good to me."

"Okay. One. Two—" Ainslon jumped back when green splattered across Justin's chest and he fell back, stunned. She didn't have time to comprehend what had happened by the time Lauren had dragged her away.

Lauren patted her on the shoulder and kept glancing behind her. "Good job distracting him. Now all we have to do is take Callie and Brandy out. They're not even on the same team, but for being so small they sure are quick. But, babe, we've got this. The two of us." Lauren held up two fingers.

Lauren looked so earnest Ainslon didn't have a choice but to go along with whatever plan she had. That's how she found herself plastered to a tree. A young boy had run past her twice and told her it was a lot more fun to play than to stand around. She took his wise words to heart, but Lauren had specified she stay here and wait until she drew Callie out in order for Ainslon to shoot her.

The size of the paintball park, over twenty acres, should have been daunting, but Ainslon quickly learned there was a method to all the madness. Maybe she could have enjoyed it more if she knew what she was doing.

Ainslon seriously considered making her own plan when she spied Callie ducking behind an ammunition box and lifted her gun, ready when Callie popped back up. But she never showed herself. Ainslon lowered her gun and jumped back, startled to come face to face with Callie. How the hell had she snuck up on her?

"I play to win," Callie said. At the same time Callie pulled the trigger, Ainslon was pushed aside and landed on the ground. She lay stunned for a moment, but quickly picked up her gun and shot at Callie running away from her. She expected to see Lauren but was surprised to see the kid from earlier.

"That's illegal, you know?" Ainslon stood and wiped herself off, only a bit pissed the little shit saved her. Justin was more than likely devouring pizza at the moment.

He shrugged. "I'm a rebel. Now go get them." He jumped up and took off running.

His confidence in her gave her the courage she needed. Ainslon made her way toward the center of the field. She knelt, settled her gun on top of the box in front of her, and scanned the area. A flash of orange caught her eye. She took aim at the small piece of orange hidden behind the tree and pulled the trigger. She heard a curse but didn't wait around. She lifted the small device they were given to check what team members were taken out, but her grin faded when she saw Lauren was out. Shit. Fuck. She and Brandy were the only ones left. She couldn't lose now.

It took another twenty minutes, and a fist-bump from her buddy before she noticed Brandy. They both eyed each other across the field. This was it. Ainslon had never felt so pumped before and relished the feeling. Brandy darted to the right and Ainslon the left.

Quickly but quietly, she made her way to a tree to hide behind when a paintball whizzed past her face. She fell to the ground, crawling the rest of the way to the tree. She could make out a piece of Brandy's vest and decided the best defense was a good offense. She wasn't sure she could make another shot like the one with Callie. That one was pure dumb luck.

Ainslon took a deep breath, thanked Lauren for all her teachings, then jumped up, steadied her gun, and ran at Brandy. Brandy peeked out from behind the tree and flinched. That's when Ainslon pulled the trigger.

Ainslon slid on the ground in front of Brandy

and raised her gun in case the first shot hadn't hit its mark. The paint splatter on Brandy's chest confirmed a hit.

"Damn, Ainslon. Good shot," Brandy said, conceding defeat.

Ainslon accepted Brandy's hand and stood.

"That's right. That's my girl," Lauren shouted at Justin and ran toward them as Ainslon and Brandy walked to the lounge area after handing in their gear. Ainslon squeaked when Lauren picked her up and twirled her but beamed at Lauren's smile.

"Take that, losers," Lauren said, holding Ainslon with one arm and pointing at Justin with the other.

Ainslon gripped the collar of Lauren's shirt and pulled her down into a kiss. The touch of Lauren's lips sent fireworks through her body. When Lauren groaned and deepened the kiss, Ainslon wound her arms around Lauren's neck and slipped her fingers into Lauren's hair.

Lauren was the first to pull away. "Oh, my." She rested their foreheads together. "You're—Kapow!"

"Yeah?"

"Yeah."

"Nice job. The win and the girl." Ainslon chuckled as her accomplice walked up to them and held out his fist for her to bump.

"I never got your name."

"Player one." He pointed at Ainslon. "Player two."

"I can live with that." She bid him farewell, then she and Lauren walked arm and arm to join the others at the front of the course.

"Is he the little punk that foiled my shot at you?" Callie asked, eyeing the boy across the field.

"It is."

"You're lucky, O'Neil."

Ainslon slipped her arm around Lauren's waist, who was busy taunting Justin. "Don't I know it." Ainslon and Lauren trailed behind the others, heading to get some pizza.

"This weekend has been wonderful, and we still have tonight. I plan on making the most of it."

"What do you have in mind?" Ainslon eyed the pizza.

"Jeffrey, Justin." They both turned to Lauren. "How about karaoke tonight?"

Jeffrey jabbed his finger at her. "You're on, Millán."

"Sounds like a plan, Stan," Justin said, joining Jeffrey in an impromptu dance session, soon followed by Charlie.

That did not sound like fun to Ainslon, and she shook her head when Lauren danced toward the boys and held out her hands toward Ainslon. "No."

"Come on." Lauren smirked. "You know you want to." Lauren beckoned her with her hand and after a moment's hesitation, Ainslon grasped it and let Lauren dance her toward everyone else. It wasn't until after they were done, and she had bowed toward their onlookers, she realized Callie had recorded it.

She sidled up to Callie. "I want a copy."

"Not going to threaten me to destroy it?"

Ainslon slipped her arm around Callie's shoulder and relaxed when Callie rested her arm around her waist. "Nope. I'm sure I looked like a dork, but I'm happy."

"I agree. You all looked ridiculous but happy."

They joined the others for the group photo.

She smiled when Lauren wrapped her arms

around her shoulders, pulled her back against her chest, and held the winner's sign in front of them. She even made the others take a step to the right to separate the winners from the losers.

At the moment Ainslon laughed and leaned back into Lauren, the photo was taken. Yes, what a perfect day.

Chapter Thirty-five

Lauren walked around the fairgrounds, taking in all the booths set up for the food festival. Almost two weeks had passed since their paintball outing. She knew Ainslon felt apprehensive about playing but was a great sport, and they had won. Lauren made sure to put more of those type of outings in, what she had dubbed, their date jar. At this point, she had no complaints about her and Ainslon's relationship. No, everything was moving along nicely.

The streets of Garriety were already congested with tourists, but she wouldn't complain because the store saw a massive spike in sales. Though she had declined to sit on the board for the festival, she still wanted everything to go off without a hitch. The almost eighty booths took up every available space of the fairgrounds. One of those was Ainslon's booth.

Just thinking about Ainslon left her breathless. They'd spent the night together but had gone their separate ways after breakfast.

Lauren glanced down at the festival map. Ainslon's booth should be up ahead. At the next turn, she looked up and smiled. Ainslon had one of the larger tents that was equipped with fans, thank goodness. That would allow the children to be out of the sun while they enjoyed story hour. A large sign hanging at the top of the tent read Turn the Page. An easel was placed on one side of the opening with their schedule for the day. The tent itself was multi-colored and as she walked around it there was a mural on all three sides depicting a different children's story. Lauren couldn't help but be impressed.

She waved at a few people she knew, pushed the sunglasses up and into her hair, walked through the tent opening, and groaned in relief. The cool breeze from the fans instantly refreshed her. She kept her eyes closed as arms snaked around her and a warm kiss planted on her lips.

"Open your eyes, sweetheart."

Lauren did and was met with the mesmerizing green ones of the woman she loved. "I love you." She could tell it took Ainslon aback since she usually wasn't this open with her I love yous in public, but it pleased her.

Ainslon slipped her arms out and around Lauren's neck. "I love you, too."

After a few minutes of holding each other, Lauren reluctantly stepped back, then took Ainslon's hands. "Quite the set up you have here."

"I know. It's great." Ainslon slipped away from her, then held her arms out to her sides. "Since our tent was so popular last year, we were allowed a bigger one this year. Thank goodness my request for fans was approved. Otherwise it would be miserable."

"Since I was a platinum donor, our booth got fans. I feel sorry for the poor bastards that don't have them. Though, I suppose most of them are used to the heat."

"If they're not they should get out of the kitchen," Justin said, walking around them with bags in his hands.

"You know, Justin. You keep eating tacos, you're

going to turn into one."

"Don't even get me started," Brandy said as she walked up.

"It's all he wants to eat at the store," Ainslon chimed in.

"Hey now." Justin planted his hands on his hips. "You don't have to eat them."

Ainslon held her hands up in surrender. "Let's not be so hasty."

"That's what I thought. Lauren, can you stay?"

"I'm afraid not."

"That's too bad." Ainslon took a taco out of the bag and put it in Lauren's hand. "That way I'll know you ate something." She tucked a bit of stray hair behind Lauren's ear.

Lauren leaned forward enough to rub their noses together, then pecked Ainslon on the lips. "Call me if you need me."

"I will."

Lauren stepped out of the tent, unwrapped her taco, and took a big bite. Justin was on the right path; they were fantastic. The quicker she got her work done, the quicker she could join Ainslon.

Tonight, they were having dinner with Edna. Tomorrow, Ainslon's parents were flying in and Lauren knew she wasn't looking forward to it. But she knew Ainslon wanted Edna to have this time with them. She could see how tired Edna looked and acted lately. No matter what, she would make sure Ainslon was always available for Edna and Easton.

After another round of the grounds, she headed back to her tent. Her stomach dropped when she spotted two people in a heated conversation in front of her tent. Carrie and her mother. After a quick call to security, she headed in their direction.

"Mom, please."

"You listen to me, young lady, I raised you better than this."

"Better than what? I'm happy. Larry and I have an apartment and we've both got jobs. I've got good healthcare. We're okay."

"You're having a baby," she spat. "You know what the bible says."

Lauren took that moment to step up. "Carrie, you okay?"

"You." Janice raised her finger. "Stay away from my daughter. You did this."

"I can assure you I didn't, and before you sprout off your bullshit, you should know I've already informed security and they're on their way."

"You people. I won't stand for this, Carrie. You're not even married."

"Mom, I'm not coming home. I'm staying with Larry."

Larry stepped out of the tent and walked up to Carrie. "I love your daughter and plan on taking care of her and the baby."

Janice sneered. "You're trash and you've dragged my daughter down with you."

"That's enough." Lauren stepped in front of the teens. "Since you don't want to have anything to do with her, leave. Now." Lauren nodded at the security officer.

"Ma'am, I'm going to have to ask you to come with me," the officer said.

"I'm going. But I will say this. Carrie, I'm so disappointed in you, and your father would be too." After she stormed off, Lauren waved away the small crowd that had gathered. When she turned, Carrie had tears in her eyes.

"Come here." She held Carrie until her tears dried, then raised her chin. "Listen to me." Carrie nodded. "Your mother is wrong. You're an amazing woman and this baby is so lucky to have you and Larry. You both are trying so hard and I know you'll succeed." She looked at Larry and opened her right arm to invite him into the hug. "Larry."

"Ms…Lauren."

It had taken him weeks to call her by her first name. "You're not trash. You've got a good job and you're taking night classes. I'm proud of you both. So proud."

Larry nodded, then joined their hug. He wiped his eyes when they moved apart. "Thank you for everything."

"You're welcome. Now, I'll give you two a few minutes, then Larry, you need to get back to your booth to finish setting up. Carrie, after we're finished here, you can have the rest of the day off. Mark is already covering the rest of your shift."

"You're the best."

Lauren chuckled. "I know." She stepped inside their tent, only a tad smaller than Ainslon's and, satisfied with what she saw, joined Noe at the back. "Show me what you've been working on."

Chapter Thirty-six

Ainslon hummed as she looked over the inside of the tent. At the far end of the tent was a cushioned chair for the reader. To the left was a stack of pads that the kids could sit on. The table on the right would be stocked with snacks and eight-ounce water bottles. At the front of the tent was a table ready to hold the books that would be read each day and available for sale. Each child that attended would receive a voucher for a free cookie at Easton's tent and a coupon for five dollars off at Turn the Page. They had a deal that Easton could market in her tent and she could market in Easton's. It worked out well every year.

Bright colors littered all the available space. First and foremost, this was a welcome spot for kids. This year, unlike previous years, they couldn't grab a spot on the concrete, so Justin had borrowed several tarps, at least to cover the dirt up. The last thing they wanted was the kids getting dirty.

She pulled her hair out of the ponytail, then put it back up in a messy bun. It was days like this, when the humidity was a beast, that she thought about cutting her hair, but always chickened out in the end.

With one final look and a wave to Justin, she headed to Lauren's tent to pick her up for dinner.

She wasn't looking forward to tomorrow but tonight Edna had promised to make her Irish stew for Lauren. She knew it was important to Edna to see her son and daughter-in-law again and Ainslon would never make her feel bad because she wanted to see them. However, a small part of Ainslon couldn't help but be upset with her. After everything her parents had put her through, she never thought Edna would welcome them back. Though she understood her reasoning, it still stung.

"Dollar for your thoughts?"

Ainslon turned to face Lauren. "Wow, big spender."

"Your thoughts are worth more than a penny." Lauren slipped her arm around Ainslon's shoulders and they started walking. "Is it about tomorrow?"

Ainslon raised her hand and entangled her fingers with Lauren's, where they rested on her shoulder. "I know why she wants to see them, but I don't understand why. Well, I do, but—"

"You're conflicted."

"Yes."

"Edna loves you."

"I know."

"Let me finish. She loves you, and let's face it, she's more than your grandma. She raised you. For all intent and purposes, she's your mother." She pulled them to a stop at the parking lot. "I can see both points. I'm furious for what they put you through, but I also understand her wanting to see them."

Ainslon rested her head on Lauren's shoulder and relaxed into her arms. "You're right. She is my mother. Easton feels the same way. She's all we have, and it sucks. Easton's parents died, but mine threw me away. But…"

"But?"

"But a small part of me wonders what their life has been like. I haven't had contact with them in almost twenty years. I have never, before now, felt tempted to look them up. I hate them. Or at least a part of me does. I don't know." She placed a kiss on Lauren's neck, then pulled back.

"Are you having second thoughts about seeing them?" Lauren pushed a few stray hairs out of Ainslon's eyes.

"I." She nervously licked her lips. "I want to see them, but I don't want to talk to them."

"I wonder if they know how successful you've become."

"I'll ask Nana tonight."

An hour later, Lauren pulled in front of the curb to Edna's house. Easton's car was already in the drive.

"Come on. Irish stew awaits."

"I can't wait."

As soon as Ainslon opened the back door, the overwhelming aroma of lamb and spices engulfed her.

"Good grief, Ainslon, shut the door," Edna said, motioning them both in.

"Sorry, Nana."

Ainslon kissed Edna on the cheek, then accepted the one arm hug from Easton.

"Did you get everything set up?" Easton asked, then popped a piece of carrot in her mouth.

"We did. It looks great."

"And you, Lauren?"

"We did as well. It's bound to be a good week. Most of the hotels are already filled up."

"Ainslon, Easton, set the table while Lauren and I relax."

"Sure thing, Nana." Ainslon and Easton worked

in tandem setting the table, then placing the food atop it. Irish stew, homemade bread, and for dessert, Easton had brought an assortment of cookies, brownies, and mini pies left over from the day. With vanilla ice cream.

"Everything looks wonderful, Edna." Lauren lifted her wine glass. "To family."

"To family."

Ainslon ladled a healthy amount of stew into her bowl, and took two pieces of bread. The first spoon full was a throwback to her childhood.

"Damn, Nana," Easton said. "This is the best stew you've made."

"It's amazing, Nana." It always amazed her that a mix of different herbs and spices could transform a dish into a masterpiece and Edna was a master at it.

Lauren nudged Ainslon. "Is this the stew you were going to make me?"

"It is, but no one has the touch like Nana does. I'll try, but I'm not making any promises."

"Practice makes perfect." Lauren kissed Ainslon's cheek.

"None of that at the table." Easton covered her eyes. "Is it over?"

"Now who's being dramatic?" Ainslon threw her napkin at Easton when she lowered her hands.

The atmosphere combined with the food and the company was exactly what Ainslon needed. After her second bowl of stew, she patted her stomach. "I'm stuffed."

"No room for dessert?" Easton questioned.

"I can't believe I'm going to say this, but not at the moment."

"I'm going to pass right now too," Lauren added.

"Lauren, why don't we head into the living room while my girls clean up the kitchen?"

"That sounds lovely."

Once they were out of the room, Easton turned to Ainslon. "Things still going good between you two?"

"She's the best." Ainslon leaned back against the counter. "I love her, and everything feels right. Everything clicks."

"I'm so happy for you. I've waited a long time to see you this happy."

"Me too."

"You look a lot lighter now than when you walked in."

"Just the thought of them being here tomorrow, in this house, doesn't feel right. I'm so angry with them and yet, I couldn't care less about them. I'm trying to reconcile one with the other. Yes, I would like to see them, but on the other hand, I hope I don't. The one thing I don't want to do is talk with them. It's all..." She waved her hands in the air.

"I understand. Completely. Maybe they could join Edna at her reading tomorrow. That way you don't have to talk with them, but you can see them, and it will be your choice whether or not you change your mind to talk."

"Maybe."

After the food was put away, they joined the other two in the living room. Ainslon settled on the loveseat with Lauren. "What have you two been talking about?"

"Nothing you two need to worry about." Edna chuckled.

"I see how it is." Easton raised her feet to the coffee table.

"Nana," Ainslon said. "Tomorrow you can invite them to your reading if you want to, but I want to make it clear. I do not want them to talk to me."

"Are you sure?"

"Yes."

"Okay. I'll let them know."

Even with her parents' visit looming, Ainslon felt at peace, at least for the moment, so she wasn't going to dwell on the what ifs. She was going to enjoy this night for what it was. Time with family.

Chapter Thirty-seven

Ainslon stood back as Edna captivated the kids with all the different voices of the forest animals in the book she'd chosen to read. Justin lent her a camera and tripod to record the reading.

The night before, she'd cried herself to sleep in Lauren's arms. Edna wouldn't be around much longer. She had known it for a while, she just didn't want to acknowledge it. Now she had to.

Excited kids filled the tent and Ainslon had already sold a ton of books. On the opposite side of the tent sat her parents. She felt their eyes on her from time to time. One time their eyes locked, but she had quickly looked away. Seeing them had been enough.

"Ainslon."

She turned and smiled. "Olivia." She quickly corrected herself when Olivia grimaced. "Sorry, Ollie."

Ollie winked. "Better." She slipped her arm through Ainslon's. "I wanted to purchase two copies of the book Edna's reading."

"Sure."

"And I wanted to invite you and Lauren to dinner next Saturday. I figured I'd get it in early, so you two don't make plans."

Ainslon rang up her sale. "We're free."

"Great. Look." Ollie pulled her to the side, situating them behind her parents. "I just wanted to say how happy I am you came into Lauren's life. She's so happy now and that's all because of you. You've brought a peace to her that wasn't there before. So, thank you."

"You don't have to thank me for loving her. It's as easy as breathing."

"Love looks good on you both." Ollie kissed her cheek and walked off.

"How did you know you loved her?"

The words were spoken so softly, Ainslon almost didn't catch them. She turned slowly to come face to face with her mom, Eileen. She had one of two options and considering she was in her tent, running wasn't an option she could take.

"It felt like the ocean crashing over me, but I was never afraid of drowning."

"That's what your dad says."

"I know." Shortly before she came out to him, she asked what falling in love felt like and he'd told her.

"From what Edna has told me about her, she seems like she has a good head on her shoulders," Eileen said.

"She does."

Eileen nodded. "Is she the marrying kind? Does she want children?"

"Yes, and yes," Lauren said from behind them. "But all in due time."

Eileen nodded. "I want to know she's taken care of."

"Very much so. When Edna is gone, she'll still have Easton, Justin, me, and my family. I fear she'll never know another day of peace for the rest of her life."

"It sounds amazing." Ainslon cleared her throat.

"Mom, this is my girlfriend, Lauren. Lauren, this is my mom, Eileen."

Lauren held out her hand. "It's nice to meet you, ma'am."

"You as well." Eileen fiddled with her necklace, looking from Ainslon to Lauren. "Well."

Out of the corner of her eye, Ainslon watched as her dad, Greg, walked up to Eileen.

"Let's wait for Mom to finish up over there," Greg said, taking Eileen's hand.

Ainslon waited with bated breath, but he never addressed her, only took Eileen's hand and walked off. Good. She didn't want to talk to him either. Ainslon turned from watching them and slipped her arms around Lauren. "What brings you by?"

"Noe kicked me out of the tent. He said everything was handled and I would only muck up his pace."

"And the store?"

"Taken care of. Trying to get rid of me?"

"Never."

"Good. I was hoping we could grab some lunch. I'm sure there's something we'll like around here."

"Sure. Once Nana finishes, we can go."

"I'm all yours." After Edna finished reading and greeted everyone, Ainslon and Lauren went in search of lunch.

"What are you in the mood for?" Ainslon asked, slipping her sunglasses on.

"How about egg rolls?"

"Sounds good to me."

With food in hand they continued their walk until they found a picnic table to settle down at.

Lauren leaned forward. "How are you feeling?"

"I…" she shrugged. "I was angry at first when she

spoke, but it quickly vanished. I've had my fill of them. I don't want nor need to see them again." She slipped her hand under Lauren's and entangled their fingers. "I'm okay."

"That's what I like to hear." Lauren lifted her hands and kissed Ainslon's knuckles. "All good?"

"All good."

"So, after the festival is over, I believe I have something I need to make up for."

"Oh, what's that?" Ainslon searched her mind but couldn't come up with anything.

"I never did finish giving you the tour of C and C."

"No, I suppose you didn't. Does that mean I'll get a demonstration?"

"If you're good, you will."

"And if I'm bad?"

"If you're bad, you're still good."

Ainslon threw back her head and laughed. "So, you're saying you like all of me?"

"Better believe it." Lauren stood and extended her hand to Ainslon. "After dessert, I'm afraid we'll have to part company."

"Oh, what sweet sorrow."

Lauren rolled her eyes.

After a tasty dessert of deep-fried cheesecake, Ainslon bid bye to Lauren and headed back to her tent. Inside, Edna waved her over from where she sat beside the cash register. A quick glance around confirmed her parents were gone.

"They went to get something to eat."

"Did you eat?" Ainslon accepted the kiss on her cheek.

"I did. Justin shared his tacos with me. How are

you, dear?"

"I'm okay."

"I told them not to bother you."

Ainslon nodded. "I didn't hate talking with her, but I don't see the need to anymore."

"You do look like a weight has been lifted."

"I feel lighter. It's nice. I've held on to so much anger centered around them for so long I wasn't sure what it felt like to feel this way."

"I'm glad. The last thing I want is for you to hold on to that anger. It could eventually eat you up."

Justin walked up to them. "I'm going for a little treat for my sweet tooth. Can I get you ladies anything?"

"Well, how about one of those deep-fried Snickers, dear," Edna said.

Ainslon glanced at Justin. "Nothing for me. My sugar craving was satisfied by cheesecake."

"I'll be back." Justin turned and hurried away.

"Well, if it wasn't for them not accepting me, I would have never moved here. I would have never met Easton or Lauren and what a dull life that would have been." Ainslon wrapped her arms around Edna's shoulders. "And I would have missed out on you and what a shame that would have been."

Chapter Thirty-eight

By the time the festival ended on Sunday, exhaustion had fallen full force on Ainslon. With everything going on, she knew better than to wear herself out, but she'd failed. Edna had stopped by earlier for lunch and it'd helped perk her up a little bit. Though Edna's walk was slower, her spirits were high. It was a hard pill to swallow, but it was inevitable. Ainslon would always cherish the time they spent together and would be there for her no matter what.

Tonight, she was spending the night with Lauren and tomorrow, she was taking the day off to spend with Edna. Edna wanted to talk with her and Easton about something and they'd agreed to have lunch together. She wasn't looking forward to that conversation. At all.

Once the tent was brought down and put away, she made her way toward Lauren's tent. On the way, she stopped at a picnic table to admire the multicolored sky. Her favorite time of day would always be the sunset.

"There you are," Lauren said. "Are you ready to go?"

Ainslon turned slowly and took in the sight of Lauren. Tall and imposing, wearing a pair of gray slacks and a white silk tank top with a skull pattern, Lauren was gorgeous. Today she wore her hair down. Her ever-present sunglasses were perched on top of her head.

"How did I get so lucky?"

Lauren motioned with her hands down her own body. "I know, right?"

Ainslon laughed and pulled Lauren into her arms, slipping her hands in Lauren's back pockets. Normally, she wouldn't show so much PDA, but they were in a more secluded part of the fairgrounds.

"I wonder how I got so lucky as well," Lauren said. "Everything will be fine."

"No." Ainslon shook her head and nuzzled Lauren's neck. "Everything is changing. Nana. My parents. It's a lot, but I feel okay."

"I'm here if you need a shoulder to cry on. Or, someone to let it all out with. Or," Lauren pulled back. "If you need someone to cuddle on the couch. There doesn't have to be any talking. There's a new true crime documentary on Netflix we can watch."

"I..." Ainslon slid her hands out of Lauren's pockets and up under the back of her tank. "That sounds good. I don't want to think tonight. I only want you. No matter the capacity."

"I can handle that."

"I'm sure you can. How about a light dinner and a bath?"

"Let's get out of here."

An hour and a half later, Ainslon slid into Lauren's jacuzzi tub and reclined back as Lauren slid in-between her legs and leaned against her chest. Ainslon picked up a washcloth, dipped it in the water, then wrung out the excess water over Lauren's shoulder.

"I love doing this with you." Lauren exhaled.

"I do too. Your body was made to fit with mine." Ainslon dropped the cloth and ran her fingers along

Lauren's sides and up her arms, repeating the process several times. "Do you want me to wash your hair?"

"I would love that." Lauren raised to allow Ainslon access. Ainslon ran her fingers through Lauren's hair and scratched her scalp as Lauren moaned. "That feels wonderful."

Ainslon lathered Lauren's hair, then took her time massaging her scalp and rinsing the water out. After the shampoo was rinsed out, she kissed Lauren's shoulder, then up her neck and nibbled her earlobe. "You always taste so good." She ran her hands down Lauren's smooth back, then kissed the other shoulder before reclining back and bringing Lauren with her. She lifted her hand and Lauren entangled their fingers. "I love everything about you, sweetheart."

"The feeling is mutual. Do you want me to wash your hair?"

"In a minute. I want to enjoy the feel of you in my arms right now. It's been a long week."

"Then that's what we will do."

When the water cooled, they climbed out, dried each other off, and dressed. Lauren directed Ainslon to the bedroom while she made them both a cup of tea.

Ainslon slipped under the covers and leaned against the headboard. She smiled when Shady jumped on the bed and settled down at her feet. The longer they dated, Lauren insisted Ainslon bring Shady over since it wasn't fair for her to always be alone. Shady had quickly taken to Lauren's condo and Ainslon had a feeling she might not be able to get her home. It didn't help that Lauren had bought her a cat tree and several toys to play with. One window in the living room even had a small hammock hanging by it so Shady could see outside.

"Now, that's what I like to see," Lauren said. "Two of my favorite girls." After giving Ainslon her tea, Lauren kissed Shady on the head, then climbed in beside Ainslon.

Ainslon loved these quiet moments. Even face freshly scrubbed and wearing a pair of silk pajamas, Lauren was still breathtaking.

"You're staring."

"Sorry."

"Don't ever be sorry for looking at me. You can look and touch all you want."

She finished her tea, then deposited her empty cup on the nightstand. Lauren did the same and they settled in for the night, Ainslon's arms firmly wrapped around Lauren's middle.

"Do you want to talk about it yet?" Lauren held tight to Ainslon's arms.

"I'm not looking forward to lunch tomorrow. I'm not ready." Why did everything have to be thrown at her at once?

"Edna loves you. You and Easton very much. She's still here. It's okay to be sad." She dislodged Ainslon's arms and turned, then cupped her cheeks. "It's okay to cry. You're going through a lot right now. I don't want to smother you, but if I could, I'd be with you twenty-four seven just so I could comfort you. I know you're all right with seeing your parents, but darling, it's all right to cry. Sometimes a cry is what the doctor ordered."

Ainslon buried her head in Lauren's chest. For the first time, she let it all out, knowing Lauren would keep her safe. She clung to Lauren as she smoothed her hands down Ainslon's back.

"I've got you and I'm not going anywhere."

As Ainslon calmed down and accepted the Kleenex from Lauren, she knew she was never letting this woman go.

Chapter Thirty-nine

After a simple breakfast and a kiss from Lauren, Ainslon left for work. It wasn't easy to stay focused, but she succeeded by the time Easton came by to pick her up for lunch. Ainslon stared at the passing scenery on their way to Edna's. Even though Edna said it was just going to be the three of them, Ainslon breathed a sigh of relief when Easton pulled into the empty driveway.

Easton cut the engine and pulled the key out of the ignition, staring straight ahead.

She looked like Ainslon felt. "I'm not ready either." Ainslon had a feeling this talk wasn't going to go the way she wanted it to. Recently, Edna had been clingier with them. It was nice but wasn't normal for the older woman.

"Fuck. I knew we wouldn't have her forever, but…" Easton scrubbed her hands on her face. "I… fuck." She slammed her hands on the steering wheel. Ainslon pried her hands away and pulled her into her arms.

Ainslon clung to her as she cried. "I know."

When Easton pulled back and wiped her eyes, Ainslon handed her a Kleenex. "She's not gone yet."

"No," Easton said with resolve. "She's not and we best not keep her waiting." Easton turned to face her. "Remember that time we were late for our curfew?"

"Do I ever. She didn't even say a word when we

walked through the kitchen door."

"No," Easton said. "Her face said it all. She didn't talk to us for a week."

"It was the worst." They both sobered. "Let's not keep her waiting then."

"Nope."

Ainslon clung to Easton's arm even when they walked through the back door. Tears pricked her eyes when the smell hit her.

Easton sniffed loudly. "Is that cinnamon rolls?"

Edna turned from the stove. "Would I make you two anything else when you're sad?"

"No," Ainslon choked out, then got herself together with the look Edna directed at her. "With icing," she finally said.

"I may be old, but I would never forget both of your favorites. Sit down."

Ainslon and Easton sat on one side of the table. Edna sat across from them.

"Now," Edna said, when they'd both taken a bite of their roll. "There are a few things I want to say, then I don't want to talk about this again, since we've already talked about this once. Okay?" They both nodded. "I love you both. More than words can say. Just because I'm not here with you doesn't diminish it one bit. Some people never get the chance to express themselves before their death." She took a deep breath. "I don't know when, but I can feel it. I'm tired. More than I have ever been. I know you are both sad, but please don't be. I've made my peace with dying." They held hands across the table. "I've had a wonderful life. More so because of you two." She patted their hands, then pulled away. "Now. As I said, all my papers are in the living room. Everything's arranged. No matter what you might think or want, please abide by my wishes."

Ainslon shared a look with Easton, then they looked back at Edna. "What do you have planned?" It would be like Edna to go out with a bang.

"Now, never you two mind. I've lived the life I want and I'm going out the way I want to. You've both made me so proud." Edna stood and motioned for them both to do the same. "We are only going to do this once." She held her arms open and both rushed into them. "It's all right." When their tears dried up, Edna pulled back and cupped their cheeks. "No more tears. I forbid it."

Ainslon sniffled but nodded.

"Okay," Easton said.

"You two go get yourselves cleaned up because I want to play Chinese checkers. Can you both stay?"

Nothing would have stopped Ainslon from saying yes. Thankfully, she had already made plans with Justin for this. "Yes."

Easton nodded. "I've been practicing, so you two won't stand a chance."

"You wish." Ainslon bumped her as they both walked out of the kitchen and down the hall. Ainslon stopped when Easton touched her arm. "What?"

"I'm okay now."

"Me too." She hadn't felt this much at peace all week. Yes, losing Edna would be hard, but she felt so much better after hearing Edna's feelings about it.

A few hours and dozens of games later, Edna had broken out the wine. Ainslon dropped to the floor and leaned back against the couch. Edna was seated on the couch and Easton was sprawled out in the recliner opposite them.

Ainslon sipped her wine. "Thank you for this, Nana. I feel so much better."

"I do as well," Edna said. "I invited someone over for dinner. I hope you two don't mind."

"Would it matter, Nana?" Easton said. "You already invited them."

"Watch your smart mouth."

"Sorry."

Ainslon chuckled at Easton. She had a feeling she knew the recipient of the call. "I don't mind you inviting Lauren, Nana." She knew it wasn't her parents, so that only left Lauren.

"I don't either," Easton said.

"Good, because she is supposed to be here at six-thirty. I was going to order take-out, if that's okay with you two."

Easton rose up and swung her legs off the coffee table. "Do you know us at all? Of course take-out is fine."

"Truer words have never been spoken." Ainslon raised her glass and they all clinked them together. Ainslon downed the rest of hers when she heard a car pull up outside. She jumped up. "I'll get it."

"All right, dear. She's early."

Ainslon opened the front door and stepped out onto the porch, softly closing the door behind her. Lauren was still in the car. When she noticed Ainslon, she got out and headed toward her.

Ainslon rested her arms on the railing as Lauren stepped up next to her.

"How was it growing up in this neighborhood?"

"It was wonderful."

"Did it always look like this? I don't think I ever explored this part of Garriety."

"No. There were only a few houses here, up until ten years ago. This part of Garriety had a growth spurt. Easton and I used to ride our bikes up and down this road." Ainslon rolled her eyes. "That is until Easton decided to try skateboarding." Ainslon pointed to a stump some ways down the road. "See that stump? She hit that and flew over the skateboard and landed hard. Nana and I both ran to her, but she jumped up, picked up the skateboard, and declared she would be sticking to the bike from now on. Do you know what Nana said?"

"Tell me."

"She said, 'Life wouldn't be worth living if we didn't take chances from time to time.' It changed my perspective on life. I took a chance with Justin and our business. I took a chance with you and I'm so glad I did." Ainslon felt so safe wrapped in Lauren's arms. "I love you and I can't wait to see what the future has in store for us."

"Ditto."

Once inside, Ainslon took a deep breath. Life was unpredictable but right here, right now, everything was as it should be.

Ainslon picked up her phone. "Let's take some pictures."

"Not more pictures," Easton grumbled but stood and joined the others on the couch.

"Oh, hush, you." Edna pulled Easton close.

"Say cheese."

Chapter Forty

Lauren ended her call, lay her head against the chair back, and stared up at the ceiling. The morning was long, and the afternoon was shaping up to be longer. Ainslon had spent a lot of time with Edna this past week. While Lauren missed their time together, they made time to talk or text and had lunch together three times this week.

She didn't think she could ever love someone as much as she loved Ainslon. She fell hard and fast.

"I don't need three guesses to know who put that smile on your face."

Lauren jumped up and engulfed her mother. "What brings you by?" She ushered her toward the couch in the corner of the room. She hadn't even heard the door open.

Patricia patted Lauren on the leg. "I was in the area and wanted to see you." She placed her purse on the floor.

Knowing her mother, she had another reason for dropping by. "What else besides wanting to see me?" Lauren crossed her arms.

"What's on your mind? And don't tell me nothing."

"Edna's health is declining and Ainslon, as well as she is coping, she's sad."

"Oh, little duck. I'm sorry to hear about Edna. I like her."

"So do I. It's been a hard week, but Edna is still in high spirits. She's still getting around on her own, but I'm sure it's only a matter of time until she isn't. Tonight, I had planned a night in with Ainslon, and she agreed, but…"

"But?"

"I feel selfish. Should I be taking time away she could spend with Edna?"

"Don't be silly. You're not being selfish and if Ainslon agreed, then she has no issue with it."

"What if she's just being polite?"

"Now you listen to me. Ainslon loves you. Just talk with her. Communication is key."

"I know."

"What you're feeling is natural. You feel a little neglected."

"Yes, but I know this is important to her, and I'm not even sure I should be feeling this way."

She patted the spot beside her, and Lauren sat. "You've been dating for what, five months?"

"Almost."

"For anyone else, I would say it's too soon, but not for you. I see the way you look at her and you've never been one to give your heart away on a whim. How serious is this?"

A smile made its way to Lauren's lips. "I love her, Momma. Really love her. Just the thought of her brings a smile to my face. She's everything. Everything I could ever want. She's warm and funny. Serious and silly. I can see myself making a life with her. Having a family. I…" She swallowed. "I've never felt this way before. Never thought I could fall this fast. It's like—"

"Like everything is aligned."

"Yes. I'm a grown woman. I shouldn't be feeling

this needy."

Patricia laughed. "Little duck, you're in love. Now, you're going to go get me some chocolate and later you're going to spend the evening with Ainslon. Talk to her. I know she will listen."

Lauren stood and kissed Patricia's cheek. "You do always know the right thing to say." Maybe she was overthinking this. Tonight, she'd talk with Ainslon.

❧❧❧❧

Lauren flitted around the kitchen, making sure everything was in order for dinner. She'd done a lot of thinking over the day and concluded there was only one way they would be able to see more of each other. Even if it was only at night and in the morning. Was it quick? Yes. Too soon? Maybe. Did she care? Nope. The box sitting on the table held a new origami piece and a key to her condo. She only hoped Ainslon said yes.

The business was doing well, and Lauren couldn't be happier. Everything was clicking into place. Hopefully in a few hours she would have two new houseguests. Shady liked it here, so there shouldn't be an issue.

Lauren arranged all the ingredients on the counter. Tonight, Lauren wanted to introduce Ainslon to more of the food she grew up with. Now seemed like as good a time as any and Ainslon could take the leftovers to Edna tomorrow.

At a quarter to seven, her doorbell rang. After a quick check in the hallway mirror, she opened the front door and ushered Ainslon in. "You look beautiful."

"You always say that."

"I must not tell lies."

Lauren slipped her arms around Ainslon when she wound her arms around her neck. "God, you always feel divine."

"And you always smell divine."

A shiver ran down her arms when Ainslon kissed her neck. Before things could escalate, Lauren pulled back. "None of that right now."

"Later?"

"You better believe it, but right now, we cook."

"I've been waiting for this all day."

"You're not too tired?" Fatigue danced around Ainslon's eyes, but Lauren would do whatever she needed.

Ainslon smoothed out the collar on Lauren's shirt. "I am tired but being here with you is what I needed. It's been a long week and Nana forbid me from seeing her tonight or tomorrow and maybe the next day and I'm okay with that. I love Nana and I don't want to lose her, but it's taken a toll on me. Is that bad?"

"Of course not. Edna loves you and doesn't want you to wear yourself out and that's what you've been doing. I didn't want to say anything, because I didn't think it was my place, but you look worn out." Lauren held Ainslon tight when she lay her head on her chest.

"You should have. I would have listened. I love you and I want you to be concerned about me. I want to be with her every minute, and I can't. Nana already said she doesn't want us putting our life on hold for her. She and Shelly spend a lot of time together. They're getting along well."

"You don't need to feel guilty. Since you have tonight and tomorrow off from Edna—"

"And work. Justin insisted."

"And work. We are going to put off dinner for an hour, so we can run to your place so you can pack a bag and pick up Shady. I'll have to go into work for an hour or two tomorrow, but when I get home, I'm all yours."

"That sounds like heaven."

Lauren cradled her cheek and kissed her. "I do aim to please."

"Don't I know it."

Three hours later, Lauren lay back on the couch with Ainslon in her arms and Shady at her feet. She couldn't remember the last time she'd had so much fun cooking with someone, and they'd planned to cook together at least once a month.

There was another first she wanted to achieve tonight. The small box goaded her from where it sat on the coffee table. "So, I was thinking." She tightened her arms around Ainslon.

"Oh, what about?" Ainslon ran her hands down Lauren's thighs.

"Us."

"Us?" Ainslon turned in Lauren's embrace and lay atop her.

Lauren closed her eyes when Ainslon ran her fingers along her cheek.

"I'm waiting, sweetheart."

Lauren opened her eyes and lost herself in the melting gaze of the woman above her. "I love you."

"And I love you."

Lauren would never grow tired of hearing those three words from Ainslon "Darling." She placed a tender kiss on Ainslon's lips. She didn't want Ainslon to move in with her on a whim; she wanted her to move in because she loved her and was ready to take the next step.

"Sweetheart?"

"Sorry. As I was saying." Lauren cradled Ainslon's cheeks. "I love you and wanted to ask if you and Shady would move in with me?" Ainslon's eyes widened. "No pressure. I know it's soon and we have—" Lauren closed her eyes at the first touch of Ainslon's lips. She would never get tired of that feeling. She laughed when Ainslon buried her head in her neck. "Is that a yes?"

"Yes. Of course we'll move in with you."

"No doubts? No hesitations?"

"Yes, I have doubts and hesitation, but I love you and life is short and we should grab it with both hands and never let go. I want this. I want you. Being with you is as easy as breathing."

"We're going to be great."

"No. We're going to be spectacular."

Epilogue

10 months later

Ainslon stood by the front windows, admiring the inside of their finished building. It had taken longer than she expected for everything to be finished because of unforeseen problems, but everything had worked out. The whimsical decorations that Patricia and Edna had a hand in designing surrounded polished wood and steel beams. The bottom floor housed their children's book section and the top floor was dedicated to comic books, toys, and games. Tonight was the grand opening and she couldn't wait. They'd created quite a bit of buzz over the last few weeks about the opening and expected a full house. Lauren and Easton had donated the sweet treats for the event, and they were offering a wide array of beverages.

If someone had told her fifteen months ago that this would be her life, she would have laughed at them. So much had changed in such a short amount of time. Or, at least, it seemed like a short amount of time to her.

She fell in love, moved her business, moved in with said love, and buried her grandmother. Edna died peacefully at home two months after Ainslon moved in with Lauren. Per Edna's instructions, she and Easton followed her funeral arrangements to the letter, even down to the balloons she wanted floating around the funeral home and the disco music she wanted playing. It was a grand party and Edna had gone out the way she wanted to. In style.

Ainslon didn't want the house, so when Easton asked if she could move in, Ainslon had agreed. She took a few pieces of furniture from the house and they'd sold many more, but it felt right. It didn't bother her as much as she'd expected, walking into the house where Edna had died. Easton had converted Edna's bedroom into an office and liked to joke that Edna was always watching over her shoulder, making sure she didn't slack off.

Ainslon glanced back to the corner of the room where they'd set up the reading nook. A picture of Edna hung on the wall as an homage to her. It was the least she could do for the woman who had given her everything and never asked for anything in return.

They'd also welcomed a new member into their ever-growing group. Carrie and Larry welcomed a healthy baby girl that Ainslon and Lauren had babysat a handful of times. Carrie's mother still hadn't come around, but she and Lauren made sure to include the young couple in their get-togethers.

She relaxed back against a warm body when two arms slipped around her waist.

"What are you thinking about, darling?"

"Everything."

"Must be tiring."

Ainslon chuckled and tilted her head back and kissed Lauren's cheek. "Very tiring."

"Maybe you should sit down."

Ainslon rolled her eyes and wiggled out of Lauren's embrace to face her. "I don't need to rest. I'm okay."

Lauren held her hands up in a sign of surrender.

Ainslon narrowed her eyes. Lauren had been a pain in her ass for the last month and she couldn't see that changing anytime soon. "You hear me?"

"Yes, I hear you. I noticed you didn't throw up this morning."

"Nope. I think I'm over that bit for the moment." She slid her arm down and slipped her hand into Lauren's, bringing it around to rest on the small, barely visible bump. "We're both fine. I promise." A month after Edna died, the topic of children came up again. They both knew it was early in their relationship, but they also knew it was the right time, and they were ready. Ainslon had taken Lauren's worries to heart and agreed the sooner the better. Lauren had even agreed to sell her condo, citing that she wanted her child to grow up with a backyard to play in. Ollie was currently trying to find them the perfect house.

Ainslon smiled when Lauren placed both hands on her stomach. "I worry and I'm trying not to go overboard. You two mean the world to me and I don't know what I'd do if I lost either one of you."

"You won't, I promise. I'm okay."

"I'm sorry. I just worry." Lauren slipped her hands in the pocket of her pants. The tight pants that showed off Lauren's ass to perfection. "Eyes up."

"I can look."

"Yes, you can," Justin shouted from the left of them, where he was dusting the shelves for the third time. "But we don't need to see you mooning over your wife."

"Shut up." She sank into Lauren's arms. After they'd decided to have a baby, they'd also decided to marry. Not only for their peace of mind surrounding their relationship, but as extra protection for the baby. It would be easier for Lauren to adopt the baby if they were married. The ceremony was small, but perfect for both of their needs, with only a handful of family and close friends in attendance.

"You're really up for tonight?"

"Yes. I promise." She pulled away and headed toward the stairs. Before her foot could step up, Lauren spun her around and into her arms. "I promise. I'm fine." She wound her arms around Lauren's neck. Truth be told, Lauren's protectiveness was nice, if not a little stifling, but she knew Lauren meant well. "If I need to sit down, I will. If I'm hungry, I'll eat. I'm really good."

"Okay. I promise to tone down my nagging."

"I love you and love that you love us both so much." Ainslon pecked her on the lips. "Do you ever think maybe we should have jumped into the shallow end instead of the deep end?" Ainslon pulled back enough to gauge Lauren's reaction.

"Don't be silly. The shallow end would have never worked for us. We're 'jump in with both feet and hope to hell everything works out' people. Sure, we have on a life vest, but there's still the thrill of the unknown. That's us."

"We're pretty badass, aren't we?"

"You better believe it. Our bean sprout will be as badass as us. Trust me. I know these things."

"You've never steered us wrong before."

"And I don't intend to now. We're like Starsky and Hutch. Laverne and Shirley. Lucy and Ethel."

Ainslon stood on her tiptoes and stared into Lauren's eyes. "How about in our story we be Ainslon and Lauren with an epilogue including a mini-me or two?"

"We'll be a bestseller."

"More importantly, we'll be a first edition."

Ainslon squealed when Lauren dipped her, then brought her up slowly. "Every chapter is a new adventure."

"With chocolate and a little bit of luck."

"No one can say you never planned your priorities correctly."

"Your sass isn't warranted."

"You love my sass and my ass."

"I do love your ass." Ainslon reached behind Lauren and squeezed said ass.

"Now." Lauren moved away and pointed upstairs. "I know you want to do a final walk through before it's time to open. Go. I'll stay down here and monitor things."

"Not coming with me?"

"You've got it handled. Besides, I'll be here when you get back. I'll always be here."

"And that's why I'll always come back, because I know you'll be waiting." At the top of the stairs, she looked back. Lauren had already moved to talk with Easton. This was her life. Her legacy and she would do whatever it took to make sure it lasted. Not only for her or even Lauren, but also for their little bean sprout.

Life did have a way of shaking things up. Thank God for an eight-year-old boy's love of *Mary Poppins*. Though, she had a feeling they would have met one way or another. She had to believe it because any other outcome wouldn't be acceptable. Lauren was worth it, and she always would be. She turned, but quickly swung her gaze back around and met Lauren's mischievous smirk.

By this point in their love story, some would say they were at the end, but not her. No. Ainslon smiled back before turning and walking into the comic section.

No, this wasn't the end. It was only chapter one.

If you liked this book?

Reviews help a new author get discovered and if you have enjoyed this book, please do the author the honor of posting a review on Goodreads, Amazon, Barnes & Noble or anywhere you purchased the book. Or perhaps share a posting on your social media sites or spread the word to your friends.

About the Author

Born near Chicago, but raised in Southern Illinois, where she still lives, Shannon spends her free time writing. When she isn't writing, she enjoys binge watching fantasy, science fiction, or true crime shows.

You can contact Shannon at -

Website: smhfiction.com
Email: smh1981@live.com
Facebook: facebook.com/smharrisauthor
Twitter: @smhfiction

Check out Shannon's other books.

The Adearian Chronicles - Book One - The Oath – ISBN – 978-1-943353-17-0

Ex-mercenary, Lanis Welsh, is finally at a place in her life where she is content with what and who she is; High Priestess Anya's Protector and Lover. After an unexpected request, she has no choice but to leave Anya's protection in the hands of someone else and travel back to the one place that holds nothing but bad memories. When she is manipulated into signing an oath she has no desire to fulfill, she questions the very truths she has built her life on. As strangers become friends and enemies become allies, Lanis must face the demons from her past. It doesn't take her long to realize there is more going on than anyone could have ever foreseen and nothing and no one can be trusted.

Adearian Chronicles - Book 2 – Revelations – ISBN - 978-1-943353-33-0

What would you do if you were faced with finding and saving the one person who held your heart, but you only had two weeks to do it?

When the unexpected happens and Lanis's world is turned upside down, she and Elson have no choice but to align themselves with two people from a strange land. With new enemies at play, and a Goddess that seems to have forsaken them, Lanis relies on the only people she can; her friends. To fight the demons that plague her daily, she has to separate her love for Anya, from the task she must perform. On top of the unknowns, she is gifted with a small black book that changes the way she sees everything and everyone around her. As her world starts to crumble, Lanis must face her fears and the nightmares that invade her dreams. With the hours ticking away, she must come to terms with the fact that she might already be too late.

The DragonWitch Tales: An Unexpected Beginning – ISBN – 978-1-943353-43-9

Death ignited her powers. Love binds them.

Paisley's normal, boring life is shattered one evening when a strange, but sexy woman appears out of thin air in her living room and claims Paisley as her wife. Things spiral out of control when Paisley is informed by her mother that she is a witch that comes from a long line of witches, that other realms exist, and that the strange woman really is her wife.

As her choices slip from her grasp, Paisley must learn to navigate her new life, a new world, and a new wife. As if that wasn't enough, Paisley must deal with a growing attraction for a new woman in her life. Throw in a dragon egg, an angry queen, a traitor, and Paisley realizes she's going to have to learn to watch every move she makes.

As the push and pull between two women and her powers reach a standoff, Paisley makes a choice that will change the course of her life and the future of the world she calls home even if that means destroying her own happiness in the process.

The Details in the Design – ISBN – 978-1-943353-79-8

Every stitch tells a story.

Avery Michaels has longed to work in the fashion industry since she was six years old. Now at thirty-two she's fed up with her job as a food critic and signs up with an employment agency that promises to find anyone their dream job.

She is thrilled when she gets an interview with the fashion house of her choice, Catherine Davenport Designs. There's only one problem. For the past six years, Avery has had a massive crush on Catherine, one of the hottest fashion designers of the past two decades.

In the midst of a new job, nosey friends, Catherine's meddling daughters, difficult co-workers, and a dachshund named Polly, Avery also has to contend with a new woman that enters Catherine's life.

From the start, Avery knows winning Catherine's heart will be no easy feat. When curve ball after curve ball is thrown her way, does she scrap her design or make it work?

Add Romance and Mix – ISBN – 978-1-948232-06-7

Briley Anderson hasn't been in a serious relationship for the past two years. The pain of her last breakup has made her weary of giving her heart away again. She spends her days flipping houses and her down-time baking treats for her neighbors. Falling in love wasn't in her plans, but then again, neither was her next-door neighbor.

Leah Daniels is a divorced mother of two and a grandmother at the age of forty-nine. Love was the last thing she was looking for, especially with a woman sixteen years her junior. All she was hoping for was a quiet neighborhood to raise her fifteen-year old son.

What she hadn't expected was the unavoidable draw she felt toward Briley.

Through laughter, heartache, love, and fear it's up to Briley and Leah to figure out if what they've created is strong enough to make a relationship last and if taking the chance on love is really worth the risk.

Blueprint for Romance: A Garriety Romance – ISBN – 978-1-948232-71-5

After the death of her husband, Dylan Lake's ability to trust in others is shattered. Her life is thrust into turmoil between caring for Emma, her seven-year old handicapped child, and working hard to make ends meet. Dylan doesn't have time to pursue a romantic relationship. Finding that one special person only happens in dreams. When fate keeps throwing Dylan and Kat together, Dylan finds her attraction to Kat something she can't ignore. Will her trust issues stop her from letting Kat into her and Emma's life? Leaving her old job and moving halfway across the country were the scariest things Kat Anderson had ever done. Starting a new life and career takes priority over any foolish notion of a fairy-tale future of romance and love. Kat's attraction to Dylan is time taken away from building a new business. Can Kat juggle love and duty to find her Happy Ever After? Welcome back to Garriety, the town with an open heart, and home to some of the quirky and warm characters from Add Romance and Mix. Join Kat and Dylan on their quest for true romance with a little help from Kat's sister Briley and her family, along with a host of new characters.

Other books by Sapphire Authors

Highland Dew – ISBN – 978-1-948232-11-1

Bryce Andrews, west coast sales director for Global Distillers and Distribution, is tired of the corporate hamster wheel. She needs a change.

A craft whisky trade show offers her inspiration and a chance to revisit Scotland and the majestic scenery of the Speyside region—best known for the "Whisky Trail." Bryce and her coworker, Reggie Ballard, need to find a wholly original whisky for their international distribution division by visiting a number of small distillers.

A blind curve, a dangling sign, and weed-choked driveway draw Bryce directly into a truly unique opportunity. She discovers a struggling family, a shuttered distillery, and a spitfire of a daughter called home to care for her confused father.

Fiona McDougall—the only child and heir to the MacDougall & Son legacy, had her career teaching in Edinburgh curtailed by fate…or serendipity.

When the stars finally align, the two women work together to resurrect a dream for themselves and the family business—if they can weather the storms of unscrupulous business practices in the competitive whisky market.

Cigar Barons: Blood isn't thicker than water - it's war!
- ISBN - 978-1-948232-83-8

Legends aren't built overnight. In fact, they take decades of hard work, long days, and selfless sacrifice—if one is lucky. Huerta Cigars is a result of the combined passion of patriarch Alejandro Huerta, who emigrated from pre-Castro Cuba to Nicaragua, and his sons Roberto and Manuel. Their unwavering dedication to their dream of producing the best cigars made for a success. Upon Roberto's passing he left the cigar empire to his only daughter, Sofia, who took over the family business.

Sofia Huerta is Don Roberto's daughter, and she is making a name for herself with her own line of fine, boutique cigars. One late night phone call will change Sofia's life forever. Rushing to Nicaragua from San Francisco, her only hope is that it isn't too late to save her father.

Roberto Huerta, Jr. might be a Huerta in name, but his womanizing, drinking, and carefree lifestyle have kept him at arm's length from his father. RJ think's his father's freak accident will leave him as the rightful heir of the family empire. He couldn't have been more wrong.

A turn of events will pit brother against sister as they fight for control of the Huerta empire. Sometimes secrets and lies aren't the only thing living in the closet, and there is only one Huerta that can continue the family legacy of excellence in this romantic mystery with a twist.

In Cigar Barons, blood isn't thicker than water—it's war.

Faithful Valor - ISBN - 978-1-948232-85-2

Sometimes danger isn't found on a battleground—it's sitting at your front door.

Nic Caldwell is back Stateside, working the job she was supposed to have before her most recent deployment, and living her best life at home. At least she thought she would be, except her PTSD is always in the background, dragging her back to her tour in Afghanistan. As she struggles to control her demons privately, her public life with Claire is almost picture perfect. However, a picture can't show everything hiding just under the surface.

Claire Monroe has the love of her life back in one piece—almost. She's trying to help Nic adjust to her new normal both physically and emotionally while also going back to school and raising their daughter, Grace. With all the difficulties Nic's re-entry poses along with the new challenges of being an adult student, she wonders how she can guide them back to their old life while building a new one for herself.

Cece Ramirez has decided that the Army has served its purpose and she is ready for a new chapter in her professional and personal life. Retiring from active duty and moving on to a new role as a police officer on a college campus, she realizes that she's traded camo, discipline, and rifles for book bags, bikes, and rowdy post-adolescents. While she and the students at Cal State Monterey Bay might be the same age, their pasts are vastly different, and the transition from soldier to college cop may not be as smooth as she hopes.

When a chance encounter at a near-base shopette challenges Nic's authority and leaves her and her family in potential peril, Cece and Claire must pull together to back Nic up in peacetime, and right at home.

www.ingramcontent.com/pod-product-compliance
Lightning Source LLC
Chambersburg PA
CBHW051643180726
48284CB00006B/1851